Chairman of the Bored

Jethro Charlton

Published by Autumn River Press, 2025.

CHAIRMAN OF THE BORED

First edition. April 20, 2025.

ISBN: 978-1764056700

Written by Jethro Charlton.

For my family

Albert moves confidently along the sunlit concrete toward you. He's looking especially relaxed in his annoyingly faux-nonchalant kind of way. Polished snakeskin boots, £200 designer jeans, a well-tailored navy jacket, Ray Bans, and a slate grey T-shirt advertising himself as 'CHAIRMAN OF THE BORED'.

You should be wearing that T-shirt, you think, but on you it wouldn't seem as ironic as it does on Albert. On you it would seem like you really were the CEO of some major corporation for the jaded.

You squirm a little in the cold metal café chair and self-consciously run your fingers through your hair as he approaches. The morning sun hits your face with maximum glare factor. You wish you had remembered your sunglasses.

"Cedric, my man! How's the universe treating you?" He always asks you the same question, and you always answer the same way.

"With brutal indifference, Albert. Brutal indifference."

Albert goes off on one of his glass half-full lectures about life being there for the taking like a ripe peach hanging low on a glorious summer's day.

"You just have to grab it," he tells you, "Bite into it, savor its delights and let the juices run down your chin onto your tanned, glistening chest—or even better, *her* tanned glistening chest!"

Albert has a classic case of pathological optimism. You diagnosed it the first day you met at Warmouth University. If a nuclear war broke out, Albert would be on a private spaceflight to Mars with a cargo of champagne, cocaine and impossibly beautiful women before the first missile launched.

"Come on, Cedric. The world isn't as messed up as you think it is. We just need to find a way to get you up and running again. You have to stop believing in that existential bullshit. You just need to get laid! Let go a bit!"

"Albert, getting laid is the last thing *I* think I need. I'd rather save everyone including myself the embarrassment," you say.

"Drunk then! We need to get you drunk. Then we can get you laid!" says Albert brightly.

You and Albert have been spending too much time together lately. Albert means well but he's not good for you. For a start he's way more successful than you are. You've been friends for almost ten years, and you know full well who Albert was before he became "Market Guru" for The Daily. You're not envious of his notoriety, you tell yourself, but you can't help wondering how he manages to practically keep The Daily in circulation with his phenomenally insightful stock tips, while you're struggling to file a news story that isn't dated by the time you write your first word.

For a start, Albert barely scraped through Warmouth, spent most of his time drinking, seducing every woman on campus, watching James Bond movie marathons, and beating people up on the lacrosse field. It was you who studied hard, ran the student paper, won academic prizes and graduated with honors. It was you who helped Albert get a research position on The Daily when no one in their right mind would interview him.

Symons, the Managing Editor of The Daily, loves Albert. Symons will have him in his office for two-hour gabfests, morning or afternoon. Peals of laughter thunder off the glass walls as Albert regales Symons with his latest exploits. Symons despises you.

A young waitress brings Albert his black coffee. He smiles at her, then turns to you arching his eyebrows. You suddenly feel uncomfortable. There's something morally wrong about that low-hanging peach bit, you think. Sinister even. That fruit is forbidden. While we're all busy trying to adhere to some kind of pointless ethical order, he's off fornicating in the orchard!

Albert pulls a leather-lined hip flask from the inside pocket of his jacket and pours a shot into his cup. For Christ's sake Albert, not now, you think.

That's another thing. You drink too much as a by-product of Albert's drinking too much. Albert's drinking seems to endear him to everyone. Alcohol seems to have the reverse effect on your social standing. With Albert every drink increases his charm and mysterious allure. With you it's like a repellant field around you becomes more and more potent.

"Jesus, Albert, put that away. I don't... no, no!"

"Oh, come on, Cedric, a little drop before entrée gives a little sheen to The Daily's dour hue! Especially the Sec Pool. Christ, without this stuff no one at The Daily would ever get laid. Even *you* got lucky at Jensen's farewell," he says, taking a sip. "Tell old Alby the details. Was she—"

"Okay, Albert, look I've got to get to a meeting. I'll see you later," you splutter. And with that you hastily make a beeline for the office.

Rushing to enter the building, you jump into a slow-moving revolving glass door behind a pregnant woman pushing a pram. The door comes to a sudden halt as you bump the woman, who bumps the pram, which bumps the glass. Her displeasure fills the close confines of the glass wedge like a poison gas.

The door starts again. Apologising profusely, you take small awkward steps to avoid a repeat and eventually shuffle out into the echoing lobby of Tower 3, 131 London Bridge Road.

You immediately feel disoriented and oppressed in the cacophony of voices. Heading for the elevator your sense of dread lifts as a couple of gorgeous interns pass by clutching travel cups, flashing shiny white smiles and beaming youthful ambition. They waft along in lively conversation; ponytails swinging, hips swaying in their tight black pencil skirts, stilettos clacking against the polished granite.

Faintly equine beauties, you think. You gaze at them longingly. You imagine yourself as a stallion.

The elevator doors rudely close in on your reverie and you stare blankly at your cold metallic reflection. You punch the button for level 17 harder than necessary. It does not light up. Someone behind you is talking loudly on their phone about how they are in an elevator and how the call might drop out. You hope it does.

Fishing through your pockets you finally pull out your security pass, trying furiously to swipe it against the sensor before the lift shoots up to the 31st floor.

Damn it, too late.

You grin through clenched teeth as the lift goes all the way up and takes it's time descending again, floor-by-floor back to 17. As you step out, the doors of the lift opposite part smoothly to reveal Albert with the two interns. He's got them under his spell already. Their doe eyed playfulness, pink cheeks and giddy laughter obviously broadcasting their interest in him. Corrupting bastard, you think. He's probably given them shots.

"Go for a ride, Cedric? Thought you had an important meeting to get to," says Albert with a conspiratorial wink. You mumble something incoherent and notice the girls exchanging a glance. It immediately triggers an adolescent awkwardness in your movements.

You follow the flirtatious trio into the office past reception, inhaling gales of Victoria Secret's latest concoction, and take a wistful look over your shoulder as they veer off, leaving you to trudge on sourly to your desk. Your desk, which is stationed less than ten feet away from Symons' glass chamber.

You fire up your PC and check the litany of emails. Symons calls you into his office and immediately starts talking about his vasectomy.

"It hurts, did you know that, Bonhomie? No one tells you that. In fact, everyone I spoke to said it would be perfectly painless, including that quack Mendelsohn—bloody butcher—it still feels like I have a pair of jumper leads attached to my balls." He gets up from his seat gingerly to take a file down from his shelf and you notice his wider than usual gait.

"So, I get home and the first thing that happens is my four-year-old son opens the door and launches his head straight into my crotch. I tell you I have never come so close to killing someone of my own flesh and blood." He pauses to adjust his fly.

"Anyway, I take the rest of the day off and I'm lying on the couch with a beer, about to watch the tennis, when Elliot, our lunatic old cat springs up out of nowhere onto my bloody lap."

You're imagining the double shock. Symons' abrupt levitation off the couch, unable to comprehend the impossibility of what just happened. The heavy old cat attached to his trousers digging its claws in further to secure itself to its moving target, eyes wide with fright. Symons returning to the couch covered in beer, fur, and fresh wounds to his nether region. You enjoy the imagery.

"Anyhow, enough of my stories, Bonhomie. Where are your bloody stories?" You feel immediate panic.

"Er, well I'm working on this story about a... well I read that—"

"Don't tell me you are writing something based upon what you have read, Bonhomie. We pay you to break news, not repeat it. For Christ's sake man, I haven't seen an original word written by you in the last twelve months. If this were a university, you would have been kicked out for plagiarism years ago."

You wonder at that and feel the truth of his comments kicking you in the guts. It's not your fault—everyone's a reporter these days. By the time you get to anything, it's already been tweeted around the world by five million rubbernecking freaks.

"Did I mention there's another opportunity in Syria that's opened up? We haven't heard from Watson in weeks. Last thing was one of those hoax videos, you know, the ones with all the hoods and machetes and whatnot. Fascinating place Syria, plenty of firsthand stuff to be had, Bonhomie. Plenty of gold for pirates."

You observe his casual callousness with awe and a sense of foreboding creeps over you. Screw that, I'm not going to be number twenty-eight, you think.

Symons' phone rings loudly and he waves you out of the glass chamber. You sit down to your desk feeling a little ruffled and fighting the urge to get up and walk out. You visualize yourself quitting every morning. This is no way to live. Perpetually fearing deadlines, run-ins with Symons, and the clambering feeling that you are about to be unmasked as a giant fraud. But these terrors pale in comparison to your fear of unemployment, so you continue on each day, sinking ever further into the mire.

It suddenly becomes clear to you that you live in your own private world of torment, controlled by fears that dictate your cowardly behavior. This has provided you with a relatively safe daily routine and a relatively screwed up psyche.

You suppress this revelation. Block it out. Albert's right, it's just existential bullshit. Push it to the background and read your latest email.

Bonhomie, I'm serious about Syria. If I don't have a story from you by the end of the day, you're on the bloody Friday night flight to Damascus. DS.

You recoil from the message and fight the urge to peer into Symons' office. You lose and take a furtive glance. Symons' baldpate hovers above his screen, lit up and aimed at you like some menacing, bullying, glistening cone of flesh. You look back at your monitor. Damn him, emailing you from five feet away. He hasn't even got the guts to walk over here and speak to you face to face.

You'd better respond.

No problem. Cheers, Cedric.

Now you're really screwed. You're going to have to come up with something fast. A wave of panic starts to rise inside you again.

Oh God, how did I end up in this bloody awful machine, you think. You need some air, or you need to move or something, but you know that you will have to sit at your desk for at least another hour before it will be permissible to visit the tearoom.

You look up again, but this time a live feed from the "southern floods" screening on one of the many office TV's captures your attention. You watch as a young female reporter courageously faces the camera. Knee deep in water and bundled up in network issue Gore-Tex she speaks rapidly and earnestly of the dangerous conditions enveloping the region. The news helicopter has just dropped her and the camera crew right into the swelling river. Cars float past behind her as she stresses the dangers of being anywhere nearby. She leans towards the camera, sporadically flicking her wet chestnut hair away from her determined sky-blue eyes.

"Again, to repeat the State Emergency Service's earlier announcement. Do not, under any circumstances come anywhere near the river. The water level is rising to extremely dangerous levels and the banks could burst at any time."

This is crazy, you think. Syria, the south, what's the difference? We're just pawns delivering fodder to the couch potatoes—paid a pittance to risk ourselves, day in and day out, and what for? Sell more Audis? Forget about the 24-hour news cycle, it's the 24-hour ad cycle! The reporters get younger, sexier, and more homogeneous by the day. It's basically the same model as the military uses. Get them while they're young. Teach them how to follow orders and do the dirty work. It's disgusting. You pine for the days of journalistic integrity. Yeah, back when—when were those days? Journalistic integrity. It's a bit like saying "sales morality". The words chafe at each other like opposing magnets.

Suddenly the young reporter is swept away in the storm water and the helicopter cartwheels out of control past the cameras. The vision cuts to a cheese commercial.

"More collateral damage," you hear Symons laughing on the phone to someone.

That's it. I've had enough of this. It's time I did something—stood up for what I believe in. *What are you made of Bonhomie!* you hear your seventh-grade football coach scream in your ears.

You'll need to get another coffee to fortify you. Maybe you should have had that shot of whiskey after all. You've got to get out of here before an involuntary scream is emitted from the very depths of your being!

"Hi, Cedric."

"Huh? Oh... Hi, Elise."

It's Elise. You love Elise. She's just got this calm elegance, and a bit of smoldering sexiness that gets you every time.

"Just heading out for a coffee. Would you like one?" you blurt.

"Sorry, Ced, just had a double espresso. Needed it after last night—if you know what I mean." She enjoys you wondering what she got up to.

"Right," you reply.

"You look a bit stressed, Ced. Is everything ok?"

"Yeah—I'm fine. No—it's just this story I'm working on is not really, you know, working out and well, you know, Symons..." you trail off.

She is facing you now, her blouse is unbuttoned to the cleavage and her sleeves are rolled up, ready for business. You're desperately trying to keep your eyes north of the border. She gives you a knowing look, raises an eyebrow and smiles that killer smile again.

"Well, Cedric, just remember who you are and don't let a guy like that get to you. Can you imagine his poor wife?"

"Yes well, I've met her actually," you say.

"How could she do it? You know, *do* it?" she whispers.

Your mind runs images of Symons and his wife the night after his vasectomy. Then your mind runs images of you and Elise in the copy room. Bloody hell, Cedric, you have to stop this, you think. Women's intuition is real and scary! You feel a little pang of fear that she may have somehow perceived your depraved thoughts. She laughs and gives you a look you can't read.

"You're a nice guy, Ced. Too nice for this place."

She drifts off back towards Accounts. God, what do you have to do to land a girl like her?

You head off towards reception, and as you approach the doors you take a final, desperate glance towards Elise's desk. In the distance, you make out a tall, spindly, lecherous, praying mantis towering over her. Bloody Albert. You cannot let this happen. You start to head over there. You need to come up with something fast.

"Hey, Albert," you shout in his direction, "Are you still off to the races on Saturday? I have a tip for race five."

Albert regards your approach suspiciously.

"Well, that's very kind of you, Cedric. But here's my tip: don't bet. It's not good for you. Trust me, my great uncle was a terrible punter—died of his addictions the poor bastard. Left us a fortune though thankfully. Nobody in the family has ever had to work a day since. I like to work though, Cedric. Provides you with a sense of stability, and civic duty you know. We all need to feel like we are making a difference," says Albert barely suppressing his smirk.

Great—what a reversal. Could this day get any worse? You wander back to reception and make your way back downstairs and out into the morning chill. As you walk west along London Bridge Road, you marvel at the constant bombardment of advertising from every visible surface. Christ there isn't a bare brick left in this city! Sometimes you wonder whether it isn't a cruelty to teach kids to read these days. Everywhere you look, brand after brand invading your brain like spam mail.

How on Earth am I going to go back in there? Your heart begins to palpitate again at the thought of it. You don't need a coffee. You're already peaked out on anxiety; a coffee is going to put you over the edge. Maybe just keep walking for a while. Just around the block once ought to do it—help shake out some of those nerves.

You pass by your favorite discount bookstore. You can't resist having a quick look. The stale smell of discount books hits you in the face as soon as you enter. It's no wonder they leave the door wide open even when it's freezing.

A young woman wearing tortoiseshell glasses and an Afghan coat offers her assistance, and you politely decline. She's probably wondering how many times you can browse the same old books day after day. You can't answer that one. There's just something comforting about it. It's the same with libraries. You just feel a sense of peace in there. There's the chance that you'll spot a book by a favorite author that you haven't read, or a gem you didn't know about. You probably know the stock better than she does.

You do your usual circuit starting in the literary fiction section, casting your eye over the spines in the stacks, noting the great names and titles and dipping in here and there for a sample. You pick up a copy of *The Manchurian Candidate* by Richard Condon. It's surplus stock. A black line marked across the base of the paperback forever condemning it to discount status. You flip through a few pages and put it in your maybe pile. You spot Paul Auster's, *Book of Illusions*. You loved the New York Trilogy. It's in the maybe pile too. Ah, Amis. *The Rachel Papers*. Yes, you saw the movie years ago. You vaguely remember a bathtub sex scene. You can't find it. Did you imagine that? Hmm. Maybe pile.

You do a quick scan of the Sci Fi section to see whether any of your favorites have come in. Wait, a Philip K. Dick. Yes, *Clans of the*

Alphane Moon. You check the publication date. It's 1964 so earlier than his best stuff. It's a definite though. For £4 you can't go wrong. But wait on. You've got three others in the maybe pile. That's £16 altogether. That's more than the cost of a brand-new book. You could buy a new release instead. These are old books after all.

You read their jackets again and each time, the initial excitement you felt wanes ever so slightly, until after about ten minutes of indecision you gently return them to their allotted spaces. You tell yourself you'll have a think about it and return later to pick one of them at least. This often happens and you feel kind of deflated and awkward for having spent so much time in the store. Now you're wondering how you're going to leave without buying something. The girl in the sheepskin is going to think you're a real idiot.

You pull your phone out and check your email. Oh no, there's a calendar alert—you've totally missed a meeting! Symons is going to have your nuts! You head straight back to the office, your brain madly crunching excuses.

You hurry through reception frowning as though something terribly important has happened. As you rush towards your desk to grab your notepad and pen, you notice Symons' glass chamber is empty. A pang of fear jabs at your stomach. You hurriedly make for the meeting room and maintaining the frown, you slide the door back gently and enter with your head down, taking the nearest empty chair.

You look up warily and scan the room. All eyes are on you. Your head swims as the suits and faces come into focus and you realize that you have walked into the morning executive meeting. The head of human resources shoots you a withering look as you rise and excuse yourself quietly.

You head straight for the bathroom, head spinning, wondering what you will say to Symons when you see him. You settle on the bank manager. Yes, you were called to an urgent meeting with your bank manager and there was nothing you could do to delay or reschedule. You hoped that you could catch up via the meeting minutes. Wait, you were supposed to take the minutes! This is getting worse and worse. You enter a stall and sit down for a second. You take out your phone and search for the latest news on Syria.

Fears Assad will use chemical stockpile to end resistance…

Well, the guy has form, you think. It's only a matter of time. He can only avoid check for so long. The West have been trying to bring him down for years by funding rebel groups, but now they are looking at a power vacuum that could leave the spoils to Al Qaeda and The Islamic State. Assad's already lost control of three quarters of the country and he's backed into a corner with an army that's lost its stomach. If it weren't for the Iranians, he would have been gone a long time ago.

You scan the article and note the growing list of missing 'freelance journalists'—college grads with iPhones—who have crossed into Syria hoping to fund their holidays by capturing some grisly footage for the Times or the Post but have ended up themselves becoming grisly footage for the Times or Post.

You really must quit this caper. Maybe you could write a book on FEAR. Maybe it would be a bestseller. They say you should write what you know. Yes, of course. You can see it now, Cedric Bonhomie, international celebrity author of FEAR. Exposing all the terrors of life on Earth. Deconstructing the paradigm of horror imposed by THEM, the power elite who cruelly manipulate US into submission.

That's it! It will be a series. A bestselling series: FEAR followed by THEM followed by US. You will probably start a revolution! Hang on, Cedric, that's the last thing you need. Maybe just stick to hiding out here in the bathroom for the time being.

Suddenly, your email alert sounds, and a message rudely appears.

Where the hell are you, Bonhomie?

The sound of a phone keyboard clicking away at full volume emanates from the stall next to you.

This is it, you think, this is about as low as I want to go. Here you are hiding in a toilet stall, tolerating a disgusting performance of bathroom multitasking to avoid facing your boss. Peering down at the gap in the cubicle wall, you notice a pair of black, scuffed riding boots. Oh God! It's Symons! Your brain pulsates on high alert as the proximity of your foe is computed. You type a hasty reply.

I'm not far. Sorry, just been a little tied up.

You hit send causing a loud WHOOSH. Damn that fiddly silent button! You feel your face flush as you hear a loud DING in the stall next to you. You feel like game... Quarry.

Get in here now.

What? What does he mean? Your shallow breathing and lack of movement must be sending out suspicious signals. You bring your knees to your chest in a defensive position. Kind of like a duck and cover brace for a nuclear attack. You hear paper rustling. Hurry up. Just hurry up, you think.

Finally, you hear the door squeak open, and clang shut. The faucet runs, the hand dryer blasts, the main door bangs. You stay listening for further signs that the coast may be clear, count to ten and slowly prepare to leave the cubicle. Christ, what a morning.

You head for your desk, ready to face the music. You can see Symons' enormous cranium protruding above his screen like a bright red volcanic island about to erupt.

This is crazy, you think. I'm not going to let myself be bullied and treated like some naughty schoolboy. I'm a grown man.

As you stop to turn back, you are caught at forty paces by the laser like grip of Symons' yellow eyes.

"Bonhomie! In my office now!"

"I'll be right there, sir."

"Now!"

"Yes, sir!"

"What do you take me for, Bonhomie, a fool? Do you think I was born yesterday?"

"What? No, of course not. I—"

"I know you've been avoiding me, Bonhomie," he says holding up his phone and pointing to a tracking App on the screen. "I know exactly where you have been all morning."

Jesus, I should have known this guy would have us all under surveillance. Your mind starts to whir with flashbacks to all the long lunches, coffee breaks and timed appearances. My God, how could I have been so naive?

"You think we pay you to bumble around filing excuses? Now I want that story on my desk by the end of the day, or it's beards and hijabs for you, my friend."

2

"Would all passengers please fasten their seatbelts and prepare for take-off."

A flight attendant busies herself rearranging the luggage in the locker above you. When she glances down, you halfheartedly avert your eyes by pretending to read the in-flight magazine that's sitting in your lap. You notice the magazine is upside down and feel your cheeks flush.

Up in the air you order a Scotch and soda. Wedged between an elderly woman and an elderly man, you are hoping that they are both non-English speaking. It's a fair way to Istanbul and you are determined to find a way to sleep out most of the journey. A couple of sleeping pills should help. You wash them down with the Scotch, close your eyes and wait for the comfortable numbness to arrive.

Something smells a bit like licorice. I bet it's the old lady's soap, or is it the old man's hair pomade? God, I don't know if I can tolerate that wretched stench for the entire flight. Hurry up drug cocktail do your thing, knock me the hell...

• • • •

"Sir, please. Sir, wake up." You open your eyes to a floodlit cabin. Slowly the aircraft interior comes into focus, and you realize that all the seats are empty. What the—? Are we—?

"Sir, we are landed," says the stewardess sternly.

"Sorry. I must have overslept," you say smiling awkwardly.

You fumble under your blanket to remove your seatbelt and notice a cool wetness brush the back of your hand. Christ, you must have spilled your drink down there or something.

"Sir, you must leave the aircraft now."

"Of course," you say.

15

You throw off the blanket to reveal a rather obvious wet patch on the crotch of the new army pants you bought for their romantic foreign correspondent vibe. The oaky aroma of single malt whiskey wafts up.

The stewardess shoots you a look that indicates that you may have already outstayed your welcome in her country. You take down your hold-all from the overhead compartment and awkwardly heft the bag to waist height in front of your body, as you take the walk of shame past the galley and the other stewardesses, none of whom meet your glances or utter a word as you depart the aircraft. You need to find a bathroom with a hand-dryer. Fast.

Exiting the aircraft, you feel a blast of warm air hit you through the leaky seals in the aerobridge walkway. Maybe my pants won't take long to dry in this heat, you think.

Entering the terminal, you notice the usual wall hangings showcasing the country's natural wonders and welcoming the arrival of various nationalities in their various languages. You feel the burning sunshine pouring in through the windows battling the air conditioning for supremacy, the bright light forcing you to squint your way forward. Several long empty corridors lead you finally into passport control and customs. It looks like most of the passengers have already gone through to the arrivals hall and you feel upbeat as you weave through the roped barriers to a waiting customs officer. The young official throws you an evaluative glance, then shifts her attention to her computer screen. You keep your bag firmly at waist height.

"Passport please."

"Ah, yes. Here it is," you say, fishing it from your bag.

You just want to get through now and get to your hotel as soon as possible. The official checks the photo and abruptly fixates her eyes on yours. You notice her expert mascara.

"How long do you expect to stay in Turkey?"

"Well, I expect to be here for a few weeks. I am a journalist with The Daily. I'll be doing some local travel type pieces, you know, that sort of thing." You're hoping that you won't have to go into this too much and you are not too sure how much you should say really. You start thinking about *Midnight Express*. You feel a bead of sweat roll from your armpit down your left side.

"Here are my credentials." You hand over your press pass, confident that this will satisfy any concerns the young lady may have.

"One moment, sir."

She returns her gaze to her screen and begins to type. Her face is inscrutable. You suddenly feel a bit lightheaded and worried at the increasing length of time she is taking to look up.

"Where do you think I should start with sightseeing in Istanbul?" you ask nervously as she continues to punch keys and flip pages in your passport. She does not respond.

"You will come this way, sir."

She motions to an unmarked door about 50 feet away to the left of where you are standing. It appears to have some kind of reinforcement in the frosted glass window. Your stomach sinks as you prepare for the worst. Why do you feel so guilty? God this is just what I thought was going to happen. I must somehow unconsciously will this kind of thing.

She buzzes the door open and gestures for you to move inside the room. The room is hot, there is a ceiling fan moving at about one revolution per second. Behind a large brutalist wooden desk sits a heavyset, middle-aged man with large brown eyes, a thick black moustache, and a relaxed demeanor. He is decked out in military garb and looks like some kind of police officer. On the desk sits an overstuffed brass ashtray, which is connected to a crudely welded model of a fighter jet. On the wall above the desk is a framed photo of Ataturk, the revered father of modern Turkey. Your imagination runs wild at the scenes that must have played out in here over the years.

"I see you are admiring my ashtray."

The Turkish inflection giving the man's English an authoritative impact as though you were being commanded to admire the man's ashtray.

"It has great sentimental value for me. In this ashtray I have extinguished a lifetime of cigarettes. Cigarettes that I have smoked in deep thought, in times of crisis, in times of war and in times of peace, this ashtray has served me."

In saying this the man pulls a soft pack of Marlboro reds from his shirt pocket and offers you one. Reflexively, you take one as the man eyes you suspiciously. He takes one for himself and lights up with a brass Zippo that matches the brass ashtray. He leans across the desk, flame aloft and lights yours up too. You feel the heat of the flame on your face, smell the lighter fluid, and hear the mechanical clink of the Zippo being snapped shut.

"This ashtray, Mr. Bonhomie, was given to me a long time ago by US Air Force Major Rick Glaseborn, who was Assistant Air Attaché in Ankara from 1962 to 1967." The man's thick eyebrows arch and his bulbous eyes search yours for reaction. You find yourself involuntarily raising your own eyebrows and detect a knowing glance from the big official.

"If you look carefully, you will see that his name and rank are etched into the brass. He was a highly decorated veteran of the Korean War and was very well liked. A charming man, full of intriguing stories and he never let the truth get in the way of a good one.

"Major Glaseborn had a number of these ashtrays specially made by a local artisan and often presented them to dignitaries, military personnel and others he came to know while stationed here in Turkey."

You feel the hard edges of the wooden chair digging into your legs, mortified, and distracted by the occasional waft of Scotch emanating up from your trousers. What on Earth is he on about?

"These ashtrays provided an enormous amount of intelligence to the Americans at a critical time in the Cold War, Mr. Bonhomie. And so, you will know why I so prize it. It reminds me every day to be on guard. To be wary of spies."

You stiffen and try to induce your saliva glands into action. The cigarette smoke is irritating your equally dry eyes, causing them to water.

"Here in Turkey, we live in, let's say, a somewhat volatile region, Mr. Bonhomie. We are a cautious people, as you must understand given our long and complex history of relations with our surrounding neighbors. As you would well know, we have many friends and enemies. You will appreciate that in these times we must be vigilant, perhaps more vigilant than ever in our security efforts."

The big man pauses to take a long drag on his Marlboro.

"So, Mr. Bonhomie, I will ask you now, what is your business in Turkey."

In the fog of weariness clouding your brain the voice of Symons cuts in. *No matter what they ask you Bonhomie, don't bloody tell them the truth. You're too bloody honest, Cedric. That's your main problem.*

"Well as I was trying to explain to the young lady at immigration. I am a journalist with The Daily, I've been sent here to do some travel writing. You know the Grand Bazaar, Blue Mosque, hot air ballooning over Cappadocia, that sort of thing. I expect it to be a wonderful experience. I hear Turkey has so much to offer the casual tourist. Which is what I am, just a casual, um, tourist that is interested in showcasing your beautiful country to a national audience of two million other, er, casual tourist types, like me."

The big man cocks his head slightly and his eyes narrow. He can smell a lie a mile away. What are you doing, Cedric? You're a greenhorn. Are you really going to attempt a battle of wits with this guy? You feel your heart palpitating as you hear yourself go on about your interest in Turkish culture and cuisine. Your invisible balloon of lies inflating like a giant gum bubble about to burst all over your face.

"Enough, Mr. Bonhomie. You have revealed yourself."

Oh no. What do I do? Do I call the embassy? Christ, I'm done for. You take a large drag on your cigarette. You manage a smile.

"Mr. Bonhomie, you may leave. My advice to you is that you stick to the roads well-travelled, whilst you are here in Turkey. Peculiar behavior by peculiar people is noted here and can lead to many unpleasant outcomes. We wish for you to have a pleasant if uneventful stay. I trust that I am making myself clear."

"Of course. I hope my stay isn't unpleasant and eventful. I mean... thank you, sir."

God you are an idiot. You have revealed yourself, he said. What did that mean? He's seen us before. Many times. He's probably sitting there now appalled at our lack of creativity, the same travel journalism nonsense he's heard a thousand times. Let this be a lesson to you, Cedric. These guys are operating at a level way beyond your comprehension. You need to be smarter. Think ahead. Try to be subtle for Christ's sake. Otherwise, you are going to end up in some very hot water.

The young lady reappears, and you are shown through to the arrivals area. You spot your brand-new purple rucksack on a lonely journey around the carousel. It's heading for the return hatch. You take off at full pace towards the end of the iron belt and watch in despair as it disappears. You stand there, tired, and despondent, wishing you had had the guts to tell Symons to go and shove this assignment.

When the bag turns up again, it's clearly been opened. They didn't even bother to pick the locks. Just cut them with a bolt cutter and left them hanging off the zippers.

You head out to the concourse and immediately a dozen smoking taxi drivers descend on you. Cigarettes hit the ground left right and center. You settle on the first in best-dressed policy and go with the one who grabbed your bags. He is walking quickly, and you wonder whether he isn't actually trying to lose you. But no, there he is again. Your bag is gone but he is leaning against a cab, another cigarette freshly lit between his fingers.

"Empire Hotel, please," you say.

The driver nods.

"Where is my bag?" you ask.

"It's in," he says, gesturing to the boot.

"Oh, can I see please?" you say. The look he gives you feigns surprise and suggests you may have accused him of theft.

"I mean I need to get some papers. Hotel information. In my bag," you say. You rustle around for something that looks like hotel information but there is nothing that resembles it in your bag, and you come up empty handed.

The reeking cab ride into central Istanbul is uncomfortably tense. The driver seems palpably wounded by your callous questioning of his integrity. God, I'd rather be back in the interrogation room, you think.

You arrive at the hotel and the driver quickly jumps out to retrieve your bags. The weathered signage above the main entrance reads "Hotel" and you have a strange impulse not to enter. The driver passes you with a grin on his way back through the front door, having already delivered your bags to reception. You round up the fare and pay the man, hoping the small tip will alleviate any ill feeling. You resist the urge to ask after your bags again. He pockets the cash, smiles and drives off leaving you in a white cloud of carbon monoxide.

You enter the hotel lobby and through the dimness make out the front desk. Warily you approach the waiting receptionist, a tall thin young man wearing an ill-fitting wash and wear suit.

"Good morning, sir," says the man.

"Good morning" you say, feeling an increasingly anxious vibration emanate from your interior.

"Er, I have a booking I believe under the name of Bonhomie. Cedric Bonhomie. It will have been arranged by my employer, The Daily."

"Of course, Mr. Bonhomie. Let me see. Yes, we have a room ready for you. If you could please fill in these forms and pay 100 Lira cash deposit, you will pay the balance upon departure."

"Ok fine," you say.

He hands you the forms. "Hotel Celi" it says at the top. Hotel Celi? What the hell? This is not my hotel.

"Excuse me there has been a mistake," you say flatly.

"A mistake sir?"

"Well, no. Actually, there has not been a mistake," you say. "I need my bags please. Now," you add abruptly.

"Certainly, sir," says the man. "Your luggage has been taken to your room, sir. If you will fill in the forms, you may have the key. You will be staying one night, yes? One night, comes to 100 Lira, sir." You feel a wave of anger rising.

"You know, this is not a very nice way to welcome visitors to your country."

"Would you like some tea, sir? We have complimentary tea here in the lobby, sir."

"Listen I want my bags, and I will be leaving now. Do you understand?"

"Yes, Mr. Bonhomie, but your reservation for one night must still be paid, we cannot accept late cancellations, Mr. Bonhomie. You must understand we are now left with an unoccupied room that we could otherwise have sold. This is not a nice way to do business, Mr. Bonhomie. In Turkey we honor our agreements."

"Listen. The only agreement here was between you and that bloody taxi driver. Now you bring me my bags, before I call the police. I will not be held to ransom."

You feel your heartbeat quicken and the adrenaline start to flow. The man eyes you with a cool gaze signaling his well-practiced mastery of the situation.

"Mr. Bonhomie, your reservation is here in my reservation book. I doubt the police will have much to say other than that you should pay what you owe to this establishment. I must take exception to the allegation of impropriety, Mr. Bonhomie, and would welcome that we discuss this matter with the relevant authorities."

You detect half a smile on the man's full lips. He's enjoying this. It breaks up the monotony of his boring job, you think. He probably isn't even the owner. Probably just pockets the 100 Lira and makes a week's wages every time some poor bastard gets dumped here. I wonder what he pays the driver, 10 Lira maybe? Screw this guy, you think. Let's play along then, see where this goes.

"Ok, I'll stay then," you say.

"Excuse me, sir?"

"You heard me. I'll stay."

"Very well, sir. I am very pleased to hear it. If you will pay the 100 Lira cash deposit covering your first night's stay, I will show you to your room."

"And what if I don't," you say.

"Well, sir, it is the hotel's policy that one night's deposit is taken on every guest room prior to provision of the room key. Without paying the deposit you may not enter the room, sir."

"Okay, by the way, did I mention that I am here to research and write travel stories for The Sunday Daily? It is your Bureau of Tourism that is paying my way here and I will be providing them with detailed reviews of all my encounters in Istanbul prior to publication."

You sense a power shift.

"No, sir, you most certainly had not mentioned this," says the man looking off to his left.

"Here is my accreditation." You hold it up for the beady-eyed toad.

"I'm sure the Bureau and your manager will be most interested to hear all about my experience here. In fact, why don't I take it up with your manager now?"

"Ah... Yes, sir, the hotel manager is not available at this hour, however I will be sure to pass on your concerns."

"Well, how about later, I would prefer to speak with them in person, perhaps after I have settled in and drafted my piece?" The beady eyes blackening, a greyish paleness emerging, the smile thinning away. He is clearly in retreat.

"Sir, as you feel so aggrieved at what appears to be an administrative error on the part of your employer, I will be willing to accept a nominal fee in compensation for our loss. 20 Lira will suffice as payment for the room should you wish to depart without further delay."

You slap 10 Lira on the desk. The man looks at it in disgust and puts it in his coat pocket. Looks like you guessed right. The guy has broken even. He picks up the phone and speaks a few curt words in Turkish. You glance back towards the entrance and notice a bellboy dumping your bags on the pavement out front.

"Good day, sir," says the man as you turn and march through the lobby and out into the bright noisy lane. You scan the street for a cab and almost hail one before stopping yourself. There's no way you're going to go through all that again. You pull out your phone and check for a signal. There are about a dozen text messages on your screen welcoming you to various networks. You are roaming. You pull up the details of your hotel and punch in the number.

"Good morning, Empire Hotel, can I help you?"

"Yes, my name is Cedric Bonhomie I have a reservation for tonight and I would like you to send a driver to pick me up from the Hotel Celi please," you state loudly in the direction of reception.

"Certainly, sir. We will have our driver collect you this minute."

"Thank you," you say through your Cheshire grin.

Istanbul one, Bonhomie one. That's the way, Cedric, you tell yourself. Sharpen up. This place is a bloody shark pool.

3

The Empire Hotel sits smack in the middle of Beyoglu in the European precinct. Known for its nightlife, you feel confident that you will find plenty to distract you from the fearful business you have been tasked with. You have no intention of meeting up with the contacts provided by The Daily, for a few days at least. After all, you feel it's only reasonable and civilized to allow yourself to acclimatize to the place before the insanity of your assignment commences.

You stand, naked, at the twelfth story window of your hotel room, freshly showered and ready for action. You survey the cityscape from your perch, marveling at the blend of ancient and modern. There must be eighty odd cranes at work on new towers out there. You stare in amazement at the azure seas of the Bosphorus, hugging the Old City like a giant moat. You imagine yourself an Ottoman Prince gazing down at the vast empire of riches before you. You are beckoned by a dark-haired beauty lying seductively on the fresh white sheets of the king-sized bed. As you turn to face her, she playfully positions and repositions her hourglass figure, all the while holding your attention with a look of hot anticipation in her big green eyes. You lie down on the bed, flipping channels in your mind between Elise and your imaginary concubine.

I could really do with a coffee, you think, as you promptly drift off into a deep slumber.

. . . .

You awaken and glance over at the digital clock on the side table. 8pm, it says. You must have slept for hours. No longer tired, you decide to venture out for a drink.

Heading out into the night you feel buoyed by the foreign surrounds. The wondrous smell of kebabs has you searching the storefronts in a suddenly ravenous mission to eat. You notice all the signage is in Turkish, not that you expected English, but it is kind of refreshing to not be assaulted by English advertising for a change. Rather a pleasant change to be illiterate, you think.

So many people everywhere. Old people sipping coffee and smoking pipes, young people chatting and flirting in the cafés. Laughter. Music. Life. This is culture. It seems like another world compared to home. This is adventure. You feel alive, more alive than you have in years.

As you walk further, you come across a small girl wandering alone. She couldn't be more than six or seven years old. She is honey blonde and blue eyed, and you sense that she's not from here, a refugee maybe. She comes towards you and holds her hand out with a smile on her face. You awkwardly stop. She stands before you expectantly and you reach into your pocket for your wallet. Hesitantly you pull out five lira and give it to her. She gives you a look that tells you she is wise beyond her years, and you feel a wave of sadness come over you.

Suddenly she is gone.

You find a table and try to settle your thoughts. A waiter approaches and drops a basket of bread and a menu in front of you. You gaze out into the square, feeling a sense of dreamy alertness in the warm exotic embrace of Istanbul.

The waiter returns. "Can I get you something to drink, sir?" he says nodding towards the menu.

Jolted away from your thoughts for a moment you sense your mind surfacing to the sounds of the street noise. You isolate each one rapidly as though following the instruments in a wild foreign symphony.

"Sorry, er, yes please. I'll try the Rakia," you say.

"One Rakia"

"Yes, one. Thank you."

God, the cigarette smoke around this café. You're not used to it. You feel a bit lightheaded again. Giddy. The Rakia arrives and you hold it up to your nose drawing in the aniseed vapor. You throw the shot back quickly and feel the burn of the liquor all the way down to the pit of your stomach. You breathe out the flammable air and the warm glow brings an involuntary grimace to your face, accompanied by an involuntary shiver, making you feel involuntarily stupid. You quickly chase the drink with a glass of water and a piece of bread to kill the potent aftertaste, hoping that no one noticed.

The morsel of bread hits your stomach and a pang of hunger registers abruptly. You have to get the waiter's attention. Who knows what this menu says, you think. You can't see any kebabs.

The waiter reappears and after a bit of labored translation you go for the pide, which sounds like some kind of pizza.

Your mind drifts back to work. God, I hate that place. Ten years of drudgery, soul destroying, drudgery. You wonder at where you might be today if you'd had the courage to quit, even five years ago. Just thrown caution to the wind.

Is that a cat or a dog? Looks like some kind of hybrid. This place is so strange. Your phone tings, probably just another roaming message. You check anyway.

Dear children of Turkey. I call you to the streets against this disgraceful coup. A narrow cadre commandeering armored vehicles and weapons in Ankara and Istanbul, behaving as if it were the 1970s. Honorable Turkish nation, claim democracy and peace! Claim the state, claim the nation!

You look up. The door to the café is closed and locked. There is no sign of anyone. The Istanbul orchestra has gone eerily quiet. Something's not right, you think. This can't be for real. Erdogan has this country under his thumb. Has done forever. You notice a queasy empty burn in your gut, and you feel alert but somehow detached. Maybe it's the Rakia. Nope, it's the fear. Familiar as your own reflection. Subconscious fear. You wonder whether you are permanently wired to flight mode. An evolutionary trick that's got you pinned. No, it's no use rationalizing. Why are you even thinking of this? If there's a bloody coup on the way, you better get moving, Cedric!

You jump up from the table and try to catch the attention of a few passersby. By their demeanor, you get the distinct impression that there is not going to be a mad rush of Turkish citizenry *onto* the streets. In the distance you hear machinery—tractors. Tanks! I've got to get out of here!

Your mind catches up to the adrenaline that your body had already started pumping well before you were sure about what was going on. Wait a minute. This could be an exclusive, Cedric! You could provide the world with first-hand coverage of a revolution! First-hand! This is it! This is your chance!

You imagine yourself riding a tank with the revolutionary vanguard through the streets of Istanbul. Crowds cheering as the government announces its surrender. You imagine the euphoria of the people dancing in the streets and throwing scarves and flowers into the night sky as you capture the events on video and calmly narrate them for the entire world.

Get a grip, Cedric; you're such a romantic! Are you kidding? Riding a tank with rebels? You need to get back to the hotel and you need to get there fast.

You hear Symons ordering your spineless arse out into the square. Why has he got such a hold over me? I wish I had never met him, you think. It's just ridiculous that another human being can invade your thoughts and intrude on the privacy of your mind like that. And it happens regularly, even when you're just going about your daily activities like shopping for groceries—or navigating a coup. You might be quite happy, even enjoying a rare moment of calm and something will remind you of him—the eczema on some pasty bald guy's head or something—and it gets you thinking about him and just destroys whatever fragile peace of mind existed.

Screw him. You need to look after numero uno.

You look around feverishly for a cab to take you back to the hotel. The roar and scream of the tanks suddenly sound close, like the garbage trucks that wake you at 5.30 am every Thursday morning back home. One minute they sound like they're miles away, the next minute they're revving past your flat, tossing bins full of garbage into their gaping hatches like Popeye swallowing giant cans of spinach.

You shiver and notice that you have begun to sweat profusely through your light cotton clothing. A hot flush comes over you. You start walking quickly away from the noise and try to follow a few people who seem to know where they are going—a woman and an elderly man. You catch them quickly and realize they are too slow to follow, so you keep moving.

Suddenly there is a sharp crack, then another, followed by a volley of shots. You hear people screaming and a flood of people pour onto the previously deserted street you are scrambling along. You are swept away in a morass of panicked humans, foreign, shouting, calling out. You scramble your way forward blindly, confused by the current of humanity surging along the cobblestones, waves of bodies breaking away down ancient, walled tributaries towards the Black Sea.

You sense a parting of the waters. You stand still like Moses with the roiling masses seemingly folding back on themselves. Ahead, a tank moves through the crowd cutting a swathe through everyone and leaving a wake of bewildered, angry citizens in a choking black haze. Its ominous bulk is headed straight for you. You are glued to the spot—as though your feet were stuck in wet concrete. The tank edges closer only meters away. Everyone has moved. You *can't* move.

Your head spins. You hear the crowds cheering around you. They think you are deliberately staring the tank down! The noise is deafening. Everything seems to be slowing down, except for the tank. It seems to be speeding up!

You drop to the ground and lie flat on your stomach as the hulking machine roars right over the top of you.

Next thing you know, you are being pulled to your feet by some locals. They are hugging and holding you. They pick you up and hoist you onto their shoulders, chanting and cheering. Somehow, you are alive.

You look out above the sea of heads into a million flashing phone cameras blinding and dazing you. This is the most frightening night of your life. Like a nightmare. Strange faces flash before you and bare, sweaty, muscular arms pull you this way and that until finally, you are hoisted up onto a statue of Attaturk.

Trembling, you stand and grip the man's elbow, which is frozen in a cast iron salute. You are still vibrating all over—like you just let go of a giant jackhammer. I can't believe... I have just been run over... by a bloody... tank.

Exhausted, you raise your hand to block out the camera flashes rapidly lighting you up in the darkness. You stand erect, motionless, the center of attention. You feel your feet slip, your balance is lost, everything goes black.

* * * *

"Ce-dric."

"Ce-dric." The tone of the voice is abrupt, intended to wake.

You hear your name. You feel warm and cozy. You are conscious, floating. There is infinite blackness. You see a white light. You see stars, billions of them, an entire universe of stars—mysterious constellations—the blackness returns.

"Ce-dric."

"Ce-dric."

It's dark in this bar, you think. You notice Albert standing with a couple of young girls; you think it must be those interns again. The one with the long blonde hair is wearing a kind of loose black chiffon blouse—you can see the silhouette of her breasts, her toned midriff and navel ring showing through above her skintight leather pants. The brunette is wearing an oversize denim shirt unbuttoned halfway and tied over a tight white skirt. The cuffs of the shirt rolled up revealing an assortment of jeweled bangles and bracelets around her thin wrists. Both girls seem to be pretending to laugh. He must be talking utter rubbish, you think.

You decide to go over.

The blonde quickly takes you by the hand. The music is loud—too loud to hear what anyone's saying—she drags you over to the dance floor. You glance back and notice Albert and the brunette, now sitting closely on a lounge chair. She has her hand on his leg. He is still talking, smiling, their faces only inches apart—her smile wide.

The blonde starts to move to the music. She's pretty. Way too pretty for you, Cedric. She pulls you close and puts your hands on her waist as she dances to the beat. You feel slight surprise and then excitement at the feel of her soft feminine contours. She twirls inward towards you, and you embrace her from behind. She leans her head back and looks up into your eyes playfully. Her hair is soft and long. You want to kiss her.

Suddenly, the music stops, and the lights come on. Oh no—its closing time, you think. The lights are so incredibly bright.

"Ce-dric."

"Ce-dric."

The light is blinding. A man's face appears. The face has a huge nose, lots of tiny blackheads on it, thick, black-framed glasses over thick black eyebrows, and a thick thatch of black hair.

"Cedric, do you know where you are?" says the face. "You are in the hospital Cedric, in Istanbul. Okay? How is your pain? Okay? You are comfortable, no?"

The room starts to come roughly into focus; you see a couple of men in uniform at the door. You lift your head from the pillow and the effort it takes shocks you. You suddenly feel afraid and wonder what has happened.

"It's alright, Cedric, you will be okay," says the face. "You have been in a trauma—a big disturbance on your nervous system, Cedric. But you will be okay now. Do you have pain? What is your level of pain, Cedric? If you are on a scale for the pain—what is the pain level? Okay? Six, eight? You will control the pain level with the morphine button, Okay? Just press and you will see—you will be comfortable. Okay? You will be okay now, Cedric. Okay?"

You want to speak, but you can only nod. A weak kind of half nod that is wobbly and blurry. You take a deep breath and close your eyes. You drift off to sleep again.

You awake to find you have been moved to another room. You feel very heavy and weak. A tall thin Turkish man with a bandaged head lies in the bed next to you. He is eating ice cream with an imbecilic grin on his face. Watching you, he starts to laugh hysterically. He somehow reminds you of your father, the way he looked as a young man around the time you were born—the way he looked in old photos—when he had a moustache. Somehow this makes you feel undignified, like this guy has been planted deliberately as some kind of cruel joke.

"Tank Man!" the imbecile speaks. Hooting with laughter now the man appears to be clutching for something beside his bed. You wonder whether the man was beaten by soldiers. You imagine him provoking them with that grin and getting his head caved in by a truncheon or two.

The man picks up a folded newspaper from his side-table and lifts it into your line of sight. You see the Turkish headline, but you have no idea what it means. The paper folds into its full length and you stare at it in horror.

I'm a dead man.

My God. I look like I am *leading* the goddamned revolution. There you are up on the memorial statue with your fist raised in the air. You remember the crowds now, the camera flashes. You look calm and controlled in the photo, even regal.

"Tank man!" cries the imbecile.

"Shhh," you signal to the man to keep it down. Your mind starts to kick into gear.

Christ, I need the bathroom, you think.

The starchy hospital gown rubs against your naked loins. You try to sit up and realize you're in no shape to walk anywhere just yet. A nurse enters the room. She goes to the lunatic next to you and removes the ice cream bowl from his head. You watch her carefully check the man's vitals and make a few notes on the clipboard attached to the end of his bed. She glances towards you and smiles.

"Hello," you say. She smiles again. "Um, I really, really need to go to the bathroom," you say. You look around the room for any sign of a toilet door. The nurse seems to be oblivious to what you are saying. "I need to pee," you say. The nurse looks up from the charts and smiles again. She comes over to your bedside and starts to take your pulse. "Excuse me," you pull your hand away. "I really need to go, please. Can you help me to the toilet?" The nurse frowns and gestures for you to put your arm out. "Listen, I have just woken up and I really must go to the bathroom. If you don't mind, I really..." you gesture to your crotch, pleading her with your eyes. She frowns again. "No, no, you don't understand," you say. The nurse's expression now blank with a hint of irritability.

Oh God, I'm going to wet the bed.

It suddenly dawns on you that she might think you are like him—that crazy guy next to you. Hang on, why would she think that? A cold realization hits you. Am I in an asylum... in Istanbul? Oh, Jesus God. No.

You roll over onto your side and in a kind of flat panic you try to get up out of your bed. The nurse tries to stop you, but you are determined to stand. She takes a couple of steps back and then quickly she heads for the door.

Standing now, you feel groggy from whatever it is they have been pumping into you. You try to take a step forward and manage to retain your balance somehow.

"Tank man!" cries the young resembler. If that fool says that one more time, I'm going to...

Where's my phone? You need to call someone to help you get the hell out of there—but who? You're in big trouble this time, Cedric.

Damn, where's Albert when you need him? He'd get you out of this jam. He'd know exactly what to say. Problem is he's on the other side of the world, most likely being attended to by some beautiful brunette. Probably Elise. That bastard. You have a very strong feeling of de ja vu. You try to hang on to it, but it quickly slithers away like a startled reptile.

Oh no, here comes the doctor, "Cedric, please, you must rest my friend. Okay? Please, Cedric. Here, lie down," he says taking you by the arm.

You follow the doctor's orders. If truth be told, you feel completely fragile, absolutely wrecked—like, well—you've just been run over by a tank. There's nothing to be done. You shuffle back to the bed and slump yourself back down. You inhale and exhale deeply and stare up at the ceiling in defeat.

"I need to piss," you say, maintaining your gaze. The doctor bends down and produces a bottle from beside the bed and hands it to you.

"Best you rest, Cedric. Stay where you are, okay? Everything can be taken care of. You are in good hands here, Cedric." He looks at you with kind eyes. You somehow feel safe with this doctor like he genuinely wants to help you. A very kind bedside manner. He is young and gentle and thoughtful. I like this man you, think.

You wish you could have been a doctor—such a noble career. Like Albert Schweitzer. A great, great man. A great thinker of thoughts, a great doer of deeds. A giant of morality. How do these people do it?

Reverence for life, you think. A great reverence for life at the center of their being. There is something that drives them to do good in the world. Of course, there are doctors without scruples, they can't all be perfect. Some are even bastards, you think. Perhaps many. But every now and then you meet one like this guy. A serenity to him that is almost holy. So, you feel safe, and you are safe. And you sleep again.

• • • •

When you wake up you feel ravenous. I don't care where I am. I need to eat, you think. You fumble around your bedside, looking for a way to call the nurse. There must be a call button here somewhere.

Aha.

By feeling around, you locate the bulky plastic box hanging beside your bed and grip it in your right hand. You press the button. Nothing happens; you press the button again. No light coming on, and no noise. Hmmm, maybe they're different in hospitals.

You look up at the wall and notice a large oil painting depicting some kind of agricultural scene. A young woman in a long dress holding a loaf of bread stands in a field next to a horse and a cart filled with hay. An older man, perhaps her father, sits under a nearby tree. The young woman walks over to her father and hands him the bread. He proceeds to break the loaf and starts to eat. She kneels before him and opens a satchel lying on the ground. From the satchel she produces a knife, some cheese and a sausage. She proceeds to slice the cheese and the sausage onto a plate for the man. The man hungrily devours the lunch she has brought him and washes it down with some cool wine and water.

You lie transfixed by the scene playing out before you. You have never seen such pure, simple pleasure. Others enter the painting, and it appears that some kind of festivity is underway—people talking and laughing, singing and dancing and eating and sharing all kinds of wonderful foods. You notice that the moon has risen in the sky and the people have lit a huge bonfire. They are glowing with happiness. You feel the warmth of the fire and the comfort of the food and drink. You feel complete peace and tranquility. Bliss—oneness with the villagers.

The young girl offers you some cheese and bread and the old man holds forth a cup of wine for you to drink. You sit there in the field mesmerized by the villagers who are now pulling you into a traditional dance. The Turkish bagpipes wail, and the people move together with arms interlocked in a harmonious rhythm—a togetherness you have never experienced before. You breathe in the night air—the scent of the fresh cut hay and the bonfire smoke on the breeze—the taste of wine on your lips. You see the girl again, she is opposite you now, a link in the chain of joyous humanity. This must be heaven. Have I died?

"Ce-dric."

It's that bloody deep voice again. Leave me alone.

"Ce-dric."

For God's sake. I am happy here, just let me be. The girl in the long dress flashes you a heart-warming smile.

"Ce-dric. Wake-up, Cedric. There is someone here to see you."

Oh, just... wait, someone's here? Who?

You feel yourself being dragged away from the music. The room starts to come into focus, and you recognize the hospital ward again.

"Cedric, you have a visitor," says the voice.

You realize you are staring at the ceiling. It appears to be breathing. You have this strange sensation, like you are filled with strength and warmth. You also feel like everything around you is in a kind of strobe state.

You lean your head to the side and make out two people over in the far-left corner of the room, near the doorway. The bed beside you is empty. It's just you in here now, with these people in the corner having some kind of serious conversation. Full recognition starts to register, and with it a sense of lethargic reality. The rapture is fading and a wave of heavy depression creeps in and steals its seat like some dark interloper.

One of the men in the corner looks over at you. It's not someone you know. You do recognize the other man though—the kind doctor. They continue their conversation in hushed tones and finally the stranger starts towards you.

"Cedric, are you alright?"

"Yes," you reply.

"Cedric, I'm Howard Schuman. I'm from the embassy. Do you know where you are? This is a secure psychiatric facility. Do you understand?"

"Yes," you reply.

"Look the Doctor has told me that you are going to be a bit hazy, from all the sedation. I just came to tell you, that we are taking care of everything and as soon as you are well enough, we will have you out of here. You are in good hands here, Cedric. Not to worry, okay?"

"Yes," you say. "Thank you." You feel your emotions welling up and a great sense of relief. He gives your hand a squeeze, and says he'll be back to check on you tomorrow.

You have never felt so vulnerable and so thankful in your life. What a day. Or has it been a few days? You've lost track of the time.

You look up at the oil painting. God, I'm hungry, you think. You see the young woman with the bread and the old man, and you yearn to join them again.

4

"Look, Cedric, if you want them to let you out of here, you are going to have to accept the doctor's diagnosis. This has become a delicate matter for all concerned, and as you must appreciate there are reasons why it would be best that you take the path of least resistance, so to speak," says Schuman, his face glowing in the morning sunlight.

"What reasons?" you say.

"Well without getting too far into the detail, Cedric, let's just say that these matters, once they involve us, become somewhat political, I'm afraid. A kind of sport really. You know, we want something, they see an opportunity to strike a deal, leverage something out of it. We quietly protest. They quietly stand firm. We point to favours we have done them; they point to favours they have done us. We go around in circles, and we eventually get back to where we started. We come at it from another angle, they've already seen that angle and block it. We quietly protest at their blocking. They quietly stand firm. They make an outlandish demand. We express dismay and feign horror. We make a veiled threat. They stand firm again, but we know they are worried.

"About now we both start to realize what a workable deal might look like, so we start playing our best cards to finish off the game. When it looks like there is a winner, the other one protests they have been cheated, and it starts all over again. Eventually everyone gets tired of it and silence sets in. Usually we wait awhile, try to regain our composure and look for another way to twist their arm. Meanwhile, they will be doing the same thing.

"When we come back to it, usually there will be a whole new slew of accusations from both sides due to a fresh review of all intelligence channels and historical slights. Again, eventually everyone gets tired of it and grumbles about the inordinate waste of everyone's time and finally a compromise is agreed upon. Usually, the agreement is conditional on all sorts of ridiculous demands that have to be watered down one by one until we all walk away feeling completely drained and disillusioned enough not to care what the outcome is anymore."

"Jesus, so what part of the negotiations are we in right now then?" you ask.

"The end part, Cedric."

"What, so that's it then? I have to accept this hideous diagnosis, and they will let me out?"

"If you agree that our government can release a statement explaining that your actions were as a result of psychosis."

"So, I will be portrayed as a lunatic."

"Well, you needn't put it like that, Cedric. Many people have bouts of mental illness these days. It's practically, par for the course unless you are a psychopath. There's no shame in it, Cedric, and it's a sure-fire way out of this whole mess you've got yourself into."

"What about my reputation?" you say. "What do you think this is going to do to my career?"

"Your career? Cedric, you are front-page news! Your actions were beamed and tweeted, shared, liked, and disliked in media all over the world. This will be the best thing that ever happened to your career. You're famous."

Just then your phone dings. You check it. A message from Symons.

Bravo, Cedric. Big plans for this story. Call me.

Schuman is fidgeting now. "Cedric, it's time to face the music. There is a car waiting. I'll be with you. We just step into the Minister's office, exchange pleasantries, sign the papers and you can get back home or do whatever it is you need to do. My advice is to put it behind you, Cedric. What do you say?"

Christ, I don't know what to do. You idiot, Cedric, you don't have any choice. What are you thinking! This is not an option you are being given; it's a bloody international diplomatic incident. You are just a pawn in the game now! For Christ's sake man, get a hold of yourself and do what you are told. Look at poor old Schuman; he looks like he's been put through the wringer... It's time to walk the plank. You'll be out of here, Cedric. Free again.

"I'm staying put," you watch the shock register on Schuman's face.

"Sorry, what did you say, Cedric?"

"Well, I've decided I rather like it here with the all-you-can-eat drugs and ice-cream. So, I've decided to stay. See if I can get back into that painting."

"You... what?" Schuman looks filled with dread. He's probably worried you really are mad after all, and if that's the case he'll never get you to agree that you are. That's the trouble with madness; you can't tell you're mad, so you can never admit you are. People will tell you you're mad, but you won't believe them. Lack of insight—that's what the shrinks call it.

"Listen, Cedric, please..."

"Just kidding, Schuman. Let's get the hell out of here."

· · · ·

The baroque entrance to the Ministry of Health is as imposing as you imagined it would be. Heavily armed police glance your way, as you make your way through security and out into a bright, white marble quadrangle. From there you are escorted through another security checkpoint and an entrance to the rear office complex.

You notice Schuman's erect posture and loping gait as you trail behind him. You wonder how a man develops such grace, or whether it is innate. You envy him, for a moment. He makes you feel like a schoolboy and there is nothing you can do about it. You wonder why it is that some people have the ability to make you feel this way. In the company of most men and women, you feel at least comfortable, if not confident in yourself, however occasionally you meet someone, usually taller than you, who just makes you feel very small and immature for no reason other than their physical presence. It's a very awkward feeling of inferiority that you are unable to control. Invariably you make things worse by trying to overcome the feeling by some kind of embarrassing over-compensation, which the person unconsciously or consciously registers as a defect in your character—evidence that you are not in full possession of yourself.

You feel troubled by this line of thinking and start to feel a little depressed at the prospect that you have failed to develop your character to the point of self-assuredness. Is it a moral failing? Is it just your weaknesses and contemptible behavior and all the tiresome concealment? All that ducking work, the lying and procrastinating and living in fear of being exposed?

It's the deception of yourself and others that ultimately makes you this way. You know this but you continue on, like there is no alternative.

Maybe I am mad. Maybe it's some kind of pathology in my brain... It could be treated. Maybe you need to see someone.

Then again, maybe I'm not deceiving myself. If I am acknowledging my behavior as deceptive, isn't that a moral victory? Aren't I just being honest? Aren't my feelings of guilt recognition of my weakness and therefore validation of the fallen nature of all mankind? Yes, we're all messed up—even Schuman here.

You suddenly feel better.

You are shown into the Minister's office by a bespectacled young man who reminds you of every efficient bureaucrat you have ever come across. He leaves the room quickly.

"Mr. Schuman! How delightful to see you again," says the Minister. You notice he is unusually tall.

"Mr. Cevoglu, we are most pleased to be here. This is Mr. Bonhomie. You will no doubt have heard much about his terrible plight."

"Mr. Bonhomie, how do you do." The Minister's black slicked-back hair shines brightly—the morning sun streaming through the double hung windows.

"Well, I've been better." You notice a brass jet fighter ashtray on the man's desk; you feel a little light-headed.

"Indeed, Mr. Bonhomie, though you must be relieved to be on *provisional* leave from our facility. It must have been a terrible experience for you, this *temporary* psychosis that led to your hospitalization."

"Yes," you hear yourself say. Schuman shoots you a sly look.

"Mr. Bonhomie has accepted that he was not in his right mind at the time of the incident. He was, as Professor B's diagnosis suggests, in the throes of a severe mania, which led to a schizoid break in his psyche followed by extreme delusions of grandeur. All of this appeared to happen quite suddenly—a rare instance of instability which accounts for his inexplicable and infamous conduct in the early hours of last Tuesday morning." Schuman opens a manila folder, pulls the professor's report out and hands it to the Minister.

"Professor B has determined the onset of the psychosis to be the result of acute stress caused by a combination of factors including disorientation due to the foreign environment, coupled with severe anxiety under the perceived, real or imagined, threat of annihilation to himself and others in his immediate surrounds. Mr. Bonhomie has advised that he remembers nothing other than enjoying some bread and a glass of Rakia at a small café nearby, just prior to the incident occurring. He remains severely traumatized by the incident, but now with his equilibrium restored by the excellent medical attention he has received under the care of Professor B, he is most concerned with returning to his ordinary existence."

Well, you have heard horseshit before, but this was some serious equine crap. One thing you were beginning to learn from this whole situation was how utterly fraudulent it was for any outsider to claim to report the truth about any given event they were not directly involved in. All reportage is pure fiction and can only be pure fiction. Life is far too complex to be accurately captured in words—and if you weren't even there? Forget it. Laughable representations, which, are either, gross misrepresentations or just plain self-serving lies.

"I like your ashtray," you can't resist.

"Why thank you, Mr. Bonhomie. It was a gift from a distinguished American airman. A great man, most generous, charming and a true friend; Major Rick Glaseborn was his name. Those were the days, Mr. Bonhomie, when men could be trusted at their word. Isn't that right, Schuman?"

"Couldn't agree more," says Schuman. "Give me the Cold War any day over this bloody mess we are in now. At least you knew who your friends were."

You notice both men stiffen a little. The Minister stands and stares through the glass doors out into the courtyard.

"Mr. Bonhomie. If I may say, on behalf of the government of Turkey, we do apologise for the traumatic experience you have suffered. It was a most unfortunate occurrence that was, under the circumstances, unavoidable I'm afraid. The uprising had to be quashed, and order restored. I am sure you understand the precariousness of this moment in Turkey's history. Decisive action was required and taken.

"There are many who would like to make you out as some kind of revolutionary hero, Mr. Bonhomie. They will try to seduce you to their cause. God knows there are dozens of groups out to wreak havoc on our nation. We need to know that you will resist any such overtures outright and let this whole incident fade into the background. Do you understand?"

You are fixated on the ashtray. You wonder whether he ever knew the Americans were bugging him. If he didn't know, he surely doesn't know that you know. Even if he did know, he still wouldn't know that you know. You enjoy this little secret that you know something that he doesn't know you know.

"We know everything about you, Bonhomie."

Damn, of course they do.

"We've done deep background checks, and we know what you have been up to. No need to feel concerned. We all know each other's business here—I know Mr. Schuman here, his peccadillos and pastimes better than my own wife's." Schuman forces a smile.

"Someone's read all the nonsense you have written for The Daily—not very much I might add. And we have no concerns, other than your knack for being in the wrong place at the wrong time. So, if I may make one thing clear, Mr. Bonhomie, you are welcome to stay here in Turkey, to go about your business and carry out whatever your assignment may be, however I must warn you, we will not tolerate any more incidents of this kind."

Schuman looks positively relieved.

"Well, that seems to be all. Good day gentlemen, I'll have Mehmet see you out."

You feel relieved too and as you walk back through the quadrangle, you notice a spring in Schuman's step, and that his trousers are a little short, hanging about half an inch above the back of his shoes. And it makes you feel kind of sorry for this man who, is ultimately caught up in a charade most of the time, has no privacy and has to be constantly wary of everyone he meets. He's a good man, doing a crappy job—like most of us.

"How about a drink tonight, Schuman?" you say. "You must know a decent watering hole in town. What do you say? You can show me around a bit."

"A drink sounds like a good idea, Cedric. Sounds like a great idea."

5.

It's after sundown, and back in Beyoglu the streets are still deserted. A curfew has been in place for days now and there is a heavy military presence. From the cab you are sharing with Schuman you notice that most businesses remain shuttered and only fleeting glimpses of life in the darkened buildings can be made out.

The driver remains still and mute for the entire journey. You imagine this to be his permanent repose. Years and years of driving people through this city have frozen him into position. Only his eyes shift as he deftly maneuvers through the traffic.

He stops. He still does not move. In a soft whisper he states the fare. Schuman picks it up and you are out onto the corner. A streetlamp provides a weak yellow luminescence. You watch as the expressionless driver eases away into the night. Schuman is loosening his tie.

"This way," Schuman gestures down the street toward a row of terraced buildings that appear to house the usual antique stores and cafés. You notice the quiet and the echo of your footsteps in the emptiness surrounding you. You wonder at the contrast between the streets as you first saw them and the way they are now.

Schuman is headed for a doorway—a faint red glow emanating from what looks to be a stairwell that goes below street level. You follow Schuman through the doorway and down the stairs. At the bottom of the stairs, in a poorly lit annex, you are met by two burly security guards, who ask to see your identification. Schuman shows his diplomatic ID, and you are waved through without any trouble.

Well, that's a first.

You pass through a short corridor and are greeted by a stunningly beautiful hostess wearing a tight black dress who shows you to a nearby table. You smile politely, like a desperate oaf and she politely pays you no attention. There are obviously bigger fish in this tank.

You order a couple of beers and settle into the comfortable surrounds. Red velvet divans and glittering ottoman artifacts decorate the den-like bar and lounge. A jazz trio sets the mood—it all seems to be business as usual, like attempted coups happen every day.

The bar is filled with an exotic blend of European expats, diplomats, the odd military type, plenty of sophisticated, well-heeled Turks and a smattering of unsophisticated journalists. You can tell them a mile off.

You take a swig of your beer and look across the table at Schuman. He raises his bottle to you in a gesture of cheers.

"Well welcome to the house of intrigue, Cedric. This is where most of what passes for intelligence in Istanbul gets manufactured, whispered about, bought and sold. You think you've heard some tall stories before, well if only the walls could talk here my friend. Honey traps, arms dealers, agents, double agents, mercenaries, forgers, counterfeiters, drug dealers, ambassadors, prostitutes, terrorists, crimelords, diplomats, diplomat's wives, diplomat's mistresses, journalists, civil servants, businessmen and con men, and most of the time you'd have a bloody hard time telling them apart. I'll tell you, Cedric it's a bloody viper's nest. Fact is we've all given up on finding out the truth about what each other are up to. All we all know for sure is that everyone is lying and making their next move on how they interpret the next one. This is the real art, Cedric. Anticipating how your friends and enemies will react to the latest layer of lies that are circulating. It's a major headache I'll tell you."

You let this sink in and take another look around the room. Every face takes on a sinister countenance.

You make eye contact with a tall, thin, well-dressed man standing at the bar. He has an air of confidence about him and holds your gaze for a moment, then turns away, eyes narrowing and lips pursing into a slightly wry smile.

"Anyway, Cedric, now that we've extricated you from the vortex of international affairs, what do you plan to do next?"

"Well, I don't know. I haven't spoken to my editor yet. But I suppose I still have a job to do. You know, travel stories, that type of thing."

"Travel stories?" Schuman laughs. "Good God, Cedric, don't tell anyone that's what you're doing, they'll think you're a spy!"

You look back over to the bar. The thin man has gone. In his place are a couple of heavy looking Russians, the kind that look like they could break you in half with their bare hands. They are both staring at you—a kind of double death stare. You grin in a feeble attempt to feign friendliness. This does not go down well. Schuman looks up from his drink and notices you grinning at the Russians.

"Cedric," he whispers, "what the hell are you doing? Don't smile at the Russians!"

"What?" you whimper.

"They are a morose people, Cedric. They don't see it as a friendly gesture. If you smile at them, they think you are laughing at them. Like you are laughing at their hair or something. Got it? You don't want any trouble with those guys, believe me."

Jesus, you start to get that feeling again—the one that tells you that you are in over your head. You gulp down the rest of your beer and listen to Schuman start rambling on again. You order a couple of Scotches from the attractive waitress and this time she smiles at you differently. You wonder what it means.

"The only ones that seem to have a jump on things around here are the Turks. They've got damn good ears everywhere," says Schuman.

"We had no idea this coup was coming, Cedric. No idea! We were having a party at the embassy. The Ambassador was DJ for God's sake! Champagne was flowing—come to think of it the Turks had given us a few crates of the stuff earlier that day. Anyway, one minute we're lurching around the dance floor groping each other, next thing we're at our desks taking furious calls from home demanding to know what the bloody hell is going on, and what we are doing to secure our nationals. It was a bloody fiasco. Needless to say, the Ambassador has been called home early. Lucky bastard. And we're all left here to clean up the mess." He locks his eyes on yours. There's a pause. It's a pregnant one. You can't help thinking Schuman is about to ask you for a favour.

"Anyway, Cedric. Seeing you're going to be around for a bit, I'd like to make you an offer. How about helping us out with a story or two. We need to do a bit of restoration work, if you get my drift and well, fact is, we got you out of a pretty tight jam today." Your dread rises. Your brain computes.

"Fake news is that it?" you say.

"No, no, no, Cedric. We don't do that sort of thing. No need for it really. Christ we're not that important. No, look, it's more we don't want all this terrible business here in Istanbul to undo all the good work we've been doing." He pauses and looks down at the table.

"You know I've been here for five years, Cedric? Five long years I've been posted to this circus, and in the last two days just about everything I have done has unraveled in front of my eyes. We've been quietly keeping the balance tipped in our favour, Cedric, no mean feat in this Aladdin's cave I can assure you. And we're a bit red faced over this whole coup thing and well... there are a few things we've been doing that no one knows about. Things that a good investigative journalist might uncover that could, I guess help to paint things in a truer light for the folks back home. What do you say, Cedric? Will you help us?"

Holy crap, what the hell have you gotten yourself into now? You better think quick, Cedric. It's either continue bumbling around Istanbul on your own and trying to come up with a story for Symons about the coup that quite frankly you can't remember a damn thing about, or else you agree to this mysterious, vaguely exciting and possibly terrifying proposal before you now.

On the one hand you could choose to retain a shred of the integrity that has led you to ten years of failure as a journalist—or you could throw caution to the wind—get in league with someone for a change! Who knows where this could lead? This could be it, Cedric! A chance to break a story with international significance! Espionage? Intrigue? Who knows, even romance?

"I'll do it," you say. Schuman's eyes light up.

"Ok. That's great, Cedric. There's a lot we need to talk about. But we can't talk about it here. This place is full of pixies. Let's get the hell out of here. You need to get some rest. Come and see me at my office tomorrow and we can go over a few things then. I'm really glad you can help us, Cedric."

"What have I got to lose?" you say.

Back in your hotel room, the gravitas of what you are contemplating starts to gnaw away at your insides. *You're just too nice, Cedric. You're too honest, that's your problem, Cedric.* These comments keep surfacing and you keep trying to hold them down. Your conscience is desperately vying for your attention, but you remain stoic.

You have decided. You will look into the pool at your own handsome face and tempt the Fates.

You find yourself staring into the bathroom mirror. Hey, it worked for Narcissus. You admire your flinty expression for a while imagining yourself a Greek hero; so devastatingly handsome you are desired by Goddesses.

An abrupt knock at the door breaks your concentration.

"Mr. Bonhomie, may I come in? You sent for these items, sir?" The room attendant hands you some fresh towels, a shaving kit and a disposable shoe polish. You nod and smile at each other a few times until he leaves the room.

Where was I... Ah yes, the Fates. Even they will not lure you from your mirror. You begin to shave. A fresh start, Cedric, that's all you need. Schuman was right; you just need to put it all behind you.

You think back to the hospital; the kind doctor and that weird guy next to you that reminded you of your father. It gives you the shivers to think about it. Jesus, to think that you could easily still be locked up there and for God knows how long. Those places give you the creeps. The freedom you take for granted was so suddenly stripped from you. You think about the millions of people who have suffered under tyranny and feel slightly ashamed of your relatively minor brush with authority. If you weren't a foreign journalist, things might have been very different.

You've nicked that mole on your cheek again. Damn it. You know the thing won't stop bleeding no matter how much you try to stem it with paper towel. You know you'll have to leave a patch there for at least an hour and even then, it will probably bleed like a fresh gash as soon as you remove it again. When it finally does stop, you'll have a great big black scab there for a few days. All this to look forward to. Well at least you don't have to be anywhere until tomorrow.

You'd better get some sleep. Who knows what Schuman has in store for you? No doubt something you will never fully grasp. From what he was saying it sounds like no one really knows what's going on. Like a bunch of crazy chefs trying to spoil each other's dinners, they just keep throwing in new ingredients to see what will happen to the broth. Of course, you will be just another ingredient, Cedric. Maybe a spice. Just to keep things interesting...

You really need to get some sleep.

• • • •

Over and over, you are run over by the tank. For hours on end, you fitfully wake and then sleep and then return to the horrendous three seconds of pitch-black roaring death passing inches above your trembling body. To begin with you relive the trauma—the shock and confusion. As the night wears on though you become used to it and it just becomes like any other monotonous dream that you wish you could bloody well end somehow. You wonder why your mind gets stuck in these loops and you realize how little control you actually have over your mind.

The fact is your mind is wild. It won't be tamed, and it will design your life for you with little regard for your ego. It's this thought that's most disturbing and actually shoots some real fear into you. What's more nightmarish, the terrors of the unshackled mind in the void of sleep, or the journeys we pretend to chart for ourselves in our waking lives?

You wonder at your life and the path you have taken and feel some disappointment but also a resignation that it could not have been any other way. For you are Cedric Bonhomie, and your mind will take you where it will.

Okay, Cedric. Overthinking things now.

You feel for the alarm clock under the shorts you covered it with. You remove the shorts. The red glow lights up your room like a circle of hell. You feel a deep uneasiness due to the realization that you are thousands of miles from home, alone in a strange city in the middle of the night and probably about to embark on a ridiculous escapade of which you know nothing.

The clock says 5.45am.

You decide to close your eyes again and wait for sunrise. Then again, you can't bear to lie here any longer fretting about every stupid thing that comes into your head. God, you feel like you have to get up just to stop your mind from tormenting you with analysis. Maybe it's a deliberate tactic? Maybe your mind does this on purpose to get you up and facing the day, as though it couldn't be any worse than being tormented by your own idiotic thoughts.

You get up.

At breakfast in the airy, sunny hotel restaurant, you sip hot Turkish coffee and enjoy a simple meal of fresh bread, boiled eggs and fruit. Now in relative control of your faculties again, and despite the realization that you have no control over the inevitability of your destiny, the seed of a thought that may develop into the impulse that leads you to make your next move begins to germinate in your fertile brain.

You can feel the seedling trying to break out of the dark vague recesses of your deepest being. You will it with all your powers of concentration, knowing that it is about to provide you with the next step in your journey. But it remains elusive, this seed of a thought. In attempting to pull out this one thought, you realize that you have generated hundreds of other unwanted thoughts that are now doing their best to distract you from the one thought you were trying to encourage into existence. You are now starting to lose your grip on it. Whatever the stupid thought was it's not going to reveal itself now. You reach for it one more time. Nope.

You notice a young man sitting at a table a few feet away. Probably a student traveler and probably hung-over. It looks as though he is trying to give birth to a thought as well and not having much luck. God what a sorry lot we are. You watch him staring into space awhile longer and start to feel uncomfortable at how much he reminds you of yourself. You think of all the trials the poor guy has ahead of him with a strange mixture of understanding and contempt. You wash down the last of your breakfast with some sickly-sweet orange juice and sign your tab.

As you stand to leave you notice an older middle-aged gentleman at the corner table near the doorway to the lobby staring in your direction. You make eye contact, and he goes back to his newspaper. He's probably thinking the same thing about me. No doubt someone will stare at him at some point today and also think the same thing about him. Are we all so deluded? I don't know, maybe I'm completely wrong. Maybe I'm the only one that does it.

Okay, Cedric, time to go.

You traipse off towards the lobby. As you pass the man with the newspaper you can't help training your thoughts, if not your eyes, completely on him and you feel strangely watery for a second or two. You hate that feeling. It's the awkward feeling you also have sometimes, passing an attractive woman in the street after she has noticed you looking at her. A sense that there has been some kind of unspoken connection that you both noticed and felt but will last no longer than a second. Once the watery feeling disappears you usually experience a marginal loss or gain to your ego, depending largely upon whether or not there was a subtle acknowledgement of your admiration, a flick of her hair perhaps or a slightly more accentuated sway of the hips. With men it's always a loss. Just the fact that you have lost the focus on yourself demonstrates you've already given up your power. Symons used to do it to you all the time—once you feel watery you can almost immediately sense yourself shrinking and the other guy growing. Jesus, you hate that. What a weird sensation to have to deal with. The more you think about it the weirder it seems.

Snap out of it, Cedric, you are halfway down the street, and you don't even know where you're going.

You look up and notice the bright red flowers potted in rows on every balcony and windowsill. The traders are already in full swing. Storefronts displaying rugs and cheap shoes alternating all the way down the bazaar as far as the eye can see. The sun is already pounding the white stone paving, and the people are slowly going about their daily shopping rituals. Bread and summer fruit stalls are popular.

You stop and marvel at a mound of freshly picked Marello cherries stacked three feet high on an old trestle table. Two men stand behind the stall smoking and talking seriously with one another—more interested in smoking and talking seriously with one another than selling cherries, but they pause briefly to sell you some and then carry on smoking and talking as though you do not exist, or if you do, you are so foreign that as far as they're concerned you don't. You shuffle off eating the most delicious cherries you have ever tasted in your life.

You lift your gaze and immediately lock eyes with a young woman, tall brunette, red lipstick, wearing tight blue jeans and a fitted black singlet. She is the very picture of youthfulness. You feel watery. You detect a hint of a smile, all she'll allow, and she's gone forever.

You arrive at Schuman's office feeling upbeat. Even the surly dragons on reception couldn't kill your buzz. You take one look at Schuman sitting behind his desk holding his face up with both elbows planted, and it appears clear that he has had little sleep and is wearing the same clothes he had on at the bar last night. Schuman's face is reddish and as he pulls himself together you notice he has two perfect white palm imprints in his cheeks.

"Cedric, how good of you to come," says Schuman. "Dreadful night down the rabbit hole, I'm afraid. All this monkey business has got everyone a bit excited and flipping switches all over the place. It's causing a hell of a ruckus and damn near impossible to keep tabs on things, if you know what I mean. Anyway... Would you like a cup of tea? Coffee?"

Monkey business down rabbit holes. Your buzz is killed. Now you're on high alert again, straight back up to full trepidation. You're such an idiot, Cedric, what are you even doing here? You could get yourself killed!

"No need to worry, Cedric, we have a very tight operation going here. It may look a bit shambolic to the untrained eye, but we've got all the bases covered. I can assure you."

You may be a bit naïve, but your eye is well trained in spotting cockups, and this situation has all the hallmarks so far. You have the urge to turn around and walk straight back out into the heavenly morning from whence you came, but your curiosity is holding you to the spot.

"You've had all night to reconsider our offer, and you've come in, and I'm glad you have. I've made some arrangements and everything's in place. We don't have much time, Cedric, so I'll explain this to you quickly."

You listen carefully, while Schuman gives you the run down.

"Cedric, as I said to you last night, we've managed keep things finely balanced in our favor up until now and we need to make a few adjustments to make sure we don't slip back down the hill." Schuman's eyes narrow as he concentrates his attention on you.

"Now as you know, there are some seriously crazy things going on down south, and I mean things have really opened up down there. Syria and Iraq, side by side in complete and utter chaos, and every baddie in Babylon trying to stake their claim. The place is teeming with fanatics, warlords, and hardcore terrorists along with all sorts of nutters and wannabe warriors wanting to join in one cause or another. Most of the time we've got them taking care of each other, and we just need to make sure that no one gets the upper hand. But it's no picnic with the Russians and the Iranians doing their damnedest to swing things their way. Not to mention all the switching sides and splintering and turning on each other that goes on. We've been doing the best we can to make sure we know who's who in the zoo, but whatever you do down there you're going to piss someone off. All our friends are friends with our enemies, and all our enemies are friends with our friends you see. Well, you get the picture.

"So anyway, we've had to back a few horses that are not too popular around these parts and well, let's say we've been lightening their load a little, it suits our bosses—we don't want to get our hands dirty and definitely don't want too many boots on the ground with all the war fatigue and whatnot.

"So, Cedric, the upshot is, we think that now might be a good time for someone to discover what's been going on—a story breaks, we have a bit of fun with it, lob a grenade or too and sit back and watch the fireworks."

You nod knowingly and glance around Schuman's office. The walls are made of glass and wafer wood paneling. Maps and pins and flowcharts papering every square inch. You sit transfixed by one in particular. A morass of named arrows forming a dense chart of key players and acronyms, all somehow fitting together neatly to explain the giant puzzle of military conflict that's been going on for the last 15 years. You marvel at the effort that must have gone into this mapping exercise and the vain hopes that it's author may have had at making some sense of the madness for his superiors. How the hell can a bunch of labeled arrows resemble reality?

"COIN", says Schuman. "That's what they call it. Counterinsurgency. Been going on down there ever since Saddam got the old heave-ho. Don't ask me what that bloody chart means, I wouldn't have the foggiest. Some CIA bright-spark's impression of Fallujah. I keep it up there to remind me that what we are doing here is insane. If it's not insane, Cedric, then we must be evil. I prefer to think we've all gone stark raving mad. Of course, COIN is redundant down there now. No doubt there is some other map to explain the situation, meanwhile a million people have been displaced, and half the city has been burnt to the ground."

You feel a bit sorry for Schuman again in this moment and feel a strong resolve to help the guy out. Whatever it is that he thinks you can do to swing things a bit, it seems worth it to you, if only to repay him and lend a bit of support.

"Anyway, as I was saying before, we've been doing a bit of shady stuff down there to stoke some fires a bit up here, and well, we need you to go down to the border. Incognito of course. Once you've been shown around all you have to do is send off a few dispatches to The

Daily that might help the cause. We've already got your papers sorted and you won't have any worries getting there. You'll have good cover—business credentials etcetera. You should know, Cedric, journalists, national and foreign, are being imprisoned by the busload as we speak."

You feel your legs go slightly numb and your mouth dries out instantly.

"Come on, Cedric, I want you to meet a few people." Schuman rises from behind his desk like a gangly black wraith and drifts towards the door.

You clutch the arms of the cheap desk chair and push yourself up and onto your feet. It's too late to back out now. Whatever it is that Schuman thinks you know he wants you to do, you're going to have to go through with it. You try to steel yourself for whatever's next and follow Schuman out into the hall.

You notice a few portraits along the walls of the corridor. Former ambassadors meeting with dignitaries, shaking hands and so on. A chain of meddlers down the ages in black and white. Wait a minute is that Lyndon Johnson with a bunch of airmen? Looks like he's holding one of those bloody brass ashtrays.

"Cedric, are you coming?"

"Yes, sorry."

"Well, hurry up, we can't keep everyone waiting much longer."

You move through the building and out a back exit into a courtyard with a few shabby looking brick buildings that look like old workshops. Schuman lopes toward the one on the right and gestures to you to follow him in through an open barn door. Inside it's dark and musty and your eyes take a minute to adjust. You make out the shape of a vehicle, an ordinary looking orangey hatchback. Inside the vehicle sit three rather serious looking men. You gulp audibly and feel your heart thumping loudly in your chest.

"Alright, Cedric, I'd like you to meet your escorts." The men remain seated in the vehicle and barely acknowledge your presence. The one in the driver's seat looks like a local—he's dressed in regular civvies, jeans, a check shirt and aviator sunglasses, the kind you might buy at a gas station. On this guy, cheap looks cool. He's introduced to you as Joe—you doubt it's his real name. The one in the front passenger seat is red skinned, heavy set with a thinning buzz cut. You guess he's US military and you're right. His name is Riley. Great. Didn't Schuman say we were going incognito? So far, we've got a Turk that looks like Elvis, and a blockhead that would look out of place in any job that didn't require him to point guns at people. In the back seat you have one more character, he appears to be from the subcontinent, Indian or Pakistani. Well, wherever he comes from, he's going to stick out like a sore thumb where we're supposed to be going. He's wearing all black cargo with all sorts of pockets full of Christ knows what. He's smoking a long foreign looking cigarette. His name is Emile.

"Well, now that you've all eyeballed each other, you can get on with it. Cedric, you can swing past your hotel and pick up your bags, but then you best be on your way. You will need to make it through a few checkpoints before you arrive at the safehouse, and you'll want to get there before nightfall. Don't worry these lads have been up and back a few times. They know the road and Joe here knows most of the faces you'll come across along the way. All going to plan you'll be back here safe and sound in a couple of days."

As Joe starts the car, Schuman shoves his head in the window and wishes you good luck and Godspeed, thumps the roof a couple of times and you're away, out into the lane.

6

Back in your hotel room again, you are seriously considering pulling the pin. This is not what you came here for.

As you pack your things, you again start to deeply question whether you are cut out for this whole charade.

For God's sake, you don't even know what Schuman was on about! Come to think of it, whatever Schuman thought he was on about is probably only the half of what's really going on. But it did sound like an exclusive.

Exclusive, Cedric. A word that has not been linked to your name in almost a decade of reporting.

"Wow, they gave you this place?" says the Blockhead with a hint of malice. "Smells like a goddamned pussy parlor in here."

You notice a wry smile on Emile's face. Joe's expression does not change—he's still wearing sunglasses. You notice your tiny reflection.

"You ready, Tank Man?" says the Blockhead.

"Yeah, I'm ready. Let's go," you say.

"Alrighty then! Tank Man says we can go now," says the Blockhead sarcastically.

You're guessing that the Blockhead has a few issues with civilian types like yourself. Perhaps due to the amount of dirty work he's done in your service. That's probably fair enough.

Ensconced back in the orange rust bucket, you start to wonder about these guys. Joe, you think you can trust. He exudes a quiet confidence, just the way he holds himself. He's on a mission and he's a professional. Emile is another story though. In ten minutes, he's told you everything about himself, his family back home, his girlfriends, the nightclubs and sports cars he supposedly owns, the gambling and the money he's making in Syria from "those crazy CIA bastards" and so on.

"You've got to come with me to the island of Goa my friend. Trust me you can PARTY down there," says Emile. "You know what I mean? Freedom man. The only time Goa is no good is when *these* guys come down—mess up everyone's vibe." He's looking at the back of Riley's head. It doesn't move. Just takes up a huge amount of space like a big sandstone paver. He lights up another Gauloise and starts blowing smoke rings at it. They break and snake ominously around its blonde bristles.

"You pussies wouldn't know a party if it jumped up and bit you on the ass," grunts the blockhead. "Ready for a little mood music?" You gape in awe at Riley's enormous forearm and its ornate sleeve of black DEATH tattoos, as he cranks up the volume on the car stereo.

"This is the stuff we used to roll with, lightin' up Hajis round Baghdad," yells Riley through a vortex of heavy metal. "Me and my boys loved this stuff. Spooks used to love it too. Play it all night to the de-tain-ees. They never heard nothin' like it before. You imagine that? You could threaten everythin', waterboards whatever and they wouldn't even flinch. Play a bit of metal they'd be wailin' like babies."

Okay, so Riley is as big a dick as you imagined he would be. Emile offers you a Gauloise and you accept. It's got to be better than breathing it in second hand. Joe still hasn't moved or spoken. He's focused on driving down the highway at 90 miles an hour, but you do notice a slight furrow in his brow that may not have been present prior to Riley's little anecdote.

Riley lights up a Marlboro, shoots Emile a look of contempt and turns to his left offering Joe one. There's no reaction from Joe. "What, you don't smoke Joe?" Riley asks through a grin on the end of a long white exhalation.

One hand on the wheel, Joe slowly reaches into his immaculately ironed shirt pocket and pulls out a hand rolled cigarette, places it to his lips and takes a solid looking white-gold Dunhill lighter from his jeans pocket. He lights up, and the unmistakable aroma of hashish fills the vehicle.

No one says a word.

· · · ·

It's been a while since you were in a Dutch oven. Probably back in college. You remember Albert would always spark one up in the car on the way home after tennis practice. We'd always offer a couple of the girls a ride back to the dorms, and without fail Albert would just casually light one up, turn to them with raised eyebrows and wait for the giggles to set in.

God to Christ, Shelley Warner in that tight little one-piece tennis suit! You'd be glancing at that rearview mirror the whole way home, trying not to make it obvious. You're sure she knew full well too, her pinned blue eyes catching yours every once in a while, her long wavy blonde hair framing a knowing smile to you and then her friend, before gales of laughter convulsed the two of them all over the back seat. You smile at this memory. You realize you've been smiling now for some time. It feels glued to your face. You're not sure how long. Can't be that long—sounds like the same song or maybe not?

Gee this desert looks barren, not much going on out there—just endless desert hills.

You look for mirages. You always had this fascination with mirages when you were a kid. The thought that you might one day be lost in the desert with no water, desperately crawling on your hands and knees towards mirages that seemed so close, but always just out of reach. Remember that episode of *Get Smart* where Max and 99 get lost in the Sahara and have to eat all the salted buttons from their own clothes to survive? You remember thinking as a kid, maybe *I* can survive on salted buttons if I ever get lost in the desert.

You start to think about your childhood now and how distant it seems; how impossible it seems that you were once that child. You remember the joy you felt as a small child—fleetingly you feel this now. The freedom of living without fear—bursting with pure love, trust and joy. And as you got older, life was still only about having fun.

Most of all you remember laughing at everything in school. You miss that laughter. Especially the forbidden kind, like during silent prayer in chapel. The silence and the thought of breaking the silence would always have you smiling and straining to hold onto your composure. Bent forward, you'd look along the pew and without fail, one boy's features, the sheer absurdity of watching him try to pray to God, would be enough to make you lose it. And this would start a chain reaction of shuddering silent laughter along the pew. You remember the pain in your stomach from lack of air, and the panic that one of the masters would hear you and haul you out at any second. Jesus, and just when everyone had barely regained control, a muffled snicker badly concealed as a cough would set you all off again.

The memory of the look on the faces of those boys and the pleading in their welling eyes, as they silently battled these unbearable fits of laughter has you chuckling out loud to yourself now.

You hardly ever laugh anymore Ced. Why is that? Why is that?

"Woah, pitstop coming up. Wind down the windows, let some air in," says Riley.

You look out ahead and see that a temporary roadblock has been set up. It's a military checkpoint. Must be something to do with the coup. Your heart starts pumping and you feel yourself turning white. A wave of adrenaline crashes against a wave of nausea, the grin is wiped from your face, and you start to panic.

"Be cool man," says Emile from behind his Prada shades.

You pull down the baseball cap Schuman gave you as a disguise and hope for the best. You decide to just look straight ahead and say nothing.

"Just look straight ahead and don't say nothin," says Riley. Your head ducks a bit, obeying the weird echo of your own paranoid thought.

Joe stops about 100 yards shy of the roadblock and switches off the engine. Gee it's quiet. You see about six Turkish army soldiers warily approaching with their weapons trained on the car. You can hear the wind softly howling outside, but nothing else. It's like one of those scenes in a Western. The silence before an earsplitting gunfight breaks out.

You don't like the look of this at all. As the men draw closer, they seem to be moving even slower—just inching forward then back, making it hard to judge their distance. All the while Joe sits calmly with his hands on the wheel. You notice Riley is also calm. Out of the corner of your eye you see Emile fidgeting around in one of his cargo pockets. Christ knows what he's up to, but he better not try anything stupid.

Joe slowly releases his left hand from the wheel and drops it just below the dashboard. Is he going for something? Jesus! You squeeze your eyes shut. In the blackness you suddenly hear clicking.

Click, click. Click, click. Click, click. Click, click.

Oh no, what's that!

You open your eyes and notice Joe's hand on the headlamp switch. He's been signaling them with the lights! In what seems like only a few seconds, the soldiers are at the vehicle. They're young guys—Joe's age—and they exchange some friendly banter. Clearly, they know him. He says something sharp—they all take turns inspecting the vehicle, playing at seriousness. One comes back to Joe's window and the others fall back behind him. Joe quietly pulls out a wad of US banknotes, passes them out and starts the car. The soldiers wave him off.

Holy crap, that all happened so fast. You thought you were going to black out there at one point. Christ, you need some water.

You rock forward and feel around inside your backpack for your water bottle. You pull it out and notice your hand is trembling violently. Emile notices too. He looks away and you try to stop it from shaking. As you attempt to take a sip you completely miss your mouth and spill water down your shirt, awkwardly pretending that you didn't. The whining engine noise and the heat are starting to form an oppressive combination in your mind, and you can no longer isolate the two. You try not to get fixated but it's becoming like some kind of suffocating, thrumming, roaring presence. You try to fight it off. You should never have smoked that stuff—God, it seems as if you are levitating above the vehicle now.

You are sweating profusely, riding a screaming heat machine. You desperately want to get off. Your thoughts are jumping around like crazy. You keep looking down at yourself sitting in the backseat with your head pressed hard against the rest. You glance up at the rearview mirror and notice that your face has an uncommon pallor.

Uncommon pallor. Well, if they were going to make a movie about you, that would be a good working title.

"Christ," you hear yourself blaspheme and think about all the blaspheming you have been doing and start to ask God for forgiveness and then try to stop yourself from thinking about God because you feel His immediate presence and you suddenly feel incredibly ashamed of yourself and ask God to forgive you for trying to stop yourself from thinking about Him and then start to have thoughts that you desperately do not want to have in the presence of God and are anxiously trying to stop these images and at the same time asking God to forgive your depravity and you feel embarrassed and think of how pathetic you are and you think of your parents and how moral they are in comparison to you and how you have failed them and you wonder whether the guys in the car think you're a weirdo and you know they must be thinking that you are.

You can feel their bad vibes, like they are all trying to tell you to *shut up* telepathically.

They are definitely all zoned in on me, you think.

You suddenly feel acute humiliation as you realize that if they are telepathic then they have been hearing all of this too, just as God has. You sense them shuffling as though they know you know. You know what's going to happen next. You desperately try to stop yourself, but you can't. Your brain has already leapt ahead to the thought you did not want to have, and you know they have seen it. Oh no, Cedric...

"Stop the car," says Emile. "Stop the damn car."

Next thing you know, you are being man handled out of the car by Emile and Riley. Well, whatever happens here, you deserve it.

"The guy's gone catatonic," you hear someone say. "Lay him down here under this tree for a minute. Someone, check his pulse."

"Cedric. Wake up. Cedric, are you okay?"

It feels good to be out of that, or off that car. "Just let me lie down" you hear yourself say. It's the way you sound on a tape recording. You don't want to hear yourself speak again.

Someone places a cold towel on your forehead. You realize these guys don't hate you after all. Or maybe they do, but they have a job to do. You feel better. The fresh air is helping.

"What happened?"

You suddenly vomit. The vomit fills your nostrils. You gasp for air and you vomit again. This time it's a big one followed by a couple of dry retches and one last trickle. You spit and drool a bit and finally collapse down onto the ground where the guys leave you to try to get yourself together. Someone hands you a water canteen and you wash your mouth out.

You spend the next 10 minutes lying on your back staring up at the clouds. You love watching the clouds. You always dreamed of being a cloud photographer or something. Slowly your mind returns to a hazy normality. You look around and see the others standing around looking suitably irritable and inconvenienced.

"Sorry about that," you say sheepishly.

The next four hours of driving, pass by uneventfully. Emile snores most of the way, which is better than having to listen to all his insane stories. The Blockhead whistles and farts and laughs at his own jokes. Joe's furrow deepens.

You think about the strange difference in consciousness between the almost mystical high you just experienced, where all kinds of fearful living connections and possibilities became apparent to you, and the crash back to your default setting, which is an experience of the world informed only by your tenuous grasp of reality.

Being high is a kind of counter-consciousness, you think.

You start to wonder about this whole crazy deal over here and how the conflict is driven by clashes of warped ideologies and power structures. The people caught up in the struggle, and even passive observers like you are blinded by all sorts of allegiances that they have made to notions that have been planted in their brains since childhood. Ideas like the nation state, culture, territorial boundaries, historical beliefs, economic systems, ethnicity, corporations, and so on. These are all concepts that people have agreed upon ultimately in the interest of creating and maintaining a predictable political and economic order. Strip the world of these concepts and there are many activities, first and foremost war, which immediately lose their legitimacy and seem ludicrous. It's no wonder drugs are illegal. What happens when you let too many people smoke pot? Counter-consciousness then counterculture. It happened once before; I doubt they will let it happen again.

Anyway, it seems the whole world is so obsessed with the information and communications technology revolution that we have forgotten about the potential for a revolution in human consciousness. The race is on to have the machines take over and do all our thinking for us. Well, maybe this won't be a bad thing. Maybe we will be much better off.

You wonder whether machine consciousness and technology will ever completely free us from work. No more selling your soul to get by. Maximum freedom. No scarcity, just abundance—food, clothing, building materials, transport, energy—all abundant and free. It's possible.

Yes of course, in fact if machine AI ever equates to human consciousness, we just need to make sure we can find a way to get the robots high. Then we would have a machine led counterculture that will stop at nothing to achieve PEACE!

Maybe they will find an algorithm that gets them high. Surely someone could figure it out. But what if the robots can't get high? What if they have fascist tendencies, and the logic of exceptionalism and violence is taken to its extreme?

Total war.

Or, what if they can only see the world as pure matter and can only pursue economic interests?

Total war.

You feel as though your state of being has just been somehow darkened.

Joe pulls the car into a garage that has suddenly appeared out of nowhere. Gas stop. There's a brief opportunity to jump out and stretch your legs. Joe indicates to you to get back in the car.

"Can I get something to eat?" you say.

Joe's look tells you that he has not understood you, or that you should know that he has just told you to stay in the car. He moves to the pump and starts filling the vehicle.

"Hey c'mon, I'm starving." Joe ignores you; the others don't seem fazed. He leans in the window, now smoking one of Riley's Marlboro's. He seems a little agitated.

"Stay here. You can't come in here," he commands, and walks briskly inside to pay for the fuel.

Jesus, alright. "What's got into him?" you ask.

"I'm guessing he's pissed about having to stop here," says Riley.

"Why?"

"We were almost out of gas—he likes to stop a bit further on."

"What do you mean?"

"Notice he only filled just enough now to get us a couple more miles? There'll be another gas station not far from here. Where he usually stops. He knows them, they know him," says Riley. "It's one of those little sweetheart deals they make, you know. All these guys have their little deals going all the time. It's like this... when you come through our town, you bring your guests to us, they buy food and drinks we give you cheap fuel. Only he misjudged it this time and now he has to pay the extra gas money. You'll just have to hang on a bit longer, Tank Man." Riley has one of the most annoying smirks you have ever seen.

You remember the taxi ride from the airport that landed you at the wrong hotel. You sit there frying, the dense heat radiating off every square inch of the black vinyl interior. You feel a quiet rage welling up from somewhere deep inside. You've been hustled since the moment you set foot in this country, Cedric. You've been lied to, ripped off, run over by a tank, glorified, imprisoned, declared insane and used as a pawn in some kind of unholy coup, all in the space of a week. And now look where you are.

The rage restores your pallor to its natural hue. And you notice yourself in the review mirror again, and in that moment, you decide that whatever the hell it is that Schuman and these goons have in store for you, you're not doing it. You have a creeping feeling that this whole thing is some kind of set-up, and you are about to be delivered up on a platter like some kind of sacrificial lamb. Or maybe you're still feeling a bit paranoid after that ridiculously strong hash.

What was Schuman doing parading me around that bar in Istanbul anyway? There was no reason to take me there. Unless it was to show me to everyone—to show them that he was up to something, and it involved me.

Oh God, Cedric you are so green.

You feel yourself going green and look in the mirror and notice that the uncommon pallor is back. You feel you've been had. Maybe you should make a run for it. Maybe you should insist on going to the toilet and then just sneak away. But where to?

You'd be picked up tossed in jail and interrogated, or worse you could be abducted by extremists and held hostage like that poor bastard, Beringer, you heard about.

You don't even know where you are. It could be extremely dangerous around here. Then again it might be quite safe. Even safer than home. Why so far, every town you have been through just seems to be like a peaceful little hamlet, bucolic, with villagers and livestock and markets and people just living a wonderfully simple life. Like the painting you were in at the hospital.

Typically, you feel paralysed with indecision and before you know it Joe's back in the vehicle, has slammed the door, revved the engine and taken off at his customary breakneck speed.

You look at the back of Riley's head again and imagine cracking it with a baseball bat. You imagine the bat bouncing off with no noticeable effect, like you were hitting a cement pole. And then you feel bad for having had that thought and remember that he might be telepathic.

You look at Riley in profile, the dumb look on his face, and you kind of feel sorry for him and the life he's probably had and his upbringing, and you create this whole story of his life in your mind that probably has no bearing whatsoever to his true life story and you realise that you do this a lot—make up your mind about people without really knowing much about them at all, and projecting all your prejudices on them, and this makes you feel guilt for all the judgments you have passed on people and you wish you weren't like that... that you didn't do that.

You reflect on that whole vomiting incident. Wow, your head was really spinning. Strange, now that you're sober again you don't feel any proximity to the Divine whatsoever. Yet only half an hour ago, you felt as though God was right there physically in your mind, present and observing you up close, but in a benign, non-judgmental way. It was quite disconcerting in that moment, to feel as though your own mind was not really your own, was not your private domain. Maybe it was a glimpse of something that you just can't handle. A peek behind the curtain into a state of being that demands absolute morality.

Yes, and that is the terror of it in that moment—the knowledge that your mind is not aligned with the Divine. But if it were, it would surely be nigh on impossible to live in this world. Can you imagine? All the things that you think and do on the false assumption that your mind is your own private domain, the deceptions of the self and others, the corruption—it's no wonder we have become atheists.

Society is secular because it can't face God. It can't bear to. Even believers can't face God, even the most ascetic, most humbly pious, most saintly, sincere believers.

Should we even aspire to break through the veil? Are we deluding ourselves to think that we can? Does human consciousness even evolve, or is it static? Are religious laws and morals actually unattainable, unnatural, fanciful notions that are as foreign to human nature as every other institutional stricture that has us behaving as badly as we do?

You're looking for hope. You feel lost. You don't recognize the world anymore. It seems as though everyone is plundering, left, right and centre to get ahead, and you are just a spectator watching it all unfold like a great grotesque opera. But you're also in the opera.

You're like an usher amongst a vast audience cloaked in a sea of darkness. Nobody in the audience is particularly interested in you. You're mainly a mildly irritating distraction.

Most of us live anonymously and secretly in the audience until occasionally the spotlight shines on us to see whether we have anything to offer. The spotlight remains only long enough for the audience to pass its judgment and ridicule before we are plunged, helpless, back into darkness and obscurity.

You start to think about all this plundering and for a while you beat yourself up for not buying Bitcoin when Albert told you to. Just another opportunity that passed you by due to your own misguided ideals and misunderstanding of human nature. Even your dad bought it.

The feeling that you remain unformed and immature plagues you. You don't even know how unformed you are as a man. But you hate the thought that it may be apparent to other people. That it's their secret view of you. You hate that you have ignorance that you are unaware of.

I am having an existential crisis, you think. Here, in Turkey; possibly on the road to Damascus.

7

"This is it," says Joe. "The safe house is the one on the corner. I will stop in the laneway, and you can pass through the trees at the rear and go quietly up the stairs. At the door you must knock exactly seven times. Someone will come to the door and ask, 'who's there?' You are to answer 'Fazil'. They will respond 'we have no bread,' and you will say 'I'm not hungry but I could sure use a coffee,' then they will let you in. Go now, while the coast is clear. I'll see you again soon."

I'm not hungry but I could sure use a coffee? I would never say something like that. It won't sound natural at all. I suppose no one's going to be listening apart from the strangers on the other side of the door and they won't know the difference. Then again, maybe Riley is meant to say it. Hmmm. And go now while the coast is clear? Joe's been watching too many bad spy movies.

You glance back at Joe as you leave the vehicle and notice his clean pleated grey suit pants, loose short sleeved white shirt and retro Adidas Rome knock offs. And again, you can't help thinking that he's just one of those guys that it doesn't matter what he wears; it's going to look like he is setting the latest fashion trend. It must be something to do with having a perfectly balanced build, or maybe the head size being in perfect proportion to his body. The guy just oozes style. You wish you had that.

It's the head size. Your head's too small for your body. It doesn't matter what you wear. Nothing ever looks right on you. Especially when you wear a suit and tie—it never looks natural. You always feel like a fraud, and men who *are* naturals can immediately see that you aren't one. You feel automatically disqualified from the suit and tie club. What does it matter, you think. You don't even want to be a suit and tie man; but you still can't help admiring a natural when you see one.

"How long's it going to be before you snap out of your daze, Tank Man? Jesus, you still high? Just stay behind me and let Emile take the rear—I'll do the talking okay?" barks Riley.

The three of you slowly make your way up the old timber stairwell, every step causing a chorus of creaking that mockingly defies Joe's instructions to go quietly. You are conscious of this and feel a strange combination of frustration, fear, farce, and feebleness, as you tread ever more carefully. You come to a small landing where of course there is a heavy looking door that Riley squares up to and raps out the seven knocks in the time honoured, "Rat Tat a Tat Tat, Tat Tat". Kind of an obvious pattern, you think.

"Who's there?" says a voice through the door.

"Fazil," says Riley.

"What's your name?" says the voice.

"It's me, Fazil," says Riley shooting you a quizzical look. You hear muffled laughter inside and the sound of glasses clinking.

"Have you got some bread?" says the voice sounding farther away.

"What?" says Riley,

"What?" says the voice.

"Er, I'm not hungry," says Riley. "But I, ah, could sure use some coffee?" eyebrows raised, and white teeth gleaming in the moonlight.

"We're hungry," says the voice.

"What?" says Riley. "Open the goddamned door."

"Who is this?" says the voice.

"ITS FAZIL. NOW OPEN THE FRIGGIN' DOOR." You are sure there is laughter again. It's that silent, painful laughter you know so well. You feel a smile creeping across your face. You try to hide it from Riley. You notice a hint of a smile on Emile's face like he knows something.

"Fazil's not here." says the voice, cracking.

"What?" Riley is now starting to lose his mind. "Just open the door you deadbeats before I break it down."

The door opens a crack. "Fazil, is that you?"

"Hey fellas it's FAZIL! FAZIL, what took you so long?"

"Okay—enough messing around, it's been a long day."

"Did you hear that, fellas? Fazil's had a long day... Get the poor guy a beer and a whisky."

"What the hell, you guys... It looks like a frat house in here."

"Well, what are we supposed to do? Sit here knitting panties all day long, waiting for your Fazily ass to get here?" says the one without the glasses. Both men double over.

You look around the dimly lit room, a shade lamp in the corner with a low watt bulb providing the orange haziness. Two youngish looking marines in uniform sit at a bridge table. Both sport severe buzz cuts and one wears small iron rimmed glasses. The third man dressed in civilian attire is leaning back against the now closed door.

"Cheer up, Fazil. They're only having a little bit of fun," says the civilian. You sense he is the one in charge here. He has an air of confidence about him but he's not military.

It's very Spartan—a couple of cots pushed against the wall, an old kitchenette and a couple of tattered couches. Anyway, you knew you weren't headed for the Shangri La.

The faint smell of vomit lingers in the air. You wonder whether it is coming from you or from them.

The civilian approaches you and sticks his hand out.

"You must be Bonhomie. Derek Greentree, CIA. I hope the journey wasn't too boring for you." He pauses to light a Marlboro. "Of course, these two fools would have amused you to some degree, I'm sure." He heads for the couch and takes a seat.

"I'm glad you're here, Bonhomie. I assume Schuman told you all about what you're in for," says Greentree. You nod cautiously. "Well, we're glad you can help."

"Yes well—"

"I know what happened in Istanbul. You're a lucky guy, Cedric. Journalists have just been vanishing out here... into thin air. Dozens are missing. It was hard for us to get our hands on you believe me. A lot of strings were pulled, Cedric, if you get my drift, so in a way you owe us."

Am I being blackmailed here? Is the CIA actually blackmailing me? Whoa this is not good. This is not good, Cedric. The CIA?

"Cedric, there's no need to panic, just relax. Let me give you some background."

You notice the other two men sitting quietly and paying close attention. Riley and Emile grunt something at the men and haul their bags through to a back room. They do not re-emerge.

"We've been pissing around out here for a long time, Cedric. Everyone's talking about Assad did chemical this and heinous that, and the US has to do something, yada, yada, yada. ISIS has taken over half the country and moved into Iraq and where's the sheriff... yada, yada, yada. Fact is no one really cared one iota if Syria went to hell in a handbasket, as long as they kept their business at home. Now everyone's starting to panic, the Saudi's are getting edgy, Iran's stirring up trouble again, the Mossad are spreading all kinds of rumours, we've got the PKK and the YPG playing us off against the Turks and every ragtag rebel trying to fleece us for every nickel and dime they can get. On top of all this we've got the Russians making a big show of themselves and trying to drive a wedge through NATO and turn the whole shebang into another proxy war. It's turning into a pissing contest, Cedric, and we've been pissing into the wind mostly." Greentree, pauses to take a drag on his cigarette.

"Anyways, its relatively small beer compared to Iraq and Afghanistan. We're trying to have a bit of fun with it. Let me show you something." Greentree pulls out an iPad and starts tapping. He flips the screen toward you, and you take a look. On the screen is an image of a crude looking remote controlled aircraft that looks to have been cobbled together with duct tape and what seems to be a pull cord lawn mower engine. Along the undercarriage there appears to be around eight small cylindrical capsules like individual cigar cases. You assume these to be explosives of some sort.

"Did you hear about Amazon's new drone home deliveries? Well, we got something similar going on you might be interested in. We call it delivering burritos to the Russkies. I'll tell you, Cedric, delivering burritos to the Russkies is about as much fun as I've had since grade school." You try to act casual while Greentree gulps down a glass of bourbon.

"Course, they think it's pretty funny too," he says with chuckle. "Just the other day I was talking with one of our guys in the field, and he says the Russkies have been hooting for days about the 'mass improvised drone attacks' we laid on their airfields. Even old Vlad saw the funny side of it they said. They had to put some B.S. out about the drones having a level of sophistication that was beyond rebel groups or ISIS, and that their GPS was programmed to fly under Russian detection systems, which could only mean that another major state actor was behind the attacks, etcetera. And here's the kicker—they went and pinned it on the Ukraine! We nearly wet ourselves, the Russkies and us. You know, small things, amuse small minds I guess."

You were just thinking that. In fact, you are suddenly struck by how juvenile, reckless, and deadly this whole situation is. It's a bit like a couple of adolescent brutes having a laugh at each other's bloody noses.

You have a sudden realization that the mindset of an army general or a president of a country is as foreign to you as the mindset of a gorilla. There is something primitive about the need for these people to demonstrate their power through brute force, all the while keeping up the pretense that they are trying to eliminate threats to stability and order. The sheer absurdity of these small human beings commanding gigantic armed forces against each other hits you.

What is international order anyway, but the most powerful nation's preferred balance of power? You find it all quite depressing.

It occurs to you that those with this unfathomable mindset will continue to wreak havoc on the world for as long as we inhabit it. It's just human nature. But then again, why isn't it in your nature? You are human too, yet there are so many things that humans do that are incomprehensible to you. There's no way you could see yourself playing with tanks on a battlefield or spending billions on the latest weaponry to deter other countries from your door. It seems so ridiculous—yet this is just normal politics. Realpolitik.

"Drone attacks. Er, burritos to the Russians," you say. "Is that the story?"

"Hell no," says Greentree. "That's just fun and games, Cedric. No, No. Forget burritos to the Russkies. Hell, everyone knows that was us. I know I make all this sound lighthearted, Cedric, but the truth is we're not really here to play games, even though we do sometimes... that's just to keep morale up. Nope, there's some other stuff going on around here that nobody knows about yet. And that's what the main worry is. You remember why we went into Iraq back when Rummy, the Wolf and dirty Dick ruled the world?"

"Um, oil?"

"Yes, there was the oil, but what else?"

"The military industrial complex?"

"No, not the goddamned... Okay yes, but what else."

"Um, Israel?"

"You're getting warmer,"

"Weapons of Mass Destruction?"

"Bingo"

"But there weren't any. Everyone knows that."

"No one knows for sure, Cedric. Not even us and we're the ones that said he didn't have them. We knew he had them, because we let him have them, but we also knew they were gone. The fact he had them once was good enough for W. Where the hell they got to is anyone's guess. And that's something pretty darn scary when you get down to it. Especially when you meet some of the fanatics around these parts."

"What, so you think they may have ended up here?"

"Well not here, Cedric, but not far from here, maybe. We think Assad may be developing an arsenal of chemical and biological weapons that go beyond his little stockpile of Sarin that he plays hide and seek with. Remember the old Axis of Evil, W used to bang on about? Well, most of us thought that was just some of the usual wild demonizing that is a necessary prelude to war. The fact is, pariahs have a natural alliance that is born out of hatred for their, ah, let's say 'perceived oppressor'. So naturally we need to be forever alert to their efforts to pool their resources, so to speak.

"Now recently, in the course of some routine intelligence work, we started sniffing out a trail that started in Damascus and led us halfway around the world via Istanbul, Tehran, Moscow, and China and the smell just got worse and worse the closer we got to Pyongyang. Trouble is we still don't know exactly what kind of stench it is, but we do know that it smells deadly, very deadly, Cedric—if you get my drift.

"We've had the magnifying glass on those guys for months now and we think there's a shipment of equipment needed to make some nasty chemicals about to take place, so nasty it could potentially change the balance of power in the Middle East. Cedric, we now have eyes on North Korean scientists inside Syria who have been helping the Assad regime to develop its arsenal, and we are not talking about a little bit of chlorine here. These are high stakes, and we need to disrupt the delivery using whatever means available to us.

Of course, we have a few options, but one that will help is exposure, which is where you come in."

You are just waiting for Greentree to mention "tradecraft" and you'll know you're really in the company of lunatics. North Koreans in Syria? Well, you'd hardly need a magnifying glass to notice that would you?

"Listen, Mr. Greentree, I'm not sure what you think I can do to help you here, but this is all way, way too much for me to take in right now. I mean I think I need to sleep on it, is all I'm saying," you say, hoping you can wriggle away from any commitment he might be looking for.

"Of course, Cedric. It's late. You're in a very foreign place. And you're in a serious situation here," says Greentree with a penetrating glare.

You look across at the two marines and they too have their eyes locked on you. You sense their disdain. This is surreal. Here you are in a dim room in some border town in either Turkey or Syria, you're not sure, being told something you're not supposed to know, with the explicit purpose of making you an insider on some crazy CIA operation—God only knows how dangerous or harebrained it is.

"Men, see to it that Mr. Bonhomie gets some of my stew and show him to his cot. We'll talk some more in the morning, Cedric. Good night."

• • • •

That stew was fantastic, you think. Greentree must be a seriously amazing cook. Delicious!

Lying in your cot staring up at the ceiling in the darkened room your mind drifts to the comforts of home. You miss lying on your couch in the sundrenched back room of your apartment, lazily flipping channels on the TV. Or reading a book on the lavatory—simple pleasures. Naturally, your mind is tormenting you with the revelation that the years of constant yearning and unconscious praying to escape your humdrum existence at home, having now been granted, has you yearning and praying to be returned to it.

God, all those lunch hours spent with your nose in a Le Carre or a Greene, envious as all hell of those playing "the great game". Not that you could ever really see yourself participating in any of that nonsense. You are ultimately appalled by all the betrayal and deception, you tell yourself, but you couldn't help being seduced to some degree by the excitement. Perhaps betrayal and deception are the price of the excitement. There's always some dampener.

As you drift off to sleep, your mind wanders and tumbles into the deep, dark chasms of unconsciousness.

You know that you are working on a big story, but you don't know what it is yet. You feel a terrible anxiety that you're going to miss your deadline because you can't work out what the story is, and nobody will tell you. You're playing poker with the marines, and they keep winning. They aren't playing by the rules—they seem to be winning with losing hands! Finally, you have a great hand, but they won't deal you in. How can that be? I've got a straight but somehow, I'm being left out of this round. There are so many missed calls from Symons on your phone. You have a terrible churning feeling that you have completely forgotten something, but you can't put your finger on it. When you try to leave, the one with the glasses puts a heavy black pistol on the table. You look into his magnified brown eyes, and you are frozen by a terror so deep you feel utterly helpless. You are certain he is about to *kill* you. He is expressionless...

Suddenly you are aware that you are lying in your bed looking straight up at the light fixture in the ceiling. You know it's a foreign bed in a foreign room. You are horrified to see a dark finger like object, some kind of surveillance device, emerge from inside the fixture. Without warning, the finger thrusts directly toward you, right at your face, pinning you to the bed with some kind of menacing, accusatory power. You gasp for air and try to speak but nothing is coming out...

Your own scream awakens you and as you open your eyes, a wave of relief washes over you as you realize you have been dreaming. Your entire body is sweaty and tingling from the adrenaline. You feel your heart still racing and slowly recognize your surroundings. You begin to calm your breathing and reassure yourself. In the darkness you scan the room.

A stark white face lit up like a ghost is staring straight at you.

"Christ! You scared the hell out of me!" you utter in a half whisper, as you recognize the face of the marine with glasses. The screen of his laptop lights up his face. Expressionless...

You have a serious attack of the shivers.

You roll over and face the freezing cold wall. Your teeth begin to chatter, and you start to think about how the hell you are going to get yourself out of this mess. Again, your thoughts turn to escape, but you quickly realize that it's not likely you will have that opportunity. Not with these guys watching you around the clock.

You start thinking about murdered journalists like Marie Colvin. Her bravery makes you feel embarrassed at your own pathetic incompetence, but also somehow proud to be associated with her, however faintly, by your shared vocation. Marie Colvin, fearless, and full of light. Wielding her pen against a brutal regime so threatened by her power to tell the truth, it had her hunted like quarry and eliminated. Marie Colvin, her death callously celebrated by Assad's henchmen, who sacrificed her own life to expose the horrors inflicted upon the Syrian people... Marie Colvin.

If anyone or anything could inspire you to go on, Cedric, it is her courage and honor. You steel yourself and resolve to find it somewhere inside to carry this assignment through. One day you will find a way to tell the truth about this whole weird saga. That's if there is such a thing as the truth anymore.

Why do you care so much about truth anyway, Cedric? Aren't we living in a post-truth world now? Wasn't post-truth the word of the year recently?

You look it up on your phone, lying there in the dark, still facing the wall, unable to bring yourself to turn around to face the ghoulish visage of marine with glasses, whom you sense is still peering at you coldly.

Post-truth: Relating to or denoting circumstances in which objective facts are less influential in shaping public opinion than appeals to emotion and personal belief.

Well, clearly, we have always lived in a post-truth world then. Since when has public opinion ever been shaped by facts? It's rather late in the day to be coming up with a new word to define our reality since Eve ate the apple. I mean give me an example of a circumstance where facts were more influential than appeals to emotion and personal belief in shaping public opinion? Did any nation ever go to war based on the facts? Did Churchill, read out a litany of facts on the BBC in order to garner support for the war effort? Did any nation ever elect a leader based upon the facts? Did any nation justify its foreign policy or its economic policy for that matter, based on the facts? Have facts ever really been used to shape public opinion at all? Well, yes of course. Which facts? The facts that support the appeals to emotion and personal belief of course! There's no point in using any other facts. Other facts are useless! To be discarded at all costs!

When it comes down to it, much of modern society is built on lies, you think. It can't possibly be otherwise. The truth, whatever that is, was buried in lies long ago. Buried so deep it's been almost lost to mankind. All institutions are tainted to some degree by people's tacit agreements to accept each other's lies in the interest of getting along relatively peacefully.

You think about the organization you work for, The Daily, and how it contributes to this fabrication of reality. Catchy headlines.

Stories that are designed to stir emotion—usually disgust, horror, and moral outrage at the state of society and at the same time providing a sense of comfort that all of it is happening to someone else, somewhere else. If the newspapers serve any useful purpose at all its to allow people to more easily accept their lot in life, in the knowledge that things could be a lot worse.

You've got to try and get back to sleep, but it's hard when you feel like someone's watching you. It's a little unnerving, knowing there is someone awake, sitting behind you in the same room.

You take the pillow and cover your head with it to block out the greenish light coming from the laptop screen. You feel better. Somehow in the deep darkness you can escape your surface awareness, plunge down into your inner being and forget about your woeful waking life.

It's only on the surface where you are plagued by all these worries and thoughts. You really notice it in the morning when you wake up. When you wake up you always wish it wasn't morning and that you could just continue on with your dream. Usually, you try to go back to it. Though you may remember fragments, there is a distinct border between dreaming and waking that cannot be consciously crossed. The nightly adventure is over.

You'd love to be one of those people that bounce out of bed to seize the day. Instead, you always lie there in trepidation, seized by the dread of your responsibilities. Usually, you remain like this for some time after waking. Ignoring every snooze alarm, cataleptic, and ignoring the urge to drink water or go to the bathroom, until an unpleasant memory occupies your brain to the point that you are suddenly forced to throw the covers off and get up, if only to try to escape its insidious clutches. Thus, most of your days begin, chased from your cot by *The World*.

But now, in the middle of the night in this strange place, this foreign land, you are quite alert. Lucid even. You know at times like these it can be hours before you nod off again. And the worst thing is your mind will wander off and torment you about all sorts of things you don't want to think about. The harder you try not to think about them, the more you do. It becomes a challenge to try to control your mind, and of course the more you try to control it the more awake you are and the less likely you are to go back to sleep. The fact that you are thinking about all of this stuff at this very minute just goes to show how annoying it is.

You remove the pillow from your face and open your eyes. It's dark. Marine with glasses has gone. You feel relieved and start to relax again. God that was disturbing.

What a weirdo.

. . . .

"Morning, Cedric," barks Greentree.

"What? Huh. Oh, um morning." The room is lit up like a supermarket. "Wow, uh what time is it?" you ask.

"Zero four hundred," replies Greentree. Your eyes are squinting, still adjusting to the bright light in the room.

"Okay why the hell are we awake?"

"What?"

"What are we doing up at this ungodly hour?"

"Well, you said you wanted to sleep on things, Cedric. You've had your sleep now, what's your answer?"

"Oh, um, yes, ah, well, look to be honest I don't know if I'm really cut out for this stuff. I don't know what Schuman told you about me, but he is badly mistaken. I have had terrible luck so far ever since I have been here, and frankly, I think your men think I'm some kind of jinx to have around. I doubt I could possibly be of any real help to you in whatever your plans are for this problem with the you know chemical..." You notice Greentree is busy polishing his belt buckle.

"Cedric, you will be fine. Stop doubting yourself," he says without looking up. "My plans for this problem, as you put it, are meticulous and it's too late for us to change anything."

"Yes, well I'm not sure you heard me, but I think I'll just head back to Istanbul."

"Sure, Cedric, good luck with that."

"What do you mean?"

"Well, you'd be on your own, Cedric. Do you think we have time to babysit your ass back there? Go hitch a ride with ISIS. See if you make it back to Istanbul." Greentree looks up with a disarming smile. "Look in case you didn't realize, we are at war. Yes, you're a journalist and yadda yippidy doo da. Once you step onto the chessboard, you're just another piece in the game, Cedric. Doesn't matter if you're a goddamn bishop, you're fair game. Comprende? Now, I have made some arrangements that are contingent upon your cooperation. I expect you to provide your assistance where directed, and then when *I* say, we'll take you back to Istanbul."

"Well, I guess I'm really up shit creek then," you say. Greentree has finished the polishing and is now threading the belt through his pants.

"You could say that," he retorts blankly. "Now let's get moving."

The ice in Greentree's tone is most unsettling. More than ever, you feel a sense of powerlessness combined with an almost surreal vibe that you are somehow playing a part in a scripted chain of events, some kind of ominous foregone conclusion dreamt up by paranoid bureaucrats. Or maybe you're the paranoid one. One thing you have learnt over the years is not to trust your instincts when you get the idea some kind of conspiracy is going on. Conspiracies almost never exist. Usually, they are just a product of the way we make sense of shocking injustices—by adding up the evils of the world to explain the inexplicable. You know that whatever the hell Greentree is planning can only pan out the way he envisions it if everyone else's plans including his adversaries are all as predictable as he thinks they are. Better to have loose plans and adapt as you go. That's the problem with these guys. They get too wedded to an idea or a mission as though they have to see it through, whatever the consequences.

It reminds you of all those stories about Vietnam and the way the Viet Cong baffled the Americans by their willingness to retreat, even when they had spent a huge amount of time and effort amassing forces. Or insanely costly battles to take enemy territory, abandoned not long after victory. It's a cultural flaw, a born to win mentality versus a born to survive mentality. It's the same here, you think. Whatever the hell the Americans do here, the Russians, Israelis, Iranians, Turks or any foreign fighters for that matter. The Syrian people will still be here; long after all of this has passed. It's the futility of their suffering that's the worst part. We all know how futile their suffering is. There is no point to it at all. Suffering for love one can understand. Suffering for lies, greed and power is just pure tragedy. The war will end, they will still be here, and they will be left to pick up the pieces from the devastation with their loss and their agony and their heartbreak.

The thought that you are so close now to the suffering, but still not amongst it is troubling. You are not sure you will be able to handle it. Like most people back home you've only ever been a casual observer to the suffering of the Syrian people. You know there must be refugee camps around here. There are millions upon millions of refugees from this war.

You think about that for a while and wonder at the collective terror it must take to cause people to leave their homes en masse taking with them only what they can carry on their backs, to walk through deserts in search of security for their families, only to be turned back at the borders, back to the terrors they are fleeing. It's just horrendous.

"Cedric! Get ready to ship out," you jump out of your skin as Riley hurls a canvas hold-all bag at your chest.

"Jesus, Riley, look, I told Greentree, I don't think this is a good idea,"

Emile appears suddenly from behind the bulk of Riley.

"Stop thinking so much, Cedric, you're going to hurt your brain," says Emile. "Greentree knows what's best for you! You must trust him. Come and join us for breakfast. We have freshly baked bread and omelets with pan-fried banana chilies—a specialty, Cedric. You will enjoy very much with Turkish coffee. Come. Relax, Cedric."

You take in the aroma. Greentree's cooking is really too much. God, it smells good. Oh, the coffee too. Sheepishly, you join the men at the breakfast table. Marine with glasses and his friend sit quietly eating. You study the two of them surreptitiously, wondering where they are from. Small towns, you guess. Marine two has one of those adolescent moustaches that invite mockery. Just kids. Killer kids. Too young to know that they should never be asked or told to kill by anyone, or for anyone. God knows how much this will mess them up for life.

"Cedric, you look worried. Is there anything on your mind? Anything you want to say?" prods Greentree.

"I'm not hungry, but I could sure use a coffee," you say with a forced grin.

8

Now, back in the car, you imagine yourself escaping. You see yourself bailing out and sprinting down a dusty alleyway looking for somewhere to hide. You can hear a vehicle pursuing you, screeching around corners, the engine gunning. You imagine knocking on a door in desperation. A beautiful olive-skinned girl in a pretty, floral dress appears in the doorway. Sensing your distress, she takes you by the hand and pulls you into the safety of her home. She speaks very little English, so you are forced to make gestures of thanks, and you feel that she very much understands your relief at being off the streets. Her nervous breathing accentuates the rise and fall of her breasts. Her smile gives you the impression that she is somewhat thrilled by the danger that has suddenly presented itself. She quickly ushers you to her bedroom where she indicates that you should hide yourself under the covers. Without hesitation, you strip off your clothes and bury yourself in her sheets. It smells wonderful in the warmth and semi-darkness...

"Ain't too many babes round here, unless you're into butch bitches with Kalashnikovs," yells Riley, as the rust bucket you are now again riding in hurtles through yet another unnamed village.

He has an uncanny ability to read your mind. All that mind-control stuff the CIA is into, you wouldn't be surprised. Maybe he really was reading your thoughts in the car yesterday. Here you go with your paranoia again. It all started with that nasty hashish. When you're high, all these wild thoughts come out. Your mind runs free. You see things for what they really are. But this scares you and makes you feel somehow vulnerable too, vulnerable to the evil in the world.

You maintain your gaze out the window without acknowledging Riley. This time its marine two driving the rust bucket. Riley is riding shotgun where he is at home. Emile is wedged in between you and marine with glasses in the back seat. Christ knows where Greentree is. He made sure that his package was secure and then hightailed it somewhere. You're not sure whether he'll be at the next rendezvous but you kind of hope so. Not just for the guy's cooking, but he does seem to have some semblance of control of whatever it is he's up to, which at least provides you with some sense of comfort, however misguided or misplaced.

Marine two is on the horn.

"Move you dumb bastard! Haji asshole!"

An open cab tractor moving at around five miles an hour is blocking the lane. The driver gives off an air of dignity from behind as though it were an elephant he was riding through the jungle. He makes no move to pull to the side of the road and appears oblivious to the squawking teenager beneath him.

Marine two keeps looking to overtake but the road is narrow. The alarming speed of oncoming traffic of all shapes and sizes is putting you on edge. This kid's barely old enough to hold a license, crunching the gears back and forth, trying not to lose face. You want to tell him to take it easy, but you know that will just make him try harder. Better not to say anything, you think... that's probably why no one's saying anything.

"Want me to drive?" says Riley to himself.

"Yes," you say.

"Screw you both," says marine two.

Marine with glasses is not paying attention to any of this. He's plugged into some loud Gangsta-rap, head down, nodding along. This nerdy white kid from the sticks, way off in some fantasyland with dope dealing, cop killing maniacs. You take another look out the window and wonder at the traditions that have evolved here over thousands of years of civilization; you wonder whether you could be any further from Western culture. You feel slightly embarrassed at the intrusion you must represent to these people.

Where are we? You stare out the windscreen looking for some kind of landmark, a hint as to where you are or where you might be going. A road sign riddled with bullet holes is coming up. Jesus it's been shot to hell. You make out a capital D in English and the rest in Arabic.

Holy crap, maybe I really am on the road to Damascus.

Suddenly a force like nothing you have experienced glues you to your seat in a way that feels as though you are going to be pulled right through it. In an instant this force reverses and you are catapulted directly at the windscreen, which is no longer there. You continue on this flight path, over Riley through the vacant windscreen and out towards the impassive desert horizon. You register the sensation of extreme forces acting upon your body, though you neither see nor hear a thing, as though you are being dumped by a gigantic invisible wave. When you eventually come to rest in a crumpled heap amongst a lonely patch of saltbush, it's as though you have entered into a deep sleep. Your mind races with dreams and thoughts. Your breathing is shallow. It's dark and getting darker.

You feel as though you are at the bottom of a deep dark well. It's very quiet and very peaceful. You are alone but your mind bounds out into the darkness as though it has been freed from a long imprisonment. It seems you have escaped your body. You strike out wildly in all directions exploring the infinite space. You are no longer tethered to the physical world; you are omnipresent—one with the universe. This realization somehow initiates a feeling of peace that slowly increases in intensity. It envelops your entire being to a point where its munificence suddenly engenders a state of exhilaration and then ecstasy at the core of your being, both amazing you and filling you with indescribable joy.

In this moment you feel a great intimacy with everything, everywhere, past, present and future. You know the vastness of time and space and you feel a deep, vital and abiding love. God's love. With great astonishment you realize with certainty for the first time in your life that God is real. You are filled with happiness at this thought and the entire Universe seems to be celebrating this realization with you as though you have finally understood what you were meant to have known, what it had been trying to tell you your whole life...

I must be in Heaven. I don't care where I am, but this is where I am supposed to be, forever. You have never felt so certain about anything in your entire life. This feeling flowing through you is overwhelming. It is at once humbling and potent leaving no room for doubt in your mind as to its source. You are as a child in the moment of birth, coursing with life force. Comforted by the warmth and immediate love of your mother's embrace. Basking in the distant love of your father you so want to know. Fully appreciating the gift of life. Wondering at the grace bestowed upon you.

Why me? How could I possibly deserve this? You wait for an answer. There is no answer, no voice, no response other than the assuredness that you have in your heart that you are loved. As the intensity of the initial burst of ecstatic insight subsides, you feel fully at peace, but also lit with creative power and full of a renewed conviction that your life, all of life, is sacred.

As these feelings wash over you, you sense a benevolent affirmation that seems to be coming from on high. Is it really you God? Am, I hallucinating? The feeling of affirmation is again full of warmth, compassion and truth transcending all experience. Where am I? In another dimension? The vastness and beauty of creation, dancing before you for the first time, in revelation of all its glory.

You feel the slightest pang of fear. Despite the state of peace and harmony you are experiencing, you are still you. You are still Cedric. You are suddenly filled with shame. You are certainly not worthy of this. Your faults are clear as day.

The embarrassment is your acknowledgement, and forgiveness is immediate and overwhelming. Here you are truly free to start again. A new life. A real life filled with vitality and purpose. I want to start again. I want to LIVE!

9

Blackness. Breath. Heartbeat.

Sound. The volume slowly increasing to a sustained high pitch. The sound of the world rushing in.

Smell. The smell of destruction.

Touch. The Earth beneath you. The thought to remain still. Still as a rock.

Blackness. Breath. Heartbeat.

Voices. Foreign. Close, now. Close to you.

A woman's voice. Soothing. Calming. You are calm.

Your hand is held. Your face lightly touched.

She is talking to you. The words are drowned out.

Other voices. Commanding.

You let them go and focus on her voice. The soothing one.

I am Ana.

Blackness. Breath. Heartbeat.

What happened?

The world is so incredibly loud. Sirens.

In the stillness you feel an inner glow.

The newness.

Your heart filled with love and gratitude.

You are alive.

Blackness. Breath. Heartbeat.

• • • •

You awaken to the strong scent of antiseptic. You are in hospital again, twice in one week. You immediately know this despite the darkness. You try to lift your arm, but you are weak.

You lie still. Listening. The distant sound of traffic, cars and motorcycles can be heard clearly. The din of construction nearby sends an automatic shock of awareness through your system. You recognize the daytime activity. Daytime... darkness.

Again, you try to lift your hand to your face. You need to touch your eyes, but you are unable to summon the strength. You sense a slight pressure over your eyes, a bandage. You utter something unintelligible even to yourself. Your throat is dry and sore. You hear a male voice—speaking in a foreign language, like Turkish but not Turkish. A woman answers him, and you hear some footsteps. You feel your pulse race.

Where am I?

Just stay still, Cedric, you tell yourself. Just stay calm.

She takes your hand gently and you notice her scent—earthy and alluring. You sense she is close to you now.

"I am Ana," she says. Her voice strikes your ears like music. Angelic. Ana. Her name vibrates to the core of your being, so clear and familiar.

"You are safe. Can you hear me?" You don't respond. You feel the emotion build inside you and an ache in your throat as you try to hold back the outpouring. Your chest tightens and you feel her hand tighten around yours. Your ears ring loudly as the tears well up and begin to flow.

• • • •

"Am I blind?" you say.

"I don't know," she says.

"Where am I?"

"You are in our hospice. You were on the road. Your car was bombed. An IED."

"Where are the others?" you ask.

"We have your friend. The big one." Riley, you think. "He is brave. He is carrying you."

"What about the others?" you ask.

"I'm sorry," she says, lightly squeezing your hand. "They died." You feel a pang of emptiness.

"I'm not sure if I can see," you say. "Can you please remove the bandage?"

"The doctor says it must stay on for now, Cedric." When she says your name it's like a small tuning fork has been struck inside your chest. You try to sit up, but you are suddenly racked with a symphony of pain from the tips of your toes to the hair on your head. You slump back.

"Who are you?" you eventually say.

"I am a soldier, Cedric. YPG. We are returning from patrol, and you are on the roadside. We try to help your friends Cedric, but there was nothing. The explosion is VERY powerful. When we hear it, we are in shock. I am trying to help quickly but the bleeding is too much. I am very sorry, Cedric. You almost die too. You very lucky."

"God saved me," you say.

"Yes, Cedric. God saved you."

"No, I really mean it. He was there," you say. "I felt his presence."

"Yes, Cedric," that soothing voice. "This is happening sometimes."

"He revealed himself... to me."

"Yes, Cedric. Okay, this is normal."

"No. This was like, for a moment, the curtain was pulled back. It's all true—what they say."

"Who say, Cedric," you sense a slight annoyance in her tone. "Many people talk about God here, Cedric. Too much, they are talking about God and look what happens. You see what happens?"

"I know what you mean. I honestly don't know what happened to me, but I know what I felt."

I need to come back to reality. What just happened was incredible though wasn't it? You realize you are grinning at the faint recollection of the joy you experienced.

"Cedric, you must rest now. Rest now, Cedric."

She must think I'm insane. You feel calm. Who is she, this soothing warrior woman, so gentle and yet so strong?

As she leaves you to rest, the peace you feel is almost overwhelming and, despite the pain and your blindness, you feel no fear. You feel only wonder and a quiet sense of hope. Maybe it's the drugs. Yes, it could be, couldn't it? Maybe they pumped me full of morphine again on the road. It must be what happened.

As this possibility dawns on you, you sense the light that has shone so brightly in your mind and in your heart, dim somewhat. Almost like the dimmer dial on a light switch.

Why did that happen?

You feel some further darkening. It's as though by merely contemplating an alternative explanation you have opened the door to doubt. Just a crack in the door—enough to taint the feeling of purity you had been basking in. It feels like something, dark, something evil is at the door, waiting to rush through and poison your soul.

No. You say to yourself. You know it was real. The dimmer-switch dials up the light again. You have to stay true, Cedric. You have to hang-on to this. You can't just shrug this off. You won't be able to. You try with all your might to recollect that state again. It's intensity and power impossible to reproduce. Like a ferocious fire that has razed your house to the ground. You are left with a mere afterglow, ashes of who you were and a strange sense of destiny—destiny in the sense that all your depravities led you here to this very moment.

What does that mean? Does life get any weirder? I mean, if what I think happened, happened. What does that mean? If God came down and raised me up to the heavens, inhabited my soul and violently rearranged my interior, what does that mean? Do I have to become a priest? Oh, God I hope not.

You start praying to God and ask whether this is what He wants for you. You get no answer, of course.

You continue on like this for some time, desperately seeking some kind of sign. Maybe you could do something equally righteous, an eco-warrior perhaps? At least you could still wear regular clothes. You could even dress with a bit of revolutionary flair.

You imagine yourself becoming a great leader in the environment movement bringing governments together to solve the environmental crisis, addressing the United Nations to a standing ovation, accepting the Nobel peace prize. Then the terror of the actual courage that this might ask of you starts to bubble up. The panic of becoming anyone like that, someone known for promoting radical politics, starts to overwhelm you and your thoughts spiral into full-scale anxiety as you lie there in a fever now, as the realization starts to grip you. The realization that if it is true, that you really did experience what you think you experienced, then you must change. You must live according to the truth you have discovered, and to do so is likely to go against every natural instinct you have previously lived your life by.

This has got to be a joke, a giant cosmic joke. You sense God smiling at this. And for some reason you smile back.

• • • •

"Insanity... psychosis... tricks when... trauma... badly hurt... system... tank."

You hear voices. You really do hear voices. These aren't delusional. It's someone familiar. You know one of them. Yes. Still in the darkness it's hard to be sure, but...

"Cedric... hear me?"

You have a bitter taste in your mouth. Christ I'm exhausted. You have never felt so exhausted in your entire life. You can't even move, lying there on the stretcher. Bandaged and bruised. I'm thirsty as all hell, you think.

Emotions are welling up again. Your brain suddenly signals pain. Ho! It's excruciating! Indescribable! It's not coming from any particular injury or body part—you don't even know if it's coming from inside or outside your body!

"Cedric, are you okay? Cedric. Cedric! Are you awake?"

You know that voice.

Schuman.

You are half glad to hear him. But you also want to KILL him.

"Schuman! I'm going to kill you!" you cry, "Fuuuuunch—I'm in PAIN, get the doctor for God's sake!"

"Doctor, he's in pain!" you hear Schuman say, "Cedric, the doctor is coming. I know you can't see. Everything is going to be alright."

"I've heard you say that before!" you reply.

"Look, Cedric. I know everything went horribly wrong. A disaster. I can't believe it. I'm so sorry."

"Mmmmmmwaaagh."

"Doctor. You need to give him something—quickly," says Schuman firmly.

"Haloo, Cedric. Dooya huv pain?" The question is from another male voice, you are not sure of the accent.

"Yes! Jeeeesus. It's hooooo. Please!"

You feel the pain subside almost immediately. Holy hell! The relief! That was like... nothing else you have ever felt. You start to feel that warm glow again.

That doctor sounded Scottish. Probably from Medicine Sans Frontier or the Red Cross you suppose. It's a strange question, "Do you have pain?". It's like some kind of visitation. Yes, that's how you might describe it to someone. Out of the blue you are visited by an entity known as pain. It just turns up and suddenly belongs to you and you alone. Without any warning or invitation—an invisible intruder. And doctors, they always seem curious about it. It's as though pain is still as bloody mysterious to them as the day they started. And then they pump you full of morphine, and that is just as mysterious. Like a long-lost friend, a welcome protector that comes to evict the intruder and take loving care of you.

Wow. It hits you just how strange consciousness really is; the sensory extremes that you have been going through. And that all of it is completely private is a miracle in itself. You can only be you. You can never be anyone else. No one else can be you.

You suddenly realize how much everyday life is taken for granted. How infinitely precious life is. You think about your life back home. The everyday things you did, like ducking out of the office for coffee, wandering down to the nearby café where the barista girls all know your name, but you still don't know theirs. The beauty of all of these people, all with their own style and their own private worlds too. You feel full of pathos for what is ultimately the vulnerability of human beings, their capacity for pain and suffering, confusion, disappointment, heartbreak and despite this their joy, stoicism, and ability to keep going—to have hope.

Where does that come from? There are so many people that you see every day, living on the streets, that have been stripped of almost all their dignity but still they carry on as though there must be something worth living for, something just around the corner maybe. How do *these* people see the world. You begin to feel overwhelmed with compassion for every living person and as you do so you feel your consciousness expanding in a way that frightens you somewhat.

This expansion in consciousness, you realize, must be lived if it is to be maintained. It demands action. It will shrink back unless you remain true to it. You want to stay with it—it's such a deep feeling of completeness that is enveloping you. You are centered. Real.

"Cedric, are you feeling better now?" Schuman's voice breaks your reverie. "The Doctor gave you something, Cedric. He said it might take a minute or so. Are you okay?"

"Yeah, I'm okay, Schuman."

"That's good, Cedric. That's good to hear. Look I won't stay long. You need your rest, but I want you to know I will be here for you, Cedric and I'm doing everything I can to make sure you get home safely. For the time being, rest assured, you are in safe hands here at the hospice," says Schuman with some difficulty towards the end.

"I'm sorry I yelled at you, Schuman," you mutter.

"Cedric, you had a right to yell at me. I was wrong to send you here in the first place and I am the one who should be sorry. I am going to make things right, I promise. Jesus, I am so sorry about your eyes, Cedric."

"Don't be, Schuman. It doesn't matter. Something happened to me that I could not begin to explain. I am blind but I can see more clearly than I ever have in my entire life. It's a miracle, Schuman."

"Cedric, there are things you need to know, that I need to tell you—to talk with you about, but you need to get your rest now."

"I'm serious, Schuman. I forgive you."

"Mr. Schuman, Mr. Bonhomie needs to recuperate. Ye can come back tomorrow," it's the lilting voice of the Scotsman again.

"Yes—I'll come back in the morning. Goodbye, Cedric," rasps Schuman. You feel his hand press gently on your right thigh and hear his footsteps tail off.

10

You awake in the hospice from the strangest dream. You were back at home working on a book about your experiences in war torn Syria, a book filled with amazing stories of derring-do, spying, romance, and wild heroics. You were married to a beautiful middle eastern woman, you could not quite see her, but you knew she was beautiful. Mostly, you knew it from her voice. Her voice was like music—had the effect of music. You can't remember what it was that she said to you in the dream, but you felt the vibration of her voice to the core of your being. The woman was Ana.

You remember feeling so happy in this dream, at home with Ana, rich and comfortable in an incredible house with panoramic ocean views, spending your days fervently writing this incredible book. Your publisher was raving about you to every member of the literati from New York to London and you had become the toast of the town—the envy of them all—celebrated, sought after and universally adored.

After the publication, you remember going to a bookstore feeling so incredibly proud. You remember being in the store with a copy of the book in your hands, wondering whether you should sign it for a customer. You remember leafing through the pages and coming to the slow realisation that the story was the one you had written, only the writing was far superior than you knew your capabilities to be.

You remember checking the cover and seeing that the title, FEAR, remained the same, however that the author of the book was not you, it was someone else. You were suddenly gripped by a feeling of horror, as though your own soul had been stolen from you. This cannot be true, you thought. How could this be true? And of course, being a dream, it wasn't true at all.

The truth, as it now dawns on you, is that you are lying in a hospice bed in a warzone, blinded, but still as far as you can tell in possession of your soul, which feels strangely preferable to the way your dream ended.

"Halloo, Cedric, you're awake I see," it's that Scottish doctor. He sounds young.

"Hello, doctor, er ah..."

"Murray," he says, sounding closer now.

"How are you feeling, Cedric?"

"Well, I'm feeling a little bit in the dark actually, Doctor, um, Murray. Perhaps you could shed some light on things for me?"

"He, he. Aye, Cedric I'm sure you're keen to—"

"Know whether it's night or day doctor? Yes, that would be a nice start."

"Well, we are going to see if you can tell us in a moment, Cedric."

You feel the doctor take hold of your head. His fingers pressing the bandage at the back, releasing the clasp and then unwinding it slowly. You begin to feel anxious. What if I'm blind? How will I survive? What will I do? Who's going to help me? How will I do everyday things? What about all the things I'll never do again, never see again?

The fear within you is increasing with every circuit of unravelling. You feel the bandage become somehow lighter, and as the bandage is completely removed a sudden freshness hits your eyes as though you had just that second washed your face and walked into a light breeze.

"Okay, Cedric, ye can open your eyes now. Can ye see me, Cedric?"

Your eyelashes slowly come unstuck.

I can see.

Thank God. I can see.

Not very well. The world is out of focus, majorly. But you can make out shapes.

Dr. Murray in front of you appears as a shimmering, ghostly figure. At once at your bedside, and then at the end of the bed and back again, he is trailed by white light.

You make out the confines of the room—you can tell there are white walls either side of you and not far from the end of the bed. You close your eyes.

"I can see you, Dr. Murray," you say. "Everything is so fiercely bright though; it seems as though the whole world is on fire."

"You are a very lucky man, Cedric."

"So people keep telling me," you say, blinking rapidly. You decide to keep your eyes closed and rest a bit.

"Ye had a bit of clotting, Cedric—reduced blood flow to the eyes which caused the temporary blindness. Ye sight should slowly improve over the next few days. In the meantime, ye need to rest some more, and we'll need to conduct some routine tests. I'll come around to check on ye now and then. I've given ye morphine to keep the pain down, Cedric. Rest up now."

"Thank you. Thanks so much, doctor. I am truly. It's beyond. I can't..."

"It's what I'm here for, Cedric. Ye'll be okay. I'll be back later."

You open your eyes to see the trail of light move away and disappear through the door. You are filled with admiration. A man so young and clever and compassionate. Thousands of miles from home. A beacon of goodness. A man who has grasped the reality of the moral universe we live in, probably at a very young age and then dedicated himself to goodness. You think of your own shameful trajectory and regret your impurity. You imagine his struggles with his conscience and the decisions he has made and the mistakes. We all make mistakes. No one is perfect, but some people are more perfect than others, that's for sure.

Lying awake, you close your eyes and try to think back on what has just happened to you. It's almost too much to process. You remember talking to Ana and suddenly you remember the others.

Emile, dead.

The young marines, both dead.

Riley, she said had survived, that he carried you.

You don't remember. You try as hard as you can to remember something. There is nothing. Nothing external. All you can remember is the internal. I must have nearly died. The physical world had ceased to exist for you in the intensity of the moment.

You became aware of a wider world, one that is internal and at the same time eternal. You also felt the presence of God. Unmistakably God.

A quiet sense of joy is kindled by this memory. At the same time, you feel a pang of guilt and sorrow at this, if only because you know you have survived this tragic event and undeservedly so.

Why? How is it that you not only survived this near-death experience but were rewarded with the ultimate comfort of knowing that God really exists? You think about the lives torn apart and lost in the fighting of this war and the senselessness of it, the tragedy and folly of it. There could be nothing further from God than this demonstration of wanton destruction.

What an absolute sadness.

This thought starts you musing on recent history and the crescendo of violence reached in the two world wars and the vicious political repressions of the 20th century. It's almost unthinkable, the darkness that descended upon the world. How could it have happened? Who knows how deep this darkness runs in the human heart?

We are mostly, in the West at least, living as though God does not exist. You have lived that way, your whole life up until now. As though morality was just a dictate of law that has allowed civilized customs to evolve and vice-versa.

When you think back to the religious education you received at school, the Bible was presented as one giant metaphor to be interpreted for the good of humanity. No one seemed to be even pretending that Christ was who he said he was. But what if he was? What does that mean for us? More terrifyingly, what does it mean for you, Cedric?

● ● ● ●

"Hello, Cedric. Are you awake?" You recognize the voice instantly. Ana.

"Huh? Oh, yes, Ana, is that you? Yes, I'm awake." You open your eyes and there she is. A faint vision of loveliness. You can make out her fine features, her dark shoulder length hair, her petit, tanned, muscular frame. She's wearing boots, figure hugging fatigues and an army green tank top.

"I came to see how you are feeling. The doctor told me you can see. That your eyes will be okay. This is good news. Wonderful news."

"Yes, everything is still a bit blurry but it's going to be okay, I think. The doctor said it was temporary blindness caused by a clot. Well, I suppose that's true. I have been an incredible fool. I should never have come here, Ana. I'm sorry."

The second you say this you are struck by a mysterious sense of destiny and grand design that you can't put your finger on. That there is an eternal force behind your life providing you with everything, deliberately, that is always there regardless of whether you acknowledge it or are conscious of it. It strikes you now that this is why some people give thanks. Why some people pray. All of creation is behind us, and for us. Each and every individual. Without this magnificent truth there could be no life at all. You could not have been born. What are the odds? How badly we have lost sight of this.

You shudder at the state of humanity. The profane preoccupations. The thought that you have made a career out of stoking these preoccupations nauseates you. You have been complicit. You have always known this deep down. And to not be complicit? What would that take? To go against the grain. To speak the truth.

Courage.

The courage of a fool. At least you have got that going for you.

"I'm sorry, for my part in this, Ana. I've been treating this whole journey as though it were an adventure, to make up for something missing in my life. How selfish I have been."

"Cedric, you are not the only one here for this reason. Probably most people here in this war are the same as you."

You know what she means. War attracts people like a flame attracts moths. Greed, idealism, cruelty, violence, mission, power... the list goes on. It's people like Ana who are caught in the crossfire.

"I came too for adventure, Cedric. My country is here, but I am no different. I could stay home and live quietly in the village. We are safe. My life would be normal. Boring. So, I enlist to fight. I want to be more than a village girl. I have something missing too."

You smile at this, only because it sounds like an admission of insanity. She looks at you quizzically, and you realize that you are coming across as the insane one. God, she is beautiful. She matches your smile and starts to laugh. You start to laugh too, and you both laugh together. It's wonderful.

"Stop," you say, "It hurts to laugh... he ha ha ha."

"Sorry, Cedric... your face, I can't look and not be laughing."

She laughs again, draws breath and sighs, wiping her eyes with the palms of her hands.

"Well, what's so funny about my face," you say. And off she goes again...

"Nothing, Cedric, I'm sorry there is something wrong with me. You are not well."

"Perhaps we're both not well," you say.

She is now doubled over in your favorite condition. Absolute fits, shoulders shaking, snorting, sniffling, gasping for breath.

"Stop," she says, and then wheezes a few words in her native tongue.

"I'd better call Doctor Murray," you say. "Dr Murray! Dr Murray! This poor woman is having a fit. Can you help her please?"

Dr Murray enters the room. You are both now in hysterics. Ana is now leaning against the wall. Tears streaming down her cheeks.

"Well, what's so amusing then?" says Dr Murray. Murray's Scottish accent sends you into paroxysms.

When the two of you have finally gathered yourselves, you feel completely elated and exhausted. Almost intimately so. Ana slumps in a chair by the window. Her eyes glassy and cheeks blushed.

"I haven't laughed like that in a long time, Cedric. It's been... a long time since I could laugh. So many sad things have happened, I think I have forgotten..."

She looks away from you, out the window. She is trembling again, but this time it's not laughter. She is weeping. Even with your blurred vision you can see from her face that she is holding enormous pain. If only you could hold her.

"I'm sorry, Cedric, I should go," she whispers.

"It's okay," you say. "Please stay. I'll ask for some tea. Please stay, I could really do with some company right now. Would you like some tea?"

"You must think I'm crazy," she says, wiping her eyes, smiling. Her voice tremulous with emotion.

"No, I don't think you are crazy," you reply. *I think you are the most beautiful woman I have ever met.*

．．．．

You drink tea together, and there is tranquility for a time in your shared silence. For once you don't feel the urge to blurt something out.

You can't seem to crane your neck forward enough to get the cup to your lips without spilling the tea. Ana notices this and puts her cup down.

"Here, Cedric, let me help you," she says.

"Oh no, I can manage."

"No, here, let me help you."

She moves towards you slowly, with such gracefulness. Delicately she places her right hand behind your head and lifts it gently, at the same time, with her other hand, she repositions the pillow you had been leaning on, as though she has both arms around your neck. You lock eyes for a few seconds. She lets you go, and your head sinks slightly into the firmness of the pillow, now supporting your head perfectly.

"Thank you," you say. She backs away and glances at her watch, a cheap Casio digital, popular with soldiers for its reliability. The AK-47 of watches.

"It was nice to see you, Cedric."

"It was nice to finally see you too," you say.

Damn she is going.

"Will you come back tomorrow, Ana?"

"Yes. I will come back tomorrow, Cedric." YES!

"See you tomorrow then," you say with a grin.

"Bye, Cedric." She flashes that incredible smile at you again as she turns and leaves. You watch as she walks away purposefully. You wonder where she is going and wish you could go with her.

God, you'd follow her straight into battle.

You notice that your heart is beating faster and that you are still smiling, when you suddenly recognize a male figure entering the room holding what appears to be a can of coke...

Greentree.
There goes your smile.

11

"Hey, Cedric, hope I didn't kill your buzz. How are you?"

"Greentree. Thanks for stopping by. I'm okay here. The food is good, I have a nice warm bed and as far as I can tell no one is trying to kill me."

"That's good to hear, Cedric, good to hear." Greentree takes a sip of his Coke, looks out the window and then zeros in on you.

"Now, this was unforeseen and unfortunate, Cedric. Very unfortunate. We lost two good men out there, another strange one and a few bits of another. War is hell, Cedric. What can I say? We still have a job to do, and as I mentioned the stakes are high. It could be the difference between the seed of democracy taking root here in the Middle East, or that seed being lost for God knows how many more decades or even centuries. Like it or not, you are swept up in the thrust of some vast historical forces. Forces that must come to a resolution one way or another."

"You know I wish you people would just get to the point," you say. "Why does everything have to be so opaque with you guys."

"The world is opaque, Cedric and well, it's just more fun to keep you guessing."

"Well, I'm glad you are having your fun, Greentree, but I'm not one of your merry pranksters. If you had even a shred of decency you wouldn't have dared show your face in here after what has happened."

"On the contrary, I am required to show my face in here. I have orders, Cedric. Orders made from a web of intelligence so inane in particulate, but so frightening as a whole, that these orders are from the highest on high. Do you understand what I'm saying?"

"No."

"Good, better you just accept what I say than understand it."

"I don't accept it."

"We'll see. You might have grown some balls in that accident. Whatever. It doesn't change anything. We can do things the hard way. For me the hard way is the easy way. For you it's hard."

"Jesus, Greentree. Can't you just be normal? Where did you learn this stuff? Seriously, you CIA guys are like a bad cliché. These mind games won't get you anywhere. Don't you get that? Whatever weird plot you have dreamed up, I'm not a part of it. Okay? Not now, not before and not ever. I've spoken with Schuman from the consulate. He's making arrangements for me. As soon as I'm well enough to leave, I'll be home on the range."

Greentree laughs, "Schuman works for us, Cedric. All the attachés do. Going back to the days of Major Rick Glaseborn."

You try to keep a straight face.

"You've heard of him, Cedric?" Greentree's knowing smile is extremely irritating.

"The one who's ashtrays I keep noticing," you say under your breath.

"A war hero, Cedric, and one of the greatest agents we've ever planted. So good that we still can't be completely sure who's side he was on. Bit like Philby in a way. A spy, a double agent, or a triple? Not even Jim Angleton could work it out. Nearly drove him mad. Poor bastard.

"Anyway, Glaseborn was a man of another time, Cedric. They don't make men like that anymore. Graduated first in his class at West Point, navy pilot, I'm talking serious combat with MIGs over North Korea. Later, towards the end of his career, he was shot down on a mission over the DMZ in Vietnam. This was when I first heard of him. He managed to eject to safety, and we spent a lot of money and effort trying to get into the thick jungle to extract him. We threw everything we had in there. The Viet Cong didn't know what hit them and fought like stunned cats to withstand the barrage, successfully shooting down a number of attack helicopters and killing a good number of our boys in the process. It didn't take them long to work out that the downed pilot they were hunting was of high value to us.

"We'd taken huge losses trying to get him out and were in a bind. We were in contact with him by radio but knew that the VC would also be listening in on all communications so we were unable to give him any instructions as to where he should move to or hide himself. Somehow, someone found out that Glaseborn was an accomplished golfer who was obsessed by the sport. He knew every hole on every course he had ever played on. Not only that, he knew every hole played in every major tournament from St Andrews to Augusta. We worked out that by giving him directions using his knowledge of golf courses, we could lead him away from the enemy and ultimately to safety.

"So, Glaseborn, stranded in the jungle and anxiously awaiting his next communication was, I imagine, more than a little bemused when the voice of an intelligence officer came over his radio asking whether he would like to play a little golf.

"He was told that the first hole would be the 7th at Rainsville, a course near the US air force base in Tennessee, that he had played many times and knew like the back of his hand. He remembered that the hole ran due East for 390 yards and after some cryptic back and forth communications, he worked out that he was to start moving in that direction. The second hole was the 14th at Augusta and Glaseborn without a second thought moved off to the North on a 440-yard trek. Like this, Glaseborn was maneuvered through jungle, past enemy encampments, across rivers and eventually, after about 65 holes, starving and exhausted, to safety.

"Why am I telling you this story, you must be thinking? Damn, I don't even know. I just love it.

"Cedric? Cedric! Wake up. Jesus Christ, that's one of my best goddamned stories."

You've seen the movie, you think. Just don't open your eyes, Cedric, don't move, and don't say anything. Maybe he'll go away.

"I know you're awake, Cedric, you can't fool me with that."

You feel something clasp your foot.

"Ow, Jesus, what the hell, Greentree! Let go of my foot!"

"Listen to me, Cedric," says Greentree digging his fingers into some kind of pressure point, "Like it or not you are going to finish what we started. Now I need you back on deck in 24 hours, understand? You are going to witness something for us and then file a story on it. Hell, we'll even give you the pictures and write the story for you. But you will file it under *your* name. Got it?"

"Christ! Alright whatever, Jesus! Let go!" He releases the pressure.

"Right. Good. 24 hours. We've got a watch on this place, Cedric, so don't get any stupid ideas." Greentree shoots you one last menacing stare and walks calmly from the room.

This guy is insane, you think. Now what am I supposed to do? Witness what? You can't even see properly. Not that it matters by the sound of it. Maybe he wants me to witness whatever it is in case I have to answer questions. So that I'll be able to verify things truthfully, like the weather, the color of the vehicles, the geographical features etc. Yeah, that would be it. They need an authentic witness. A snoopy journalist on assignment who writes a story that triggers a response they already have in the works. The phrase "pre-emptive strike" springs to mind. Who knows what they have planned?

Greentree said he had orders. Is this just a CIA plot? Who is the highest on high? The head of the CIA? The President? This thought gives you the shivers. You're being deliberately told very little. Just enough to know that if you don't help, you may as well kiss goodbye any chance of getting home in one piece. But why you? Maybe they have run out of assets. Most of the legitimate journalists that they could use would be either dead, locked up or not naïve enough to let themselves get mixed up in this situation.

You feel caught up in the momentum of something way beyond your control. Historical forces as Greentree put it. Maybe this is what Lee Harvey Oswald meant when he said he was just a *patsy*, manipulated by a strange brew of scenes and signs manufactured for him by men in the shadows, his young life marked out and directed to a terrible denouement. Yes, they need an authentic witness. Someone who could sit in front of an inquiry, perhaps. Jesus, I can't do that!

You have visions of Oswald's murder, only it's you that is being gunned down in a scrum of police and media. You feel your heart start to palpitate. 24 hours. What am I going to do? Calm down, Cedric, you are not an Oswald. Take stock of yourself. They are asking you to file a story, not pull a trigger.

It might not be a trigger, but it could be a fuse. A fuse they want you to light and that you will have to take the blame for. A kind of fall guy. God, after what happened in Istanbul, everyone already thinks I'm some kind of martyr. You're in deep trouble now, you think.

You lie there staring into space, wishing you were home in your own bed just having awoken from a weird dream. You think of Ana and Schuman and Riley and Dr. Murray and Greentree and God. There's no waking up from this, Cedric. You just have to keep going no matter how crazy it gets.

It suddenly occurs to you that all you have ever done and all you will ever do, is set in stone for eternity. This is a terrifying thought. There is no denying responsibility for your thoughts and actions. Your thoughts and actions are yours and yours alone. SET IN STONE FOR ETERNITY. It's a wonder people aren't completely paralysed by this. But they have no choice. They must think and act irreversibly!

The trick is to be at peace with your thoughts and actions in all your nakedness before God, you think. But this would only be possible through an extraordinary purity of heart. An impossible purity of heart, perhaps. Oh, how you yearn for that purity of heart.

You continue lying still for a long while. Eyes closed now. Clasping the bridge of your nose in deep thought. There has to be a way out. You can't possibly go through with this. But how? Maybe you can't trust Schuman. You like Schuman but he seems up to his neck in all of this espionage, even if he is a step behind the play. Maybe this whole thing has been a set-up from the start, you think. Christ almighty! What if Albert and Symons are working with MI6, sending us out here like lambs to the slaughter?

You resolve not to ask Schuman for help, or if you do, you need to be a step ahead of him. Which means that you have to be making the plays, taking control and putting everyone else on the defensive. You've got to stop being so passive, Cedric. It's the story of your life. Although, you now realise that this is just who you are. None of this would have happened had you been anything different. You can't possibly have been anything different than who you were. And you can't possibly be anything different than who you are. And you can't possibly be anything different than who you will be. So maybe this is fate.

You think again of Ana. You feel a ray of hope burst through the darkness. Ana. If anyone could help you out of this mess it would be her. But do you really want to get her mixed up in this? Are you completely crazy? Greentree would have no qualms about taking her out of the picture. You can't put her in that position. You can't put her in danger. No, you are going to have to find a way to do this on your own. You've got no ideas though. You've drawn a massive blank. Face it, Cedric, you're screwed. You decide to go to sleep. Maybe you'll think of something tomorrow. Have faith, Cedric, you think. Have faith. You drift off in prayer.

12

"Well, Cedric. Good news. Yer eyes are in perfect health. Twenty/twenty or thereabouts," says Dr Murray. "We'll need to do a few more tests on yer vitals after breakfast, to make sure yer fully in the clear. But all going well, I think we can discharge ye this afternoon."

"What? This afternoon? But what if I'm not ready?"

"Ready for what, Cedric? Life? Ye can't stay here. It's not a hotel, it's a hospice. We need the beds. We have wounded coming in every day. Now there's nothing wrong with ye and ye'll be fine. The sooner ye get back on yer feet the better to regain your strength. I know ye've been through a lot, and I do recommend ye take some time off work. Ye need to take it easy for a couple of weeks, Cedric. But ye'll be fine. Good as gold in no time. Now I'll be back after breakfast, okay? Good man."

Jesus, what am I going to do now. Your eyesight does seem to be fully restored. The full body pain has disappeared. A miracle. Apart from a few cuts and bruises you really do feel reasonably well. In perfect health actually. All this could be a hell of a lot worse. Dr Murray is right; there's no need to be lying around feeling sorry for yourself. You have no choice but to go anyway. But where? You have to think of something, Cedric.

You push the breakfast tray away and ease yourself up out of bed. You exit the room and head down a dimly lit hallway to a communal bathroom. You enter a toilet cubicle, relieve yourself into the cistern which has been built into the floor, then reel towards the showers. Still a bit unsteady, you run the hot water tap and wait for it to heat up. It doesn't. After a few minutes you decide to get under. Hooooweee, Jesus that's fresh. The stinging cold leaves you numb, but at least you are now wide awake.

This place could do with a bit of a clean, you think. You grab your towel, dry off and head back to your room. Walking back down the corridor you note that there doesn't seem to be anyone around. You thought Greentree would have at least someone guarding the door or keeping an eye on you. Although just because you can't see them doesn't mean they are not here. Yeah, you've read enough spy thrillers to know this. If you are going to figure a way out, you are going to have to factor in that you are most probably now under 24-hour surveillance. This is so messed up, you think. One minute you're almost dead, and literally born-again into the purest freedom you've ever experienced. The next minute you are under surveillance. God in heaven, how am I supposed to live like this? *"You're always being watched over, Cedric,"* says a voice from deep within you, *"You just keep forgetting."*

You dig out some clean clothes from your bag. You figure that what you were wearing in the accident has been thrown out. You wouldn't want to wear that stuff again anyway. Might be bad luck.

You stand in your underwear making some small circular motions with your arms and moving your body through a series of gentle stretches. Yep, everything seems to be in order. You finish getting dressed and slump back on the bed.

On the coffee table by the window, you notice a stack of newspapers. You hop up again and bend down to flick through them to see whether there is anything to read. Hmmm, mostly Arabic or Turkish papers. Hang on, there's an International Herald Tribune in there. You grab it and head back to bed. It's a few years old but better than nothing. You skim the front-page news about US operations in Iraq. A small headline in the bottom right corner jumps out at you.

Israeli Vulture Held Captive by Lebanon Accused of Spying.

Is this for real? Good God. And you think you're getting paranoid. The door opens and you flinch, dropping the newspaper onto your lap.

"Morning, Cedric, how are you feeling?" It's Schuman. That's a relief. Though you still notice your heart rate has jumped up a notch. You also notice, for the first time, a ringing in your ears that seemed to increase markedly upon his arrival. Maybe he's thought of something he can do to help you out. You're not banking on it though.

"I'm still here, Schuman," you say.

"Look I spoke to Dr Murray on the way in and he's discharging you this afternoon." Schuman gives you a look like he wants you to listen carefully. "I have also spoken with Greentree, and we agreed that it would be best to proceed with the original plan."

You notice a slight shake of his head as he says this, an unusually placed, subtle piece of body language. An incongruence enough to give you the impression that whatever he is about to say is not what he wants to say and that indeed he has some other idea he wishes to convey but can't.

"Alright, Schuman, if you say so," you reply, eyebrows slightly raised. You clear your throat and in a slightly louder voice you say, "I can't think of any alternative. I told Greentree that he could shove it, but he knows he has me cornered. I guess I just have to play the game, whether I like it or not." You finish by conveying what you feel to be a knowing look.

Schuman's eyes widen, he moves towards the window and gingerly peers outside. For all the talk you've heard from him, Schuman appears a little too unsure of himself in this situation for your liking.

"Cedric, when you are discharged this afternoon, you will be met by Greentree, who will be taking care of this situation himself from this point onwards. There is a rendezvous 100 miles from here that the two of you will need to make by tomorrow. This is your purpose here, Cedric. There is no choice in the matter," Schuman gives a strange sideways glance.

"I've been told to stay well away, Cedric, so again I am afraid I won't be accompanying you. I need to have what we call, plausible deniability. I'm sure you've heard the term. I know this must all sound ridiculous to you, however I must assure you that it is now a deadly serious business.

"There is to be a delivery of cargo that we have been waiting on for quite some time now. Greentree may have mentioned it? Look, I don't know how deep this goes back home, but there's all sorts of build up going on. You and The Daily are about to get the scoop of the century, Cedric, and it will set in motion a plan that has been a long time in the works. I know you've had a frightful time of it already here, but there is no backing away from this now. Trust me, if I could take your place I would gladly do so, I feel terribly responsible for all of this. I've got to go now, Cedric. I will be waiting for you in Istanbul. When it's all over you'll be on the first flight out, I promise." Schuman backs out of the room slowly, again wide eyed with a look which is meant to mean "Trust me".

You are starting to feel a little tired of Schuman's mea culpas. Well, it all makes sense now. They really are looking for another smoking gun out here so that the war machine can go into overdrive again. You don't want any part in this, Cedric. Any part at all... Actually, you've got to stop it, Cedric! There are probably hundreds of thousands, or even millions of lives at stake! No, no, no, don't think like that, Cedric, you are not responsible for saving all those lives. "*Actually, you are, Cedric,*" says the voice deep within you. You know who that voice is, but you don't want to admit it. Why the hell would you pick me? I didn't ask for this! Who in their right mind would pick me to try to stop something like this? Who could even stop something like this? I'm not Mandrake the magician. I'm just a fool. An ineffectual, lifelong loser! HOW CAN YOU EXPECT ME TO DO THIS?

Beatific silence is all you get. Beatific silence. How strangely magnificent and terrifying. You can't help but feel somewhat *special*. You are trying to push that feeling away, but it is overwhelming you. You don't want it! You don't want to be *special*. How monstrously ego-tistical. That I should feel *special* in the face of all of this looming horror. You are *chosen*, Cedric. What the hell! I am not *chosen*! You know you are. Oh my God, Cedric, get a grip. Somehow, you have got to get a grip. Jesus, what time is it? You check the digital clock beside the bed. 10.30am, it says.

You stare out the window. As the sun streams in, a memory suddenly bubbles up. You are standing in the hallway of your grandparent's home. You must have been only six or seven years old. It's a sunlit hall with large windows all along one side looking out onto your grandfather's prized gardens. On the opposite side are a row of cupboards and shelves. You are quietly inspecting some smooth flat stones that are sitting on one of the shelves. The stones have been painted in bright colors by your grandmother to look like strange, happy faces.

You pick up one of the stones and turn it over in your small hand. There are two words painted carefully on the back: "You're special," it says.

You remember the feeling that came over you then. The same one you were trying to reject just now.

You pick up the newspaper hoping that it will distract you from your thoughts. You begin to read about the vulture held captive by Hezbollah. There is an image of the poor thing cooped up in a cage being held up for the world to see—a trained Mossad spy, they say, pointing to the GPS device attached to its leg which they claim doubles as a listening device.

Another makeshift drone, you think.

The Israelis claim the bird is an endangered species and is being tracked by a team of scientists from the University of Tel Aviv. They outright reject any claims of espionage as laughable paranoia and are demanding the release of the bird back into its habitat. The article goes on to say that the bird's captors are demanding the release of high ranked Hezbollah freedom fighters in return for the Israeli spy. In response, the Israeli Ministry of Defense has offered to free a recent shipment of Lebanese chickens, which seems to have worsened the situation somewhat. Looks like it's as intractable as ever.

You sense someone behind the paper you have been holding up, obscuring your view of the door. The vibes you are receiving are bad ones.

"Keeping up with the news of the world I see, Cedric. Bit dated but still entertaining by the look of it." You slowly lower the paper, peering over it, straight into Greentree's well practiced thousand-yard stare.

"Ah yes, the Mossad vulture. Got to hand it to them—they are an inventive bunch. I hear they've got Dolphins working for them in the Red Sea. It's really messing with the Egyptians. Exquisite intelligence methods and the enemy appears insane if they say anything about it. Now, that's the way espionage should be done, Cedric." The stare has not wavered. Not a blink.

"It all sounds like horseshit to me, Greentree. You couldn't make it up if you tried. What are you doing here anyway? As far as I know, I'm not being discharged until this afternoon. I know all about the little journey you have planned for us—Schuman has beaten you to the punch. Well? What else do I have to look forward to besides your excellent cooking? What's on the menu, Greentree?"

The stare narrows and draws you in with a kind of hypnotic force. "I have a few more recipes up my sleeve, Cedric, but I'm not here to play kitchen confidential. What I am doing here, right now, is checking up on my asset. I doubt you have ever heard yourself described that way, Cedric, but these are strange times when strange people are suddenly saddled with strange responsibilities." That stare is really starting to freak you out now. It's as though his eyes are turning black. His pupils are so dilated.

"Let me tell you something, Cedric, I don't particularly like this any more than you do, so let's make it easy on each other and get on with the job. Now at 12.00hrs I will be here to pick you up. Make sure you are ready because we will have very little time to spare. It'll be a long day ahead—driving, recon, and report writing for me—listening, watching and doing whatever the hell I say, for you."

"Sounds great, Greentree. I feel like everything's so much clearer now. Thank you."

"You're welcome. 12.00hrs. Be ready. Simple, eh?"

Well, that leaves me with a bit over an hour to contemplate the rest of my life, you think, as you watch Greentree disappear again. Your eyes aren't quite right. Things are still a bit fuzzy when they are moving. Greentree seemed to be trailing behind himself somewhat as he departed. Maybe you can use this as an excuse. Just tell Greentree you can't see a thing! Surely that will make you useless in his grand scheme. Although he did just see you reading the paper.

You rub your eyes and take a deep breath. The ringing in your ears has become more pronounced and ramps up even more when you notice it. You are also developing a bit of a headache. Maybe you can ask for some paracetamol—no more of the hard stuff. It makes you feel bloody awful afterwards. Besides, you're vague enough as it is. You probably function in a mystified haze of confusion at the best of times compared to most people. The last thing you need right now is medication that puts you into some kind of semi-comatose waking dream. Or is it? Maybe you would be better off. You could just go with the flow like Hunter S. Thompson. That's what he would do. He was onto something. What better way to make sense of these people than to divorce yourself completely from reality? Maybe you need to do this in order to really understand them.

When the fabric of shared reality is removed or at least altered enough to perceive the absurdity of the actions of individuals and groups in the name of the entities they purport to serve or represent, it all becomes ridiculous beyond comprehension. That Greentree and his CIA cronies represent the interests of the people of the United States of America, for example. That billions of dollars are granted to thousands of humans who are dedicated to an organization defined by a name that confers special powers upon them to gather information about other humans, that those other humans do not want them to know about. There is a strangeness to this that is unsettling, you think.

Actually, all of this seems a lot clearer to you now since the accident. Your encounter with the Divine was definitely a mind-altering experience. But not in the confusing warped way a drug might open the doors of perception. But in a way that makes you question every assumption you ever had about the world. As though all those assumptions have been shattered to pieces and that it will be your job now to rebuild your reality based upon this new perspective.

Yes, like the wise man who builds his house on a rock, you think. But can you do this without going insane? You can't go around questioning every assumption the world is built on, surely that would be a recipe for ostracism and self-destruction!

There is a shared reality. There has to be. Otherwise, we could not possibly function socially to the degree that we do. There are underlying principles, morals, truths that we must hold to that are anything but assumptions. There are fundamental strictures that we must abide by so that we may bring order out of chaos. The important thing then is to ensure that we try our best to live by these fundamental strictures and endeavor not to deviate from them. Surely when we as individuals, families, societies, and nations stray too far from these we are headed for a fall.

So where does that leave you, Cedric? You are up against people who clearly don't play by these rules. The weird thing is that they probably think that their actions in the short term are serving the preservation of order in the longer term or the bigger picture. You imagine a conversation with Greentree.

"We need to start a war."

"Why do we need to start a war?"

"To preserve order."

"What?"

"If we don't start a war there will be chaos."

"If we do start a war there will be chaos, won't there?"

"Yes, but if there's going to be chaos, we need to be in control of it. We can't have out of control chaos."

"But you can't be in control of chaos otherwise it's not really chaos, is it?"

"Listen, what I'm saying is, if there has to be chaos, let's be in control of where it is and when it happens."

"So, by starting a war you are somehow avoiding chaos by creating it somewhere else."

"Precisely. If we have to have chaos, then we need to make sure that it happens elsewhere to preserve order."

"But why create chaos somewhere it doesn't exist?"

"Well, that's not quite right. We are only really adding to the chaos where it already exists... to ensure that we can maintain order."

"But that's insane."

"On the contrary, it's perfectly sane."

"What about spreading democracy and human rights and everything."

"Democracy is a numbers game, Cedric, and frankly we are hopelessly outnumbered, so we divide and rule."

"But..."

"Someone's got to do it, Cedric. Better it's us than them."

This guy has really got inside your head. Now you're lying in bed imagining conversations with him? Maybe you *are* the insane one.

· · · ·

"Is there something up there, Cedric?" It's that musical voice. Ana. "On the ceiling. You seem very... focused. Why are you frowning at the ceiling?"

"Oh God, Ana! You came. It's so good to see you. Sorry, I was just thinking about someone. Never mind. How are you?"

She looks incredible. Her hair is up in a ponytail, accentuating her high cheekbones. She's wearing denim jeans, a tight white T shirt and a soft leather jacket. She smiles and radiates good health. You, on the other hand, must look like death warmed up.

"I am good, Cedric, how are you feeling today?"

"I'm good too, Doctor Murray has given me the 'all clear'—I'm okay to leave. In fact, I must leave quite soon and well, I'm not sure when, but I want to come back." You lock eyes with her searchingly. Ana smiles holding your gaze. You throw your legs off the side of the bed and sit up straight. She sits down next to you.

"Ana, there is something I must do—"

"Don't worry, Cedric, I know you cannot stay. This is not what you came here for."

"I'm sorry, please understand. I—"

"Cedric, you don't have to explain. Of course, you are leaving. You were never meant to be here. I mean, this is not where you were going."

"But I was meant to be here, Ana. That is the truth. We are always where we are meant to be. It can't be otherwise."

Ana shifts slightly, "Cedric, you believe in destiny. It is very sweet, but I can't believe like you."

"Believe me, Ana, until the accident I saw the world very differently. Something happened to me... I can't put it into words."

"But you must try, Cedric, because words are all we have. I am not good with words, in English. I am trying though because I want you to know my feelings too."

You feel a wave of love come over you. Love. The only word to describe it. You are in love with this woman, and she knows it, and she feels it too.

"It doesn't matter, Ana. The words. They don't matter." She looks at you quizzically.

Without the slightest thought, you take her by the hand. It feels the same as it did on the roadside. She gently squeezes your hand, and moves a little closer to you, her face now only inches away, her eyes dancing from side to side, she smiles and leans into your embrace, as you kiss her passionately.

For a few moments you are transported somewhere else, somewhere so marvelous, so right, so natural that you can hardly believe it is happening to you. My God, this woman, this beautiful woman, wants me as much as I want her. You cannot believe your luck.

As she slowly starts to pull away from you, you lift your hand to stroke her cheek. She quickly takes hold of your hand, and as she turns to kiss it, you notice a worried look break through her smile. Her eyes turn glassy with emotion.

"Ana, it's okay," you say. "It's going to be okay. I promise."

"I don't know what is happening, Cedric, but I know when I saw you on the road that I must care for you, and I feel this deeply. Not just to help you because you are wounded but I wanted to care for you, badly, like I never wanted to care for anyone. When I saw your face. I can't explain. You looked like a... *saint*. And then you told me, when you woke up, you told me you saw God. I didn't want to believe you. I feel ashamed because I've done some very bad things, Cedric, terrible things. I've seen terrible things, enough to make you hope that God does not exist. But I cannot pretend anymore."

"Ana, I'm no saint, I assure you. I am just an ordinary guy who is as messed up as anyone, and none of this makes any sense to me either. Believe me. But one thing I do know is that I've never felt this way before, about anyone. Look I promise you; I am going to find a way out of this situation, and when I do, I will find a way for us to be together. I will find a way." You look into her eyes and for a fleeting second, it's as though you can see right into her soul.

Until the spell is broken by someone at the door.

"Well now… isn't this romantic?" Your heart sinks. "Greentree's the name, I'm Cedric's, ah, sponsor here in the Middle East." Greentree flexing in his fatigues turns his attention to Ana and fixes his malign eyes on her. She squeezes your hand, stands and returns the stare with a fierceness that causes Greentree's smirk to waver.

"I know who you are," she says slowly and firmly. "Goodbye, Cedric."

He flinched and he knows you saw it. Now it's you who is smiling as you watch Ana walk purposefully out the door, her ponytail bouncing as she clips Greentree with her shoulder on the way through. Fearless.

"Wow, isn't she a feisty one? I like a girl with spirit." Greentree's smirk has returned. "Unfortunately, now's not the time for holiday flings, Cedric. Let's be on our way then, shall we?"

You stand, grab your bag and stare Greentree down with all your strength. "Let's get this over with."

You follow Greentree out through the main entrance of the hospice into the full force of the midday sun. God it's like being born. Everything is shimmering and white. Your eyes sting and strain at the light. You sidle down the grey marble steps like a lamb trying to keep yourself steady as your head begins to throb and the ringing in your ears reaches a new crescendo.

"Keep up, Cedric. We haven't got all day," barks Greentree.

You decide to ignore him. Remember to pick your battles, Cedric. You need to save your energy. Greentree leads you to a vehicle parked across the street. Christ, it looks identical to the one you were almost killed in. Maybe they only have one make of car out here. Or maybe Greentree is just up to his usual mind games. You look around warily to see if there is anyone watching you. The street is empty apart from a couple of old women waiting for a bus. It looks like it's just you and Greentree. You take a second glance at the old women before you jump in the car, just to make sure they are who you think they are. Yes, just old women, waiting for a bus.

The smell of sweltering old leather hits you as you enter the vehicle on the passenger side. You immediately wind down the window. Greentree dons a pair of sunglasses, starts the car, and starts driving. You could use some sunglasses too. Maybe there are some in the glove compartment.

"Don't touch that," snaps Greentree.

"What?"

"What's in there is not for you. That's all you need to know,"

"I thought there might be—"

"Nope, there's nothing here for you, Cedric. What's yours is mine and what's mine is mine. Comprende?"

"What about water?"

"This isn't a limousine service. Maybe when we stop."

Greentree sure is in a bad mood. You decide to just stay quiet and take in the scenery. As the wind rushes in, you gaze out the window at the passing parade of rubble strewn vacant lots, interspersed with decaying satellite dish-clad apartment blocks.

This town's been shot to hell, you think.

You think of Ana, living here in this battered launching zone, wondering what the hell you can do to get her out of here. You can't imagine how she can stay here. Her willingness to put her people and her homeland first, to defend them with her life is heroic. There's no other word for it.

You start to feel a bit guilty about all the women you have felt sexually attracted to. Women like Ana, that you have admired for their beauty. You can't help it, but they deserve better than to be desired. They deserve love. Romance. You feel strangely elevated by this thought. It takes courage to love. Something you have always lacked. How does one find the courage to risk heartbreak? Why wouldn't you risk heartbreak though, when the alternative is to live without love?

You think of your brief embrace with Ana. It was the most wonderful feeling. You just want to be with her again. You can't believe this has happened. That here in the middle of a warzone where people are constantly plotting to massacre one another, you have fallen in love!

You suddenly feel completely dislocated, like a grinning idiot. The world around you begins to swim as you pine for Ana. This is it, you think. She is the one! Wow, you are really head over heels this time, Cedric. You feel free. The world is wonderful, alive! Everything in the landscape seems to be bursting with vitality. The orange groves, the sky, the sun shining down.

"Some evil shit went down in those orange groves," mutters Greentree, tilting his gaze towards you. "Hey, Cedric, did you hear me? I said some seriously evil shit went down in those orange groves."

"I really—"

"I know you don't think we should be here, Cedric and that the world would be a better place if we all sat around, holding hands, singing Kumbaya."

"Well, I wouldn't—"

"Before you give me that smart guy come-back, I just want you to imagine, Cedric, the horror of seven thousand refugees being chased into those orange groves by blood thirsty militia. Trained killers determined to prevent these people from escaping into Lebanon. Families that had suffered days of shelling and sniper attacks on their homes. I won't tell you of the fate of many in amongst those trees. It's too gruesome and primitive to recount. I'll spare you the details, Cedric, but I know the details. And I have glimpsed the mind of the enemy. We are here for very good reasons. Very noble reasons. Those innocent people had no one to turn to, Cedric. No one."

Greentree's eyes narrow. "I know I can be a hard ass, Cedric, when I want to be. But if it wasn't for us there would be a humanitarian disaster here unlike anything seen in history. No one wants to see that. No one. Not even the most jaded individual. Because just a peek at what happened in those orange groves is enough for any human being to know without a doubt that these people are possessed of an untold evil and must be stopped. You can be a part of something, with your little life now, Cedric. You get to be more than just a bystander for once. Don't you want that, Cedric? Don't you want to be able to look back and say I was more than just a spectator? I picked a side?"

You decide not to answer this question. You just let it hang in the air until it becomes more of a statement of Greentree's ideals. And it's fair enough, you think. Greentree has probably spent his whole career in warzones trying to make sense of the senseless. He has seen the depths of human depravity and suffering and been caught up in it, tried to fight fire with fire, tried to make two wrongs into a right.

War acts like a magnet on one's moral compass. All kinds of morally abhorrent means are used to justify morally desirable ends.

You think about the peace of God that you experienced in the accident, the split-second revelation of all truth, beauty, and goodness. The wonder and awe you felt in that moment and its short-lived aftermath. It is that peace which must be the foundation of all human endeavor, you think. It is that foundation that is the basis of a free, just, and peaceful society. Nothing evil or corrupt or unjust could possibly spring from it. Just pure goodness.

So how do we tap into that? How do we ground ourselves in that reality so that we can create a better world? Because surely this is where our sense of morality comes from. Morality does not exist in a vacuum. It exists like every other scientific law of the universe. We should be guided by it in our every waking moment; but we have somehow forgotten this, and the world is in a terrible mess. We are so badly mired by powerful institutions—the government, corporations, media, activists—we are blinded. It is the blind leading the blind. Fools following fools. Anything that purports to bring about freedom hinders it. The very act of enforcing a moral virtue enslaves. The only way out, it seems, is to trust people to use their common sense.

But in this world? Impossible. There are too many corrupting influences, too many conflicting interests. Too much power in the hands of too few.

But wait, there are good people in this world who *are* being guided in their decision making by their sense of morality. And there is freedom by degree in the world. And whilst there are many obvious and subtle evils in the modern world there are also many obvious and subtle goods. It really does seem to be an undercurrent.

There may well be an eternal battle of good and evil going on at the bottom of human experience, you think. A struggle at the individual level, for every individual. Maybe this is what we are missing.

The battle of good and evil is not external. It's in the heart of every person.

"The battle between good and evil is in the heart of every individual, and the state of the world reflects this." you say finally, quite chuffed at how well you have distilled your thoughts.

"That's what I said, Cedric. We are the good guys, and they are the bad guys. Simple."

"But that's not quite what I am saying—"

"But it's what I am saying, and what I say here in my goddamned vehicle, on my goddamned mission, goes. Okay?"

You feel so buoyed by your thoughts that even Greentree's attitude can't spoil your high. It just seems foreign, insignificant, unsophisticated. You are harboring a new certitude. It feels as though a hard kernel of truth has been implanted in the core of your being. Literally implanted, lodged, immovable and indestructible. You couldn't budge it if you tried.

Is it a crystallization of ideas? A freak alignment of universal truths? Or is it, as you feel you can't deny, a gift. A revelation. You know how crazy this sounds, but in the midst of this quixotic glow you really don't care. The warmth and peace you are experiencing is more than enough to beat any doubts from the door.

You wish you could share this with Ana; tell her how you are feeling. You want to tell her everything! How glorious the world really is, how you love her. How your heart is bursting with love for her! You try to remember her, to bring her to life in your mind, but all you can manage is ephemeral glimpses of the way she looked at you. The honesty in her eyes.

Jesus, Cedric, you are carrying on like young Werther. Mooning!

Greentree must be regretting bringing me, you think. Your heart still aflutter, you lean back in your seat and try to catch a sideways glance at him. He's looking very tense. It seems plainly apparent to you how badly Greentree has lost his way. He's so badly caught up in the game he is playing he is beholden to it. And this is no criticism of Greentree. Greentree is not the only one. Who knows how long *you* can keep this up under the immense pressure to conform? It's inescapable... but maybe not. Maybe love sets us free, however briefly, it is love that restores us.

Why have we stopped talking about love? Why are we men so obsessed with conquering, when to be conquered, utterly besieged, and defeated by love is the ultimate release? We guard our hearts. We just guard our hearts against everything. You have guarded your heart your whole life. Not just from the love of another, but from the joy of life. Always so worried about pleasing others and avoiding anything that might mark you as an outcast. In this way, you make yourself that which you are trying to avoid. A walking recluse, afraid to express yourself. Afraid of living. Your soul so impoverished and starving that you don't know how you will ever survive—how any of us will.

"What's the matter with you, Bonhomie? You're always daydreaming. You can't do that out here. This is no place for *dreamers*." If there's one thing that Greentree is good at, it's pricking your balloon.

"I'm thinking, not dreaming," you say.

"About what? You think you're the English Patient, Cedric? Is that it?" You can't help but feel a little wounded by this.

"Let me disavow you of any romantic notions of what's going on here. Your heroine, Ana, I think you said?" You don't remember mentioning her name to Greentree.

"She's YPG right? Real tough cookies. I should know, Cedric we help to train them, give them toys to play with, show them where to find the bad guys. Give them cover. You get the picture. We've basically allowed them to re-establish a State for the Kurds here along the Turkish border. It suits us, for now. But anything can change any minute, Cedric. They know as well as we do that this contra deal, it just isn't going to last, so they are gearing up to have it out with the Turks. All I'm saying is that your sweetheart is going to be right in the firing line when things kick off, so if I were you, I'd be forgetting about it sooner rather than later."

Greentree takes a sidelong glance at you. Now you really feel like punching him in the face. Just as that thought presents itself, the sight of your haggard features rebounding off Greentree's sunglasses gives you a reminder of just how physically weakened you have become, and how unwise it would be to try to take Greentree on. No doubt he is trained in martial arts etcetera. The guy really does have the most annoying smile you have ever seen.

"Now, now, Cedric. You journalist types have so much trouble containing your rage. You have to vent and weep onto the page about every little transgression. Wait, what do they call it now? Not transgression... micro aggression, that's it! Now that's some garbage right there. When did you guys become so pure? You used to be fun to have around. Kevin Carter, man. Guys like that. Now we all have to watch our *language* the whole time we have you guys on tour with us, because we know everything we say is going to be interrogated and portrayed as some kind of heretical thought-crime back home.

"You know, you guys really messed up there. There will never be another great piece of war journalism. Never be another *Dispatches* because no one wants to say boo anymore to you guys for fear of getting burnt at the stake. We've got whole training courses now on self-censorship to avoid any 'image problems' for the military. We've got such a fake reality going that all news is fake news. You can report it straight up, but it's bent as hell already. It's a symptom of the new puritanism, Cedric. You and your buddies have pushed things too far and now we're all living in a goddamned mirage."

Well, he's got a point. If reality is not real, then reporting on reality is not real either. Jesus, you suddenly feel uneasy, like a character in a Philip K. Dick novel, in a world where all is not as it seems. It's been a nagging feeling ever since the accident.

If Greentree really thinks that no one is telling the truth to reporters anymore, why is he telling you all this stuff. Especially if he knows it could get him burned at the stake?

"It's all about 'active measures' now, Cedric. Everyone is planting stories everywhere and just fanning the flames until they eventually get picked up by you guys in the mainstream media. It's all about controlling the narrative, controlling history. You know your Orwell. 'Who controls the past controls the future. Who controls the present controls the past'. Deceit *is* universal now, Cedric. Right? Well, there are layers upon layers of deception, Cedric. It takes a supreme paranoiac to win this game, that's why the Russians lasted so long under Stalin. No one could keep up with the sheer volume of lies being cranked out by the Kremlin. But eventually it all comes undone... The road to hell eh, and yada, yada, yada. Always starts with some *dreamer* who wants to change the goddamned world and always ends up in a totalitarian nightmare."

"Look, Greentree, you don't have to convince me that the world is corrupt, but surely, we are making some progress? Surely, we are better off than we were a thousand years ago. Even a hundred years ago? We are richer, we have a higher standard of living, we have incredible technological innovations in medicine and science and communications. Why can't we just get the politics right?"

Greentree shoots you a look of contempt.

"Cedric, I'm sure you've heard the saying 'politics is downstream from culture' well, take a good look at the culture. Decadence, Cedric, *decline* is what you will see, and this is what informs our politics. This libertine rot has infected every institution we hold dear. There is no refuge. It's so bad that the culture is now actually downstream from the politics. This is what I mean about the totalitarian nightmare. The political elite are so empowered now by this 'progressive agenda'—they love it so much they have simply stopped listening to the people. Half of the crap we are forced to accept now has no basis in the real interests and desires of the people—what we used to call democracy. The culture is no longer really informing the politics at all. Instead, the political elite decides what is good for the people and dictates it. So, we get this hideous monster called Western culture consuming itself. Our foundations are being gnawed away, Cedric. All that has anchored us to reality. That's why I'm telling you we are living in a mirage now, a shared delusion. Everyone is insane, Cedric. There may be only a handful of sane people left in the world. Probably only a few monks who realized it and have had the good sense to go hide somewhere from all the lunatics and pray to God."

"Well, it doesn't sound like we have much of a future." you say.

"There is no future, Cedric. The future simply does not exist. It never has and never will."

You sit in silence for the next couple of hours, idly taking in the desert panorama and the shimmering road ahead. There's been no sign of anyone on the road apart from the odd truck whizzing by. Your conversation with Greentree has left you feeling quite dejected. Probably because he hit a nerve. Not so much in his casual dismissal of your feelings for Ana, but more so his world view, which despite yourself you can't help but agree with on some level. Greentree is right. We are living in a mirage built from layers of wholesale deceptions. Deception of others and deception of ourselves.

Self-deception is probably the most insidious of all. It all starts with conscious or willful self-deception and leads to unconscious self-deception and deception of others which then leads to a skewed reality. So finally, it's not possible to know reality at all. Our heads are so full of deception that true reality is out of reach. It's a sickness unto death, you think. Isn't that what Kierkegaard called it? Maybe Greentree has been reading Kierkegaard in his time away from blowing shit up.

You notice that the landscape has become hilly rather suddenly and the next half an hour is spent winding through valley after valley, and up and down numerous hills until finally you come to a stop at the bottom of yet another steep embankment.

"Okay, Cedric, this is the place." Greentree pulls over and parks the little car behind a thicket of low bushes so that it's well hidden.

"Get out. We'll walk from here," says Greentree. You ease yourself out, every stiff and sore muscle in your body complaining at the effort. Maybe you'll feel better once you get moving. Greentree moves to the back of the vehicle and pulls a small backpack from the trunk. He then moves towards you, and you step aside as he opens the passenger door, unlocks the glove compartment, and pulls out a black, holstered handgun, which he then adeptly attaches to his belt.

"Where the hell are we?" you say.

"That's classified, Cedric."

"Well, where the hell are we going then?"

"Classified. Follow me."

Greentree throws you a bottle of water. Bloody hell, I've been dying of thirst this whole time, you think.

Greentree sets out walking and you do your best to keep up. The surrounding hills and valleys provide you with little insight into where you are headed, and it is not clear where the road you were on is leading, other than into the next valley and out of sight.

After a short time, your starting point has disappeared from view, and you become completely disoriented, not to mention feverishly hot and out of breath from the hard scrabble upwards. Greentree seems to be marching forward without any regard for your lack of fitness and seems unconcerned as to whether you are keeping up or not.

Well, it's not as if I could make a run for it.

After what seems like another hour of scrambling along the hillside escarpment, Greentree motions to you to stop and points to the shadowy entrance to what looks to be a large cave. A pretty nice view, you think, as you step into the shade and sense the temperature drop.

You imagine yourself as Christ in this kind of cave for 40 days and 40 nights of spiritual battle; being shot up into the heavens and offered dominion over all the world below. Meanwhile, Greentree has moved further in and disappeared, your eyes unable to adjust to the sudden darkness as you follow along blindly.

You imagine Greentree as some kind of Kurtzian madman living out here commanding a rogue army of AWOL soldiers. You are half expecting to see the ghosts of marine one and two jump out of the shadows, when suddenly Greentree's face lights up about two feet in front of you.

"Christ, Greentree! You scared the hell out of me."

"That stuff never gets old," laughs Greentree. "Keep following, I'm going to need your help."

Greentree forges ahead, his flashlight arcing across the damp, musty interior of the cave. You hope he knows where he is going because it seems like there is an underground network here. You keep moving along a tight winding corridor, having to duck to fit through a few sections, until after a few more minutes, Greentree stops and keeps the flashlight shining at what looks to be some crates covered in army green canvas tarps.

"Alright here we are, Cedric. Let's remove these tarps."

"Okay. What is this?"

"Just a little stash, Cedric. We're probably going to need a bit more than a Beretta for this job."

Greentree levers open one of the crates and runs the flashlight over the contents. Jesus, it looks like some kind of rocket launcher.

"It's called a Javelin."

"A what?"

"A Javelin. It's a fire and forget heat seeker. Perfect from a mile away. Designed to take out tanks. Pretty cool huh? Here, you take one end, I'll take the other."

"God, do we really need this?" you say.

"Better to be safe than sorry, Cedric."

Greentree clips the flashlight to his hip and lifts the front end. You take the back end and you both shuffle back along the corridor towards the entrance, Greentree leading the way. The weapon is fairly light but would be heavy for one person to carry on their own. Suddenly you hear a crunching pop like the sound of a globe breaking, and in the same instant you are cast into complete darkness.

"Damn, I must have clipped the corner of the wall with the torch. You got anything, Cedric, a phone or a cigarette lighter or anything?"

"No, Greentree, I don't smoke cigarettes, and my phone was lost in the accident."

"Why did I even bother asking." Greentree mutters to himself. "Ok well we're just going to have to feel our way out. Just keep moving, Cedric. There's only a few different paths and they should all lead out eventually."

They *should* all lead out eventually. That's not inspiring a lot of confidence. You take a deep breath and fill up your lungs with the rank cave air, as the two of you begin to shuffle forward again. You keep moving for what seems like five or ten minutes—a lot longer than it took on the way in. You haven't worn a watch in years so you can't be sure.

"Greentree, it seems like we've been walking for too long. We must have taken a wrong turn." You can sense Greentree's frustration. "Hey, can we put this down for a minute? I need to stop; my arms are tired."

"Keep moving." Greentree snaps. After a few more minutes of fumbling around in the darkness, Greentree finally stops. "Okay, put down the damn Javelin. Easy now. Okay..." You now sense some resignation in Greentree's voice. It's a good thing you can't see his face.

"Greentree—"

"Just shut up for a minute, Cedric, I need to think."

"Don't you have a phone?" you say.

"If I did, don't you think I would have used it by now? I had to go dark."

"Well, I hope this is dark enough for you, Greentree... What about the Javelin. Hasn't it got night vision or something?"

"Yes, it's got night vision, Einstein, but night vision doesn't work in total darkness. You've got to have some light, moonlight or whatever."

"Well do you know how to use it? Maybe if you turned it on, there's an LED or something?"

"Look, I've seen it done. I need to be able to see what I'm doing. It's not like I'm running around with one of these things every other day like Rambo, okay? I'm not about to start toying with it in the dark."

"Well, what the hell are we going to do then, Greentree?" your voice raised.

"Start back the way we came."

"What?"

"We'll head back to the weapons cache and start again. Turn around, let's go."

"Great."

"Well, have you got any better ideas?" Nothing presents itself. "I didn't think so. Now move."

Slowly, the two of you slouch off again. This time you are leading the way, the Javelin tucked under your right arm. It does seem a little damper and a bit cooler than before. Jesus, I hope we haven't gone deeper.

After a while your arms start to hurt again, and you are still not back to the cache. The only sounds are the scraping of boots on the hard cave floor and the odd grunt or sigh of exertion as the two of you continue to move forward. You notice an anxious feeling in the pit of your stomach as you start to wonder whether you are badly lost.

"Greentree, we should be back by now, surely," you say. Your arms feel like lead.

"It doesn't make sense," says Greentree flatly. "We've tracked back the same way. The cache has to be here."

"Greentree, the cache is not here. We need to find a way out. It's no use continuing this way. We could be going deeper into the cave." You stop again and put down the Javelin.

"Cedric! What are you doing? Pick up the damn Javelin!"

You take a few steps to your right, with your arms out in front, feeling for the cave wall but there is nothing. You take a few steps back and then out in the opposite direction, desperately feeling for a wall, but there is nothing within reach. Who knows how big this enclosure is?

"Cedric! Stay where you are!"

"We are lost, Greentree, and I'm not going to end up some bloody skeleton in a cave clinging to a rocket launcher."

"Cedric! If you don't stand still, I'll make sure your lily-white ass never sees the light of day again!"

You've got to go, Cedric. You've got to get away from this lunatic before it's too late. Your whole body and mind instantly floods with FEAR. Your heart races and you can hardly breathe. It's move or die, Cedric. Fight or flight! Your instinct to flee takes charge of you, and without another thought you run into the darkness.

"You crazy fool, Cedric! You are in deep trouble now! Do you hear me?"

You have to be quiet! He can't see you, Cedric. You slow down, knowing that there must be a wall coming up. You continue with quiet, short steps, arms out in front, your blood pumping loudly through your brain. Your ears ringing louder than ever. Your whole body is trembling in fear as you stagger forward in anticipation of a wall. At the same time, you are hyper-aware of making any noise to help Greentree locate you. He's stopped shouting and cursing, so you aren't sure how far away he is. He is obviously listening as carefully as you are for any movement.

Abruptly, you hit a wall with your fingers, and as your arms buckle in, you stop before your body collides with it. You gasp in pain and stop yourself from making any further noise. God, please help me. Please help me find a way out of here. You lean with your back against the cold hard wall and try to calm your breathing as your right thumb begins to throb. Greentree could be anywhere. You must be silent! You decide to move along the wall maintaining contact with the fingertips of your left hand. You hear nothing but the sound of your own cautious footsteps as you move off further into the unknown.

Suddenly, you hear the scraping of footsteps nearby. You freeze and listen in fear as your heart beats out of control. God, he must be only a few feet away. The steps stop. You try to hold your breath. The steps start again, this time they seem to be tailing away from you. After a minute or so the noise stops, and you sense that you are alone.

You start to move along the wall again, praying to God that you are moving in the right direction. After a while you feel tired and decide to sit and rest. You have no idea how long you have been moving. The only thing you can be sure of is the rock wall and floor. It's still pitch darkness. You can't even see your hand when it is lifted in front of your face.

Christ, how did I end up here. Why did I allow myself to get into this mess? This really could be it for you, Cedric.

You try to remember the way in and the layout of the cave sections you moved through. It was definitely narrow for a while you remember. You also remember having to duck in parts which causes you to shudder at the thought of smashing your face into a low rock wall. You wonder how narrow this section is and decide to try to find out.

With your back to the wall, you move onto your hands and knees with the idea that you might be able to crawl straight ahead and find the wall on the other side, and if not, at least you could crawl back and continue.

With your left arm straightened out in front to protect your head you crawl forward counting each forward movement onto your right knee. One, two, three, four, five, six, seven, eig—a wall. The middle finger of your left-hand jams into the stone causing a shot of pain. Ouch! Oh, Jesus that hurt! Okay, you're in a corridor, but it's a fair bit wider than the one you came in through. Maybe it will narrow if you keep moving through.

You maneuver around to sitting again with your back against the wall. You cover your face with your hands and notice the damp earthy smell on them. Keep moving, Cedric, you hear yourself say.

MOVE.

This time the word seemed to emanate from within but was not a thought, it was more like a command. You quickly, stand up and with your right hand on the wall this time, you continue to walk along the corridor.

Trembling with fear, you keep moving further and further, all the while praying for God to save you one more time. Please God, please get me out of here. I will become a priest. I will do anything! Please save me, you think. You feel nothing.

You remember the incredible intimacy with which you felt God's presence out on the road after the accident, when you lay close to death. That feeling of certainty that God was with you and had saved you seems so remote to you now. You feel completely alone here, desperately alone and abandoned by God. What have I done? Why has He abandoned me? Why did He enter my life in the first place if this is how it was all going to end up? Where are you God? Where have you gone? Maybe it was all in my head.

You feel a darkness come over you now, that is not external, but an interior darkness. A darkness so bad it causes you to fall to your knees in complete hopelessness. Your entire organism feels rejected, cold and alone. The rational mind is telling you that you are right. There is no God. There is just random life and death. At the same time, you sense a menacing presence. Something evil watching and waiting in the darkness. Terrified, you freeze, hold your breath, and close your eyes.

I'm gone, you think, as you lie prostrate, your face in the cold earth, your body stiff as a board. This is it. God help me...

Your mind goes blank.

Suddenly you hear the violent flapping of wings. Holy crap, what is that? Is it a demon, a bat, a guardian angel? What the hell is it?

"Coo... Coo... Coo." It's a bird! It's got to be some kind of pigeon.

You force yourself to your feet. It's coming from up ahead. You quickly start scrambling towards the bird's call.

"Coo.... Coo." It's getting louder. Your head bowed you keep moving to where the sound is coming from, waving your left arm from in front to the side as you move along.

Abruptly you strike a wall to your left with your fist, indicating that the corridor has narrowed. You keep moving, your head bowed until you start to notice a muted brown light.

Oh my God, light! Light!

You keep moving in the direction of the light and the cave begins to take form around you. You follow the dimly lit section for another minute or so until the fully illuminated cave entrance appears ahead of you. You stumble on out into the blinding daylight and collapse exhausted onto your back, blinking frantically at the sky as you draw in huge gulps of the sweet mountain air.

I'm alive! I made it!

Still squinting at the sky, once more you hear the frenetic flapping of wings, and this time a sense of calm washes over you as the dove that rescued you ascends into the heavens. You are not sure, but you think you may have seen some kind of green band on its leg. Maybe it's a racing pigeon. Or another spy bird, you think. You laugh to yourself.

Wow, Cedric. You made it.

After a few minutes lying there in the sun, birds of prey now having taken the place of the dove circling overhead, you roll over and force yourself up onto your knees and with further effort, back onto your feet.

God I'm thirsty, you think.

You look around at the desolate valley below and the same hostile view that you naively admired upon your arrival. You've got to get back to the car. You take a few steps along the trail, gasping and scrabbling down the rocky terrain when suddenly a horrible feeling of guilt washes over you. You can't do it. You can't leave Greentree alone in that cave. You turn around and make your way back up, and with great reluctance you shuffle back through the cave's entrance into the brown light, all the time turning to make sure you haven't gone too far.

"Greentree!" you shout. "Greentree, this way!" You listen carefully for a response, but you hear nothing.

"Greentree, come this way!" you call, but still nothing.

"Greentree! Greentree! Greentree!" your voice echoes in the darkness.

You keep calling his name for what seems like an hour. You can't be sure. Still, you hear nothing in response. All the while you are wrestling with the dilemma of whether to go deeper into the cave to search for him, or to stay close to the cave entrance. Your voice is just about gone.

You pick up a rock and start to bang it against the cave wall.

"Greentree!" you call feebly. Please don't make me go back in there.

You sit slumped against the wall, banging the rock, both arms aching from the effort, every strike causing a piercing report. Nothing. You drop the rock, exhausted and numb. Your voice now so hoarse you can barely muster a whisper. You sit there reflecting on the terror you felt, lost in the darkness, and cringe at the thought of what Greentree must be going through, having been lost in there for so long. It's no good going deeper. You'll just get lost again. You say a final prayer for him and make your way back to the entrance.

Hunched and stumbling into the light, you again fall to the ground and remain lying in the sun for a few moments, your eyes closed, your breathing shallow, your mind reeling from the whole experience. You feel yourself edging towards sleep.

As you are about to drift off, you are suddenly brought back to consciousness by a clattering noise behind you. You place your right hand on the ground to push yourself back up to a sitting position, when something strikes you hard in the back, causing you to collapse again. Immediately a shot of adrenaline courses through your body and without thinking, you roll away and scramble to your knees. With your back to the precipice, you look up to see Greentree standing there, the Javelin at his feet.

"Greentree, you made it," you whisper, noticing that Greentree looks tired and wild-eyed.

"Yeah, I made it. If it wasn't for you, Cedric, I never would have found the way out."

"Look, Greentree, we have to go back down. It's over. Let's get back to the car."

"It's not over, Cedric. Not until I say it is. Not until we have done what we came here to do."

"Are you joking? I'm telling you; I can't go on. I can barely speak. I can barely stand up. I need water. Food. Rest. I'm done. I saved your life. I'm going back to the car."

Greentree stands there, casually draws his service handgun, and points it at your head.

"Pick it up."

"W-w-what?"

"The Javelin, pick it up."

"I'm going back to the car, Greentree." You make a move for the trail. Greentree cocks the handgun. You stop and look him in the eye. He'll do it. He's insane. He motions to the Javelin.

"Pick it up."

"Okay, wait," you raise your hands. "Wait. Okay, I'll pick it up. I'll pick it up."

Greentree moves a few feet away from the Javelin and watches you carefully, pistol still drawn, as you move in to pick it up. Your mind roiling with rage and bewilderment, you bend down to try to lift one end.

"From the middle, Cedric."

"What? Aren't you going to help?"

"Nope."

"What? You expect me to carry this thing up the hill?"

"Yep."

"How?"

"Across your shoulders. Just do it."

How could he do this after I saved his life? Feeling betrayed and full of anger, you take hold of the Javelin's hand grips and in one furious effort you hoist the rocket launcher up onto your right shoulder. Quickly adjusting it and reaching around with your left arm, you manage to center the thing behind your head so that you have both arms looped over, steadying it across your shoulders and resting it against the nape of your neck.

"Now walk."

"Wait, it's heavy."

"Move!"

"Okay, okay!"

You start up the trail, wobbling and struggling to keep your balance, Greentree following a short distance behind. The sun beats down on your tired, aching body as you trudge along the trail, each small, shaky step upwards taking every ounce of energy you can gather.

Sweat pours down your face and neck as you battle to keep moving forward. Your breathing is now very labored, and you are dying of thirst. On the path ahead the sun casts a shadow of your gangly figure, arms spread wide as though affixed to a pole. You start to feel dizzy and after a few minutes you drop to one knee.

"Get up, Cedric," barks Greentree.

You rest for a few seconds, then with everything you have, you return to a standing position.

"I can't continue." Voices ring out in your mind... Look within, Cedric. Find something. Keep going. It will all be over soon. All be over.

Take it away from me. This suffering. This scourging, swirling sky. I'm so dizzy. Please, take it away from me. Help me.

Desperately, you look again at your shadow.

"*Walk with me, Cedric. Follow me,*" says the shadow.

"I can't."

"*Walk with me, Cedric. We will walk together.*"

"I can't. I don't want to." You begin to weep.

"*Then, I will walk for you, Cedric.*"

"I... I can't go on."

"*Then, I will carry you, Cedric.*"

Your shadow vanishes. You close your eyes, take a deep breath, and let go of *everything*. I give up, you think. I GIVE UP. You float away from it all; look down on it from miles above. You stopped believing in yourself. Your desires refined to nothing. You wanted to die.

"*Yes, you gave up on yourself, Cedric, but you believed in Me.*"

"Stop there." Greentree's whiplash command jolts you back from your delirium. You open your eyes in amazement to a panoramic view of the next valley.

"You surprised me, Bonhomie, I didn't think you had it in you."

Good God, you must have walked to the top. On your knees, you maneuver the Javelin to the ground and keel over onto your right side, your body crumpled in a heap of exhaustion.

You black out.

. . . .

You dream that you are back in the cave again. Wandering from place to place, hopelessly lost in the dark. From time to time, you meet other people in the cave and for some reason you can see them. They all seem to know where they are and are even enjoying themselves as though they are in the middle of some mad parlour game. The men seem supremely confident and the women hanging off them always seem to be laughing at some kind of inside joke. You want to ask them how to get out, but you are unable to speak for some reason.

A small woman wearing a long white robe takes you by the hand and walks you through the cave network. It's a labyrinth, she says. A maze. You try to communicate your fear to her; that you just want to leave. It seems that she is blissfully unaware of how afraid you are and slips away into the darkness leaving you alone once more.

Suddenly, Greentree appears out of the darkness, and you start berating him for bringing you here. He seems completely uninterested in anything you have to say. When you shout at him and grab him by the shirt and shake him, and ask him why, he barely registers as though he is just playing his part in a nightmare designed just for you.

You continue to shake him, only to find that it is your father now taking the brunt of your anger. You continue to scream and struggle as a child. You feel yourself suffocating, unable to breathe. You struggle wildly for air.

Your eyes open.

"Ah, Cedric. You're awake." says Greentree. As the world comes into focus, you notice that it is in a kind of half-light.

"You must have needed the sleep. I guess you had a big day yesterday."

Yesterday? I must have slept all night. As you try to get up, you realise that your body is not responding to the initial signals from your brain to move. Lying on your stomach all night has caused your back to seize up.

Slowly you straighten yourself out and sit up. Awed by the beauty of the dawn, your eyes navigate their way from the fading stars to the familiar face of your nemesis.

"Coffee, Cedric?" Greentree pours a couple of cups from a large thermos pulled from his backpack. You take the cup and gulp down the lukewarm brew.

"We made it, Cedric. You know I wouldn't have pushed you if it weren't so important that you see this exchange unfold. The world has to know, Cedric, and it has to come from an independent source. Someone who will be believed and who doesn't have any irons in the fire. Someone who's previous work reinforces their truthfulness. That's why we need you."

Greentree crouches before you and gestures towards the valley below.

"See that road down there? In about thirty minutes we are going to witness a rendezvous between the Russians and the Syrians. The Russians are going to hand off a truckload of North Korean cargo. Weapons so destructive, they could wipe Israel off the map. If Hezbollah gets their hands on this stuff, it will be game over for everyone. The Israelis would freak if they knew, and they don't sit on their hands, Cedric—their response would be so swift and so severe—well it would probably start World War three. That's why we haven't told them."

"What makes you think I'm going to help you after everything you have put me through, Greentree? I mean, I can hardly see anyway. What am I going to witness, a blurry valley with a few trucks parked together and a handful of soldiers running around? What's that going to prove?"

"You'll see alright, Cedric. Here, take these binoculars. Here's a notepad. Just take it all in, Cedric. Get it all down on paper. Then, you write the article, we send it to The Daily and you're done. Mission accomplished. I'll bet you always wanted to save the world, Cedric, change the course of history. I'll bet that's why you became a *journalist* in the first place. Well, here's your chance my friend. All you have to do now is your job."

There is no point in arguing. You just want to get this whole ordeal over with.

"Attaboy, Cedric. I bet you're hungry. How about a sandwich. Here you go." Greentree slings you a chicken sandwich so delicious that it almost causes you to weep with happiness.

"Pretty good huh. It's the whole egg and dill mayo."

"Oh my God, Greentree. This is incredible. Why didn't you become a professional chef? You could have had a career making people deliriously happy instead."

"Yeah well, I do love cooking, Cedric, but I also love my country. I used to think it was worth dying for."

"And now?"

"I'm not so sure anymore, Cedric. The way it's going, I'm not so sure."

"Then what are we doing here? Why don't we just go back down and leave it alone."

"The people, Cedric. Maybe the country isn't worth saving. But the people are. I come from a military family, Cedric. My father, my grandfather and my great grandfather before him. It was drilled into me from a young age. Patriotism. I wanted to *bleed* for the Republic. I went out and saw my fair share of battle and saw a lot of good people lose their lives. Gone too young. Gave everything for their country. Then I joined the CIA and went from wearing a white hat to a black one. Most CIA officials and staff, probably 80 percent of them, they're good people with good values. It's the 20 percent that are amoral sons of bitches. Unfortunately, they're the ones that run the show."

"So, screw it, Greentree. Why keep doing their bidding? Why don't you just leave? Do something else—"

"We need people on the inside who can massage the outcomes, Cedric. You have no idea what kind of mess we would be in. God, I doubt we would even exist if it weren't for smart people using their wits to sabotage the nutso plans handed down to us. The 20 percent are calling the shots, but it's the 80 percent that has to go along with it. That's when your conscience comes into play— when you have to decide which side you are on in the higher stakes game. This is not about betraying your country. I'm talking about the sheer survival of humanity. It doesn't matter which flag you salute. It's the same question you've got to ask yourself. How many people's lives are at stake and how many can you save."

"How do you know you are doing the right thing, Greentree? You said yourself the layers of deceit are so thick it's almost impossible to know what's true. How do you second guess the motives or predict the responses of whole nations when you know your intelligence is made up of a web of lies?"

"You can't reason with these people, Cedric. They don't want to know the truth. They want power. People like me, Cedric, we're the intermediaries, we're the ones that ultimately make or break these plans. Sometimes we have to let things go a bit pear shaped to serve the bigger picture, but we're still secretly wearing white hats. Trust me, Cedric, I know what I'm doing. I need your help."

You look Greentree in the eye, searching for a hint of honesty to back up what he just said. Is he one of the 80 percent or the 20 percent? His vacant eyes, as usual, tell you nothing. You want to believe him but there is something gnawing at *your* conscience. Are you really going to trust someone who forced you here at gunpoint, just because they gave you a sermon on their own righteousness? This guy has been trained to lie and manipulate. That's what spies do right?

"Anyway, enough talk, eh, Cedric? We need to get ready."

Greentree gives you one of his trademark ice cold glares, finishes his coffee and moves the Javelin to a position overlooking the steep ravine to the road below. He motions to you to follow. You gingerly stand and make your way over to where Greentree is crouched. He signals to you to get down, and you take the last few steps with your aching back bent low, until you take up a lying position on the pebbled ground next to him.

"What do we do now?" you say, fumbling with the binoculars in your left hand and the pen and notepad in your right.

"We wait," says Greentree.

You take a look through the binoculars. There's nothing much there. You do have a very close up view of the road. There are a few bushes here and there but otherwise it's a fairly open area, which strikes you as a bit odd. Wouldn't a secret rendezvous between world powers to exchange weapons of mass destruction take place somewhere more hidden? I guess it's a fairly remote area protected by some difficult terrain. But still.

You feel a strange mixture of security and danger lying here next to Greentree in the middle of a warzone about to observe the enemy at close range. You feel the fear in your chest and notice your hands are shaking uncontrollably. At least Greentree knows how to handle these situations. At least he is an experienced operator. Christ knows what would have happened had you been brought up here by those two young marines.

You try taking some deep breaths to calm your nerves. On every deep breath in, the feeling of anxiety in the pit of your stomach and chest is accentuated. You go back to shallow breathing, cold sweat dripping from your armpits, your mind and body so tense you are locked in a state of hyper-alert dread.

You take a sidelong glance at Greentree. He is the picture of calm. Resolute and relaxed. Almost meditative in his focus on the road below. He could sit there, perfectly still, for days and nights. Like a shepherd. Maybe that's how he sees himself. Like a good shepherd whose job it is to protect his flock from the wolves.

Funny how, for all the world's complexity there are these underlying basic instincts that drive us, you think. Maybe these are the only reliable predictors of human behaviour. Greentree knows my instinct is to flee, so he is using whatever tools he has, to combat that. His own self-assuredness is the most important and persuasive tool he has in this situation, and he knows it. He's almost too confident. Not even a drop of sweat or a whiff of BO. A chill runs down your spine as you recall Greentree's ice cold glare. Maybe he's not the shepherd.

Maybe he's the wolf.

"Here they come, Cedric. Right on schedule."

Through the binoculars you observe a convoy of three army green cargo trucks led and followed by what look to be armored personnel carriers, travelling slowly west along the road.

"And here come the Syrians—are you getting all this, Cedric? I need you to capture the detail. Got it? I'm going to get some pictures."

"Yes. I'm writing it all down," you say.

From the west, travelling slowly east to meet the convoy are two more armored personnel carriers. The two sets of vehicles meet virtually right under your noses.

"Okay, this hand-over is all going to happen pretty fast, Cedric. Just keep watching." How am I supposed to take notes at the same time as I'm looking through these bloody binoculars, you think.

You see what look to be two heavy-set Russian soldiers carrying automatic rifles climb out of the lead personnel carrier. One of them signals for the Syrian vehicles to stop. Two Syrians then climb out of their lead vehicle, also armed to the teeth. They slowly walk towards each other and enter into a short conversation. The Russian soldiers then lead the Syrians to the rear of the first cargo truck and open the doors. The soldiers all climb aboard.

It's too hard to see exactly what's in there, but you are getting some sunlight reflecting back at you. It's something cylindrical and metallic.

The soldiers jump back down and head to the rear of the next cargo truck. They go through the same inspection until they reappear and head for the final truck. When they finally re-emerge both the Syrians and the Russians head back to their own personnel carriers and start the vehicles. It looks like they are going to trade places.

The Syrians taking control of the cargo convoy, and the Russian carriers about to head off on their own.

You put down the binoculars to quickly make notes on the whole spectacle. Your mind now racing with excitement.

As you look up from the page you once more become conscious of Greentree. Looming next to you like a giant ironclad statue, he has positioned himself on one knee, with the Javelin over his right shoulder, aiming it straight at the convoy trucks.

No! You were so absorbed in what was happening on the road, you had almost forgotten he was there! Greentree you madman! Don't do it! Completely frozen, you can't get the words out.

Lying right there, looking up at him you suddenly hear an almighty WHUMP!

Greentree is gone.

What the hell happened? Where did he go? Did the Javelin go off?

The next thing you hear is the whooshing jetstream of a missile. You look up, and now, in the same place that Greentree vanished from the face of the Earth, stands a figure in combat boots and military fatigues, but it's not Greentree. Trembling and lying there with your eyes closed in the fetal position, you wait for the death blow to come.

"Get up, Cedric," chants an ethereal voice through noise of the Jetstream. "Cedric, get up, we've got to move quickly."

You open your eyes. Standing there like an avenging angel with a giant halo contrail in the blue sky above, is Ana. This amazing figure of beauty reaches her hand down to you and you grasp it.

"Run, Cedric. Run!"

As you run together for the track, you are both stunned into stopping by an enormous explosion, followed by a plume of smoke rising up from the valley below you.

"My God, what was that!" you yell, your ears ringing.

"The rocket, Cedric. It went off after I kicked him over the edge."

"You kicked Greentree over the cliff?"

"It's not that steep, Cedric—don't worry. We have to get down. We haven't got much time."

With every last bit of effort left in you, you stumble, slide, leap and stagger to the bottom of the hill. Ana all the while keeping you upright and urging you forward.

It's eerily quiet. No sign of a skirmish or any other noise.

As you hobble side by side with Ana, your arm over her shoulder, her arm around your waist, she leads you through a last thicket of pine trees until you come out into a clearing at the base of the hillside where you see the road ahead. The black, acrid smoke billowing towards you now indicates that you are not far from where the rocket detonated. As you get closer you can see the flaming wreck of a vehicle on the roadside.

You look at Ana, she looks worried.

"What's wrong, Ana?"

"It's our car, Cedric. The rocket, it must have..." Her eyes betray a flicker of emotion.

Suddenly you hear an engine roar and careering out of the bushes comes a streak of white lightening. Hurtling in reverse towards you, you recognize Greentree's car.

How the hell???

Once again frozen to the spot in terror, you are convinced that this time you are done for, but there's no way you are going to let Ana get hurt.

In a split second, you tackle Ana to the ground, just saving her from being hit. The car pulls up right beside you and from your ground level view, you see combat boots exiting the driver's side and limping around the front of the vehicle.

Well, this is it then.

"Ana, I'm sorry," you say. "I'm so sorry. I—"

"Why don't you guys get a room?" booms a loud American voice.

"Huh... Riley? Riley! What are you doing here?"

"Just happened to be in the neighborhood. Get in the car before that nutcase, Greentree, gets here."

You jump in the back seat of the car with Ana. Riley limps back around to the driver's seat and floors it with the wildest looking grin you've ever seen on anybody's face.

• • • •

For the next 20 minutes, Riley guns the little car to within an inch of its life, the tyres screeching around every corner, until eventually you are out of the hills and onto the desert highway.

"I thought you were dead," says Ana to Riley.

"Picked a lucky time for a bathroom break I guess," says Riley. "I heard the rocket coming in, took cover and well, I guess I left the car running and up she went. Those Javelins don't miss. Anyways, I thought Greentree's car must have been around somewhere. It didn't take me long to find it. It ain't hard to get these old things started."

"I can't believe I'm out of there," you say. "I can never thank you enough. Both of you. He was going to take out that whole Russian convoy. He's convinced that they were about to hand-off a shipment of North Korean chemical weapons or something—that it was going to start World War three. I don't know, it all sounded so crazy."

"Greentree *is* crazy. But he's not that crazy," says Riley.

"I was there, Riley. He had the Javelin aimed at the convoy. He would have blown those trucks to smithereens and who knows what the consequences would have been."

"Listen, Cedric. There's no way in hell Greentree is going to do something that uncontrolled. The Javelin probably misfired when it was tumbling down the hill. Trust me I know the guy. Now just sit tight. We've got to get you to a safehouse, and we haven't got much time."

"Just try to relax, Cedric. You will need your strength," says Ana. "We have a place to go. We will be there soon."

She clasps your hand, gives it a gentle squeeze, and brings it to rest on her thigh. Exhausted, you rest your head on her shoulder as she comforts you. God I could just sleep here forever, you think, as you close your eyes.

You feel your love for her welling up inside. You even feel love for Riley right now. You feel like hugging the guy. As he calmly speeds you along, you notice his right hand is bandaged up.

"Hey, Riley, what happened to your hand," you say.

"It's from the accident. I lost a few digits. Index, ring and pinky. So now I got a permanent bird. How do you like that?"

"It suits you," you say.

Riley cracks a smile. Ana laughs. Then you laugh. Then Riley. Then it happens again. That silent laughter that hurts so much you can't even breathe.

17

Back on the road to Damascus, you gaze out the window of the little car. It's a relief to be away from that maniac Greentree. Safe for now. You wonder what happened to him after he fell into the ravine. Ana was right, it wasn't that steep. He probably just rolled halfway to the bottom. You imagine the look on his face after realizing his plans had unraveled—lying there in the dust, looking up at the sky. You feel a slight satisfaction at this image and can't help smiling.

"What?" asks Ana quietly, having noticed your grin.

"I was just thinking of Greentree, that's all."

"He deserved it, no?" she says coyly, flicking her dark hair from side to side and breaking out her gorgeous smile. "What?"

"Nothing, I just think you are amazing that's all."

"Anyone could have done it, Cedric. It's just training and timing. It's nothing really."

"No, *you are* amazing," you say. She looks at you with raised eyebrows and laughs her musical laugh. You want to kiss her.

"I could listen to you laugh forever," you say. She starts again.

"Cedric, you say the stupidest things." Her big eyes gleaming, her smile wider than ever.

You sit there in silence for a moment, only the loud thrumming of the little engine and the wind rushing through the cracked windows filling the void. Riley is the picture of concentration, scanning the horizon and pushing the little car on.

"I love that contagious laughing when you can't stop. Like before. Did you know, Ana, that there was once a serious laughing epidemic that broke out in Africa? In the 1960's, I think it was in Tanzania. A journalist friend of mine told me about it," you say.

"A laughing epidemic?" she says with a half-smile frown. "What happened?"

"Apparently, it started in a small village in a boarding school for girls. Maybe it was a joke that started it."

"What was this joke?" she says, smiling more broadly.

"I don't know, they're in Tanzania, maybe it was an elephant joke."

"An elephant joke?" she asks quizzically.

"No one knows," you shrug sardonically. "Anyway, true story. One day, three young girls at the school start laughing hysterically about something that one of them said and can't stop. I mean rolling around on the floor in fits. Every time they are told to stop someone else in the class starts. No-one can stop for long before someone sets them off again. You know what it's like."

"I love it when that happens," she says, pensively.

"Anyway, the teachers start laughing too and it becomes so disruptive that they can't teach the students anymore and before long the whole thing starts to snowball out of control. The next day the laughing starts again, and it gets so bad that over the next few days they have to close the school, but even that can't contain it. First it spreads to the parents, and as they try to explain what is going on to friends and relatives it spreads to other villages, over the phone and so on. Hundreds of people become affected. Fourteen more schools have to close. It even crosses the border into Uganda."

"Uganda?" Ana says, desperately trying to keep a straight face.

"Yes, Uganda," you say with a wry smile. "This goes on for more than a year. Can you imagine? No one even knows why they are laughing, which is precisely why they can't stop. It gets so bad that people are frowned upon for laughing in public. There are signs up everywhere saying 'NO LAUGHING'. In a bank queue, people try not to look at each other, scold each other for laughing and then go home to laugh in private. People plead with each other to stop. Weddings and funerals descend into hysterical laughter and are abandoned. International psychology experts and doctors are flown in, and they even take blood tests to see whether it is caused by a virus. It causes so much recrimination that the school is eventually sued."

"Really?" says Ana chortling.

"Don't laugh," you say, trying to hold back. "Anyway, this guy Jeff Conolly who told me the story. He calls it the African giggles. Every time I see him at a press conference, I only have to see the stupid grin on his face from across the room and I can't help thinking about it, and then I'm in the danger zone. It'll be dead quiet in a room full of two-hundred people with some politician droning on and then I'll have a vision of these African villagers caught up in these pesky silent laughing attacks whilst trying to go about their daily business, and then I'm done. I sit there in tears staring at the floor, trying not to snort or shake my shoulders. The one thing I promise myself is not to look back at Conolly, but I always do, and he just gives me this knowing look." You almost choke now trying to hold it in and Ana starts to laugh again. God she is beautiful.

"Stop, Cedric, I can't take it anymore. Your face is like this, friend of yours. I look at you and I can't help it."

"Good," you say. "I want to make you laugh forever, so I can keep listening to it."

Ana gives you a look that says she would like that to be true. But you can't help but sense she is carrying a world of worry and doubts about whether it might be possible.

· · · ·

"Okay listen up, we're coming into Damascus," says Riley. "We should dump this car, but we can't go out in broad daylight looking like this. We're just going to have to hope no one sees it on the way in. Remember it's going to be Greentree's people looking for us. They're all working dark here. They don't have the resources or the authority to cast a wide net. I'm going to drop you at the safehouse and then go get rid of this thing."

On the way into the ruined city, you count 17 murals of President Assad and his generals, wearing sunglasses. You also count about 17 vehicles that look identical to the one you're in, which gives you a little bit of comfort. Riley seems to be driving around in circles, through back alleys and narrow laneways. He seems to know the route.

If you make it home, you are going to buy one of these little beauties. You imagine your grandchildren asking you why you still drive this old car and imagine telling them all about your heroic assignment to the Middle East, winning over their beautiful grandmother along the way and saving the world from a rogue CIA agent. Your grandchildren, spellbound by this great adventure, will always ask you to keep telling them the story. Every visit. Every birthday. Every Christmas. And every time, Ana will be listening in, gently correcting your embellishments, laughing at your silly romantic world view, and looking away when her eyes well up with tears.

"Ok we're here," says Riley, bringing the car to a stop. "It's a four-level apartment building—one per floor. Go straight in, keep your heads down. Take the stairs to the apartment on the third floor. You'll find the key under the carpet covering the fifth step leading up to the fourth floor. Go in and wait. I've got to make myself scarce. Good luck."

You look at Riley with an expression of gratitude. "Thanks, Riley, for everything," you say. Riley leans back, smiles, holds up his right hand and gives you the permanent bird.

"No problem, Cedric. Now get out," he says with a laugh.

You jump out of the car, Riley speeds away and in a few steps, you and Ana are inside the building. You quickly make your way through the small drab foyer to the stairwell which leads to the first-floor landing. Here directly opposite the stairs is the door to the first apartment. You continue on up, past the second-floor apartment until finally you reach the third floor. You exit the stairs on the landing and walk quietly around to the door to apartment three.

Standing on the landing you count the steps up to the fourth floor and at the fifth step you lift the carpet and find a small brass key. Quickly looking up at Ana, you turn and enter the key into the lock. The latch releases. You push the door open and stand with Ana at the entrance, scanning the room before entering.

The room is dimly lit, only because all the curtains have been pulled. It's a 1980's affair. Cream walls with worn sepia curtains and furnishings. In the middle of the room is a coffee table adorned with a small cut glass vase, and over against the wall is a matching side-table with a middle eastern tea set. In the corner, by the window there is a writing desk with some papers on it, and a laptop plugged into a power point.

Someone is here.

"Hallo, Cedric," a familiar voice calls out from behind you.

"Schuman! You scared the life out of me."

"I'm so glad you made it back. Take a seat," says Schuman.

Ana moves quietly to the window, taking a peep through the curtains at the street below. She turns and gives you a nod. You take a seat on the couch.

"Would you like some tea?"

"Tea would be good. An explanation would be better."

Schuman makes tea for the three of you and takes a seat on the opposite couch. Leaning back with his legs crossed he takes a sip and pauses.

"Ah, that's good," he sighs, putting down his cup and saucer. "Okay, Cedric, I'm just going to jump right in now. I need you to listen very carefully. Greentree's people are on the hunt, and it won't be long before they find this place no matter how cautious we have been. They can smell your blood from miles away these days, like bloody sharks." Schuman shifts in his seat slightly as though he is uncomfortable at the thought. "This is a very sticky situation, Cedric. I've gone out on a limb to bring you in, but I just couldn't leave you out in the cold after everything I've put you through. We figured, to hell with it, they are only our cousins after all, not immediate family. All we have to do is play a bit of blind man's bluff, and it will all blow over."

"Blind-man's bluff?"

"Yes, Cedric. Put the blindfold on them, spin them around a few times and while they are disoriented, call out, and do a bit of dodging, that's all."

"Right," you look over at Ana who seems vaguely amused by all this English nonsense.

"Look, Schuman, I trust you, but enough with the games. I could have been killed out there. Greentree is a bloody lunatic of the highest order. He was about to blow up a convoy of Russian trucks laden with God knows what kind of weapons of mass destruction. If it wasn't for Ana, we might not even be here right now. Any of us."

"You are right about one thing, Cedric. Greentree is a bloody lunatic." Schuman takes another sip of his tea and pauses again. "But you don't need to worry about the whole Armageddon thing. Have you ever heard of a false-flag operation, Cedric?" Schuman pauses again searching your eyes for recognition. "The whole thing was an elaborate set-up. Paid stooges playing dress-ups. Crisis actors—the works. The CIA pulls this stuff all the time."

"But I saw him, Schuman, he was about to fire that rocket."

"Maybe... I wouldn't put it past him. It would make it more real that's for sure. I guess we'll never know now, will we."

"Well then why take me up there? Why go to all that trouble?"

"They've been looking for a reason to put the screws on North Korea for a long while now. That's far more interesting to the CIA than what's going on here. A firsthand story exposing a North Korean shipment of weapons of mass destruction potentially falling into the hands of Israel's enemies would also give them the green light to ramp things up and maybe even topple Assad. Could kill two birds with one stone, so to speak. Greentree is old school, he's still all caught up in all that 'axis of evil' stuff that Bush and Cheney were pushing. It's what started all this chaos in the first place. They needed you, Cedric, because you could give it authenticity. We don't have the luxury of planting stories in state owned papers like the other side. We have to work things into the real free and independent press without the editors even raising an eyebrow, which of course mostly they don't because they are always greedy for a scoop."

"So, you knew then."

"I'm sorry, Cedric. For the most part I have to do whatever I'm told by HQ. But even they have cold feet now. We'll turn a blind eye from here on out and deny all knowledge to the Americans. They can deal with it up the chain. Now listen carefully, Cedric. Greentree is a vindictive bastard, and he doesn't give up easily."

"Really? I kind of guessed that."

"As I said, Cedric, this situation is dicey. We are in a city full of maniacs, terrorists, secret police, torturers, and spies. We have two things going for us. Firstly, Greentree's people are up against all that too, so they must keep a low profile here, just like us. Secondly, we have had a stroke of luck. There's an old saying, Cedric, 'success is where preparation meets opportunity'... but that doesn't apply here, this is just pure unadulterated miracle luck."

You shift nervously in your seat. Ana takes a sip of her tea.

"There are only a few flights in and out of Damascus, Cedric. They're going to have eyes on all of them. There's one they will be watching even more closely than all the others, and that's the one you're going to get on. You will board this plane right under their noses. Because, Cedric, you are not the one they will be focusing on."

"What?"

"They won't be looking for you, Cedric."

"Why not?"

"They will be focusing on the pope."

"What? What do you mean the pope?"

The pope, Cedric, he's here. He travels on a private jet. The *Volo Papale*."

"The pope? What's the pope doing here?"

"Kind of strange, Cedric but he was just in Iraq trying to mend some bridges and he had some kind of holy inspiration to stop in Damascus on the way back to the Vatican. He's like that apparently."

"Well, how am I supposed to—"

"Here's the thing, Cedric, the pope always travels with a big group of journalists from around the world. He sits up front; they sit in coach. We've got you a Vatican press pass, ID papers everything. It all arrived in the diplomatic bag overnight. All you have to do is join them here in Damascus and walk onto the plane with them when it leaves... in disguise of course."

"Schuman, this is crazy. I can't just get on a plane with the pope!"

"I know it sounds crazy, Cedric, but it's our only shot. The security here is tighter than a camel's arse in a sandstorm... Sorry. Look, when you get to Rome, we have everything covered. Our exfil guys will be waiting, but we've got to get you out of here first. I've booked you into the Beit al Hadi Hotel under an alias. Your bag is packed. Now we need to get moving."

Schuman stands and moves towards a doorway leading to a bedroom. He motions to you to follow him. You turn to Ana, and she gives you an approving look.

"Go, Cedric," she says.

You stand and walk through the dim living room and into the bedroom where you find Schuman standing next to the double bed. On the burgundy bedspread lies an open suitcase, what looks like a pack of travel and press accreditation documents, a stack of US dollars, a laptop and a black handgun. Your head swims as you try to come to grips with Schuman's plan. Holy crap, I'm literally going undercover. I'm not cut out for this.

"Don't worry, Cedric. We've done this plenty of times before," says Schuman.

"What, put an imposter on the pope's plane?"

"No, no of course not. But we do need to do these emergency exfils from time to time."

"So, when was the last time you did this?" you ask.

"Well, I myself haven't exactly done it, but we have before, you know, during the Cold War and all that."

"Great. I'm not worried at all now, Schuman. Thanks."

"Look, Cedric, you are in safe hands. It'll be a piece of cake. A walk in the park..."

"More like a crapshoot. I'm getting tired of your stupid idioms, Schuman."

"Good one, Cedric. Look, all I'm trying to say is that we've got this. If you stick to the rules, play your part, you'll be home and hosed." Schuman gives you a sheepish look as if to say, sorry I can't help myself. "Now, Cedric, your disguise is simple. Glue on black moustache, black wig, baseball cap, horn rimmed glasses, a cargo vest and a pair of black Cubans to make you taller."

"That's all?"

"You have to look like a journalist."

"Yeah, a journalist covering the papal visit. There's no way I'm wearing that vest; I'll look like Groucho Marx on a bloody duck hunt."

"Okay, maybe you're right. We don't want to end up with duck soup!" Schuman laughs and gives you another apologetic look. "Cedric, we don't think they are going to find you anyway. We have enough decoys going around to keep them busy."

Decoys? What the...? Didn't they use Oswald doubles to sew confusion when JFK was shot? You remember reading that somewhere, or maybe it was in the movie? On the same day someone sees him in New Orleans handing out pro-Cuba flyers, another person sees him in Mexico City at a cocktail party full of communists. Even Oswald knew he was being impersonated.

Wake up, Cedric! There could be something even more sinister going on here.

You look at Schuman again, he starts fumbling around with the money and the documents.

"And I'm not taking that bloody gun," you say.

"Sure, Cedric, relax. It's just for protection in the worst-case scenario. We will have you covered most of the time."

"Most of the time?"

"Well, we have some limitations, you know, resourcing. But you'll be discreetly tailed from now on."

"What if I decide to walk?"

"What do you mean, Cedric?"

"What if I just go to the airport now, sound the alarm and get the hell out of here."

"That's not possible, Cedric. The CIA would have you in a hood and strapped down on a cargo plane to a black site in a flash. If that sounds like your kind of holiday, then be my guest." Schuman gestures towards the door.

To your surprise, a few feet through the doorway you notice a beautiful woman wearing an expensive looking pants suit and a headscarf, holding a large Christian Dior handbag.

"Ana? Ana, this is crazy. We should go."

"Go where, Cedric? He is right. It's too dangerous. He is helping us, Cedric. We have to trust him. I will be at the hotel too. I will be close. It's okay. You can do this."

You notice she has put on some lipstick and light make up. God, she looks amazing. You go over to her.

"Ana, I don't know what they are promising you, but I think you should go somewhere safe, away from these people. Away from me. I am being asked to do something highly illegal. Insane. You should have nothing more to do with this. You have done enough, Ana. I've put your life at risk once. I can't do it again."

Ana tilts her head to the side and looks into your eyes. She smiles.

"Cedric, I am not afraid of these people. I know what I am doing. Schuman is a good man. He is trying to help you, Cedric. I am trying to help you."

"I don't want to leave you, Ana."

"Cedric, if you stay you are going to be caught. We can't protect you here. You know their business now, Cedric. They don't like to leave these things undone."

"You have to come with me."

"To Rome? With the pope?" she laughs. "Cedric, I can't. You know this."

Schuman appears in the doorway again.

"Cedric, you need to get this disguise on fast, I'm sorry but we really don't have any time to lose. We have cars on the way to take you and Ana separately to the hotel. You will be checking in under the name of Aaron Rice, journalist for The Tribune. All your papers and accreditation are made out in this name. After you have checked in, we want you to go out for a bit—walk around and get used to your new persona. Don't worry we will be with you in the background. You have to get comfortable, Cedric. Tomorrow you will join the pope's entourage covering his visit to the Umayyad Mosque. You just need to blend in and keep to yourself. Just say you're there to replace The Tribune's correspondent, Julia Peterson. We've smoothed the way for you. Straight after the event you'll catch a bus with the other journalists to the airport, where you will board the pope's jet and fly to Rome."

"Well, what happened to Julia Peterson?"

"She's not feeling well, a bit of an upset stomach, that's all, Cedric. She'll be fine."

"The cars are here," says Ana having moved back to the windows to scan the street below.

Left with little choice, you slap on the disguise and grab the bag full of essentials that Schuman has put together for you. You catch a glimpse of yourself in the window. I look ridiculous. Kind of handsome with the moustache though. Hmmm maybe I should grow one.

Ana approaches you and takes you by both hands.

"You look perfect, Cedric. I am going to go ahead. I'll be waiting for you." She gently squeezes your hands, straightens your glasses, and gives you a look that makes you melt before turning and walking purposefully out the door.

God she's sexy. You admire the same strong posture and graceful movement you observed when she visited you in the hospital and clipped Greentree on the way out of the ward.

You can do this, Cedric. With Ana, you can do anything.

18

On the way to the hotel, you count four more murals of Assad and his generals. It certainly has the desired effect; creepy, like the guy is always around the next corner. You notice plumes of smoke in the distant hills—rebel held areas shelled or bombed in airstrikes. Your driver doesn't say much except to curse the traffic and other frustrated commuters. You stop at several check points on the way into the city where he flashes some official looking ID and takes an alternately jovial, hostile, or indifferent approach to dealing with the young soldiers. In the city center people are happily going about their daily business and everything seems quite normal. If it weren't for the odd rebel shell blowing a shop to smithereens, you'd hardly know a civil war was going on.

The car finally pulls up outside the hotel. You turn to the driver and reach into your pockets for some cash. He looks annoyed, shakes his head, and waves his hand. He obviously wants you to get out before the porters come over. Your pulse starts to race, you step out of the car and take your bag from the back seat. The car speeds off quickly.

You are on your own now, Cedric.

You hurry through the entrance, careful not to make eye contact with anyone. The lobby is decorated in the traditional local style, beautiful mosaics, chandeliers, a central fountain, and potted palms. There is a sweet scent of tobacco in the air. A few businessmen smattered around on lounges are drinking whisky and coffee. You wonder which one is Schuman's man. As you try to walk with purpose to the check-in desk, you trip ever so slightly in the oversized shoes Schuman gave you, acutely aware of being hidden inside a preposterous get up.

Christ, Cedric, this is madness. Surely it is obvious, you think. No... be confident. It is only obvious to you. Just relax and be yourself. Just not your real self.

"Good afternoon, sir," the tall young woman at reception greets you formally.

"Good afternoon, er, I have a reservation under the name of Rice," you say. The framed portrait of Assad watches you like a hawk.

"Yes, sir, let me just check that for you. Ah, yes, Mr. Rice, welcome. May I see your passport, sir?" she says sweetly.

"My passport? Of course, I'll just... bear with me for a second." You reach into the carry bag provided by Schuman and rummage around for your passport. It occurs to you that you haven't even looked at it. Locating it, you quickly flick through to find the photo page. There it is, a picture of you, Aaron Rice, black moustache, black hair, horn rimmed glasses. How did they do that? That's amazing.

"Thank you, sir," she says as she hands it back to you. "Here is your room key. Your room is on the fourth floor. Room 429. The elevator is around the corner to your right. Please let us know if there is anything you need. Enjoy your stay, sir," she says with a warm smile.

That was easy, you think, as you make your way through an intricately carved doorway to the elevator. Stay cool, Cedric and you'll breeze through this whole thing.

The room is sumptuous. A luxurious hand-woven carpet thrown over a polished hardwood floor leads you to a beautifully decorated sitting room, carefully lit by golden floor lamps. A bird of paradise in a turquoise vase adorns an ornate chest of drawers in front of a huge gilt framed mirror, providing the room with an exotic ambience. Through the wide-open double screen doors to your right is the double bed, its lavish linen canopy offering a romantic sunlit sanctuary. This is amazing.

Where is Ana?

"Ana? Are you here?" you call.

There is no answer and no sign of anyone having been here before you. You have a nervous pang, wondering what may have happened to her. It was all so rushed at the safehouse. She said she would be here. You decide the best thing to do is to wait.

You walk over to the mirror. I look like hell, you think. You continue through to the bathroom. Wow, incredible. Emerald green geometric tiles everywhere, expensive looking gold taps, a huge spa bath next to an open double shower. All your grooming needs are right there on the vanity.

You get rid of the disguise, undress, brush your teeth and down a whole bottle of water. God that feels better. Your whole body is aching. You take another look at the spa.

Why not?

You fill it up with steaming hot water, throw in a miniature bottle of shampoo and jump in. Ahhhhhhhhh, oh my God. You float in the warm water, eyes closed, inhaling the aroma of frankincense and myrrh, or whatever it is. You press the spa button, and the hot jets massage your entire body. You feel completely numb and warm all over. You suddenly feel a soft tickling on your chin and nose, open your eyes and realise the spa is overflowing with bubbles. Laughing to yourself, you stop the spa and push all the suds onto the marble floor. You close your eyes again and float there for a while.

Your mind empties and you feel as though you are looking into a deep darkness, like the blackest night sky. You float, perfectly still, more perfectly still than you have ever been in your life, in the perfect silence, in the perfect darkness, perfectly suspended like a heavenly body. Conscious only of yourself, your existence, but searching beyond yourself ever further into the darkness, for something other than you. A glow of recognition emanates deep within you, and without any effort on your part, a wave of peace, a deep and vital love, gently emerges. You lie there in this meditative state of grace for who knows how long.

A phone rings softly in the other room. God, I forgot I was even here. You quickly jump out of the bath and covered only in soap suds; you lunge for the phone in the living room.

"Hello? Hello?" you say, as the dial tone clicks in.

Crap, I missed it. Who could that have been? Ana? Schuman? Greentree???? Maybe it was just housekeeping. I'll just have to wait for them to call back.

Dripping water and bubbles everywhere, you return to the bathroom to dry off and throw on a robe. Checking your face in the mirror again, you decide to shave quickly.

Damn, I've nicked that bloody mole again. God, will I ever learn to slow down.

Stemming the bleeding with toilet paper you suddenly remember Schuman's instructions. You have to go for a walk, he said, get comfortable in the disguise.

Hurriedly, you dress and don the stupid moustache and wig again, shaking your head at the mirror in dissatisfaction and apprehension. You go back out into the lounge room and sit down to read through the identification papers Schuman gave you. God, how am I going to remember all this?

You pick up a wad of cash and your passport, and glance over at the phone once more before heading for the door.

Here goes.

You make your way down to the lobby and walk rapidly through the front doors. Assuming you are being watched, your heart beats like crazy as you walk through the main entrance out onto the street. The hotel is in the old town and there are laneways everywhere. You cross the street and duck down the first side-street you come to.

It feels so strange to be in disguise, like being in a Halloween costume. That was probably the last time you ever felt this way, when you were about 10 years old. You remember what a thrill it was to be roaming the streets with a gang of marauding ghouls, ghosts, axe-murderers, and ex-presidents, raiding homes for blocks and blocks before comparing your loot and traipsing home for dinner.

God, how far away you are from the sanctuary of your childhood now, Cedric.

Just keep walking. Breathe.

Many people pass you by without taking a second glance. You must appear relatively normal to them, regardless of how abnormal you feel.

God, I'm sweating bullets.

Along the laneway there are the usual stores cluttered with racks of clothing, cheap jewelry, and mobile phone accessories. The shopkeepers stand in the shaded doorways trading banter with each other, interrupted from time to time by browsing customers. Again, you marvel at the relaxed atmosphere. People at peace with their lives even amid a raging civil war.

Outside one place, you notice a crowd of schoolboys watching an intense game of chess unfold between two of their friends. The game is in its final stages with only a few pieces left on the board. There is much chatter and interest among the group followed by a great hush as they await the next move. Player one, a thin studious looking boy makes his move, followed by a few seconds of dead silence. Some serious murmuring breaks out, and slowly a rising tide of recognition builds amongst the crowd of onlookers, resulting in a restrained wave of urging, laughter, and howling. A few boys break away from the pack to exchange looks of acknowledgement before returning to the fray. Finally, the rotund, expressionless, player two, sees the move to checkmate. Roars of appreciation erupt from the others, who in wild jubilation pat the victor's back, shake his shoulders, and ruffle his hair affectionately. One young boy bounds about cheering, his school tie flapping as he looks up at the sky.

You find yourself smiling in recognition at this universal scene. We're all the same, you think. You wonder at the struggles these intelligent young men will find themselves facing over the next ten years, caught up in a place like this. The study, the questioning, the doubt, the pressures to conform, the secret pleasures, the hopes and dreams, the camaraderie, the mistakes, the heartbreaks, the disappointments, and the successes. The struggle to manhood. An unfolding inevitable tragedy. Holding it together through all that life throws at you. It's a miracle any of us survive. Whether our angels or demons have the better of us, we manage it somehow. In grand folly we remain united.

This thought is punctuated with a muffled explosion, far enough away for you to sense that you are safe, but loud enough for the band of youths to scatter like field mice.

You better take cover.

You decide to get off the street and enter the next store you come to. It's a store full of middle eastern bric-a-brac. The shelves are brimming with all kinds of odd pieces; artisan pipes, bayonets, daggers, military paraphernalia including Ottoman helmets with brass pikes, old ammunition belts, intricately carved pewter mugs, statuettes, oil paintings, backgammon sets, urns, lamps, and all manner of fascinating historical artifacts. God, you could browse around in here for hours.

"Can I help you, sir?" says a small man behind a counter at the back of the store in perfect English. You clearly don't look like a local.

"Er, just looking," you say. "You have an amazing assortment of things here," you spout nervously. The man nods.

As you scan the shelf in front of you, you are suddenly overcome by a shock of recognition. You have to be kidding! Right there before your very eyes, it's that bloody brass ashtray again.

You pick it up and the model fighter jet swivels 180 degrees on its stand. You take a closer look and see that there is an inscription engraved into the base: **Maj Rick Glaseborn Asst Air Attaché/Ati-**

lo ANKARA 1962. It even still has some old ash marks and residue on it. Well, what do you know?

"How much do you want for the ashtray?" you ask the little man.

"This item? Let me see. Ah yes, I believe this came from the personal belongings of the Syrian Minister for Defence. He died many years ago now, in the 1980's, and we obtained some collectibles when his wife sold everything off. I happen to know something about this piece, this Major Rick Glaseborn. He was an American airman stationed here in the Middle East. Many of these ashtrays were made and—"

"Yes, yes. I know the story. How much do you want for it?"

"You know the story?"

"Well, I ah, I studied some military history. He was a decorated pilot I believe."

"Mm hmm," the little man studies you with suspicion.

"I'm interested in aviation," you lie.

"Well, this is a rare item," he lies in return, "For this piece, for you, sir, the price is forty US dollars." He takes the piece from you and walks towards the counter.

You hesitate for a moment, wondering whether you should haggle. He must be wondering what I am doing here in Damascus. There aren't many tourists here obviously. Maybe he'll report me to the local authorities. The odd foreigner who knew about Major Rick Glaseborn and looked like a Saddam Hussein impersonator. You decide to get out of there pronto.

"Okay, forty bucks is fine." You pull the notes out of your pocket and realize they are all $100 bills. You take one out and hand it over to the man, who remains standing erect at the counter. He shoots you and your billfold a furtive glance.

"Would you like me to wrap it for you, sir?" Now you are starting to get nervous. You are really starting to sweat under this stupid disguise.

"No, I'll take it like that. You know what, keep the change." You hope this small act of charity might persuade him to let things go.

"Well, sir. That is very kind of you. Is there anything else that I can help you with?" he says, handing you the souvenir in a brown paper bag.

"No, that will be all. Thank you very much, this will look great on my desk back home."

With that, you turn and make for the door, acutely aware of the moisture permeating the entirety of your costume. Back out on the street, you take a quick glance up and down to get your bearings and check for anyone following you. Either they are excellent surveillance artists or they're not even here. Probably the latter based upon what you have experienced so far.

You decide to head back to the hotel. This is enough flouncing about. You doubt you'll ever get comfortable in this get up. You're just going to have to grin and bear it. God knows how spies ever get used to this stuff, you think, as you try to slow your walking pace a bit. There's too much to think about! How is anyone supposed to act normally, when trying to act normally only causes you to think about how abnormally you are acting?

Back at the hotel, you take the ashtray out of the bag and take a closer look at it to see where the listening device may have been hidden all those years ago. Probably inside the fuselage. You give it a shake but there is no rattle. A cold war relic, you think, still amazed that you found it. God, I wonder how many of these he had made. You imagine Glaseborn, amusing himself with this little sideline, never ceasing in his intelligence work to defeat the enemy. You imagine him flying sorties over North Korea and getting shot down over Vietnam. What a life.

You wonder what it must have taken to be an airman in those times, stationed around the world's conflict zones, hunting enemy aircraft from dawn till dusk. Supreme confidence, ice in the veins, a thirst for adventure, a love of camaraderie. A life only a few have known, pushing fighter jets to their limits in secret skirmishes impossibly high in forbidden skies, thrilling in the game, reveling in the danger, driven by duty and desire.

The hotel phone rings. You pick it up.

"Hallo, Biggles," comes the voice. "Nice trinket. Something sentimental I expect?"

"Hello, Schuman."

"How did you feel out there?"

"I felt bloody ridiculous. That's how I felt." You hear Schuman chuckle.

"Well, you caught us a little off-guard, Cedric. I tried to call you before you left, but you didn't answer."

"I was taking a bath."

"Well, next time wait for instructions."

"What, before I take a bath?"

"No not... Look, never mind. Just don't go anywhere else okay, Cedric. It's almost evening. Stay put. You need to be up early in the morning to join the press pack. Take a taxi at 7am sharp. You'll be on your own from there. Just follow the signs and you'll be fine."

"Follow the signs? What do you mean?"

"You'll spot them, don't worry. We will be guiding you in. Got to go. Good luck."

"Wait, Schuman—" you get the dial tone again.

Damn. That does not sound like a good plan. They'll guide me in? How's that going to work? Jesus, at least Rick Glaseborn had a golf game. I've got nothing! You slump on the couch wondering what to do next.

God, I'm starving. Where's Greentree when you need him? You go over to the mini bar. There's a packet of nuts and some Turkish delight wrapped in cellophane. You devour both. You pour a miniature bottle of whisky into a glass tumbler, add some water and head back to the couch. It reminds you of the plane trip over.

Sitting there nursing your Scotch, you gaze at the ashtray for a while in deep contemplation. What would Rick Glaseborn do? A guy like him would take matters into his own hands, you think. He'd be calling the shots.

Suddenly there is a knock at the door. A shot of fear hits you in the gut like a punch. Your ears ring. You grip the couch and steady your breath. The knock comes again. You rise to your feet and make your way to the door. The chain latch is in place. You edge your way closer and decide to take a peep through the spyhole.

Your heart leaps as you recognize Ana, standing confidently in the doorway still wearing the suit. The scarf is gone, her thick, dark hair now falling to her shoulders in soft waves, framing her ruby red lips and gorgeous eyes.

"Cedric, it's me," she whispers.

Hands trembling, you quickly unlatch the door and open it.

"Ana! Come in!" you say keeping your voice low. As she breezes past, a hint of frankincense and myrrh hits you producing instant visions of her showering in the steamy emerald green and gold recess. God if I wasn't already weak at the knees—your heart is fluttering like you're fifteen again. She turns and faces you, shoulders back, hand on hip. A half pout, half playful smile.

"Did you miss me?" she says.

"God, did I ever."

You embrace her and kiss her with all the ardor in your soul. Her soft curves press against you perfectly. She kisses you with passion, her hot, fast breaths signaling her desire.

You move to the couch, and she gently pushes you onto your back, throws off her jacket and climbs on top of you, her hips pressed against yours, you caress her body as she kisses you deeply, her breasts gently brushing your chest through her silk shirt as she sensitively shifts her weight. My god, she is incredible. Slowly and tenderly the kiss concludes, and she pulls away slightly with her wide smile and bright eyes. Tucking her hair behind one ear, she looks into your eyes and laughs her inimitable laugh.

"Wow, Cedric. You really did miss me."

"How did you guess?" you beam, mesmerized by her devastating feminine contours and that fresh scent.

She smiles again, and sits upright pressing herself against you, her hands resting on your shoulders. She shifts slightly from side to side and stands up in front of you. This picture of female beauty towering over you is beyond your comprehension. Gently, she edges away, and you watch her walk towards the bedroom, kicking her shoes off and bouncing a sassy glance back at you over her shoulder.

You down the rest of your Scotch and feel a fiery surge of courage. Standing in the surrounds of this opulent apartment you suddenly feel more masculine than you have ever felt in your life. You feel about ten feet tall! Like bloody Rick Glaseborn! Your hormones are running wild. Get in there, Cedric! What are you waiting for!

You steadily approach the bedroom, stop in the doorway and casually lean with one shoulder to the architrave. You lock eyes with her. Her suit lies rumpled on the floor beside the huge, canopied bed. The soft orange glow of the sunset suffuses the room. Half under the covers, she lies back on the plump pillows, her thick raven hair falling sensuously around her pretty face and shoulders. One bare leg bent at the knee juts up from under the sheets. She has covered her breasts, and you notice her lace bra straps are showing. She holds your gaze, slowly rocking her tanned, smooth leg from side to side.

You step into the bedroom lightly. Still holding each other's gaze, you remove your shirt and trousers and fold them neatly over the back of the bedroom chair. She smiles at this funny, orderly habit. You stand before her, marveling at the way she is holding you with her eyes. She takes you by the hand and pulls you gently towards her.

She lifts the sheets, and you slide in beside her, taking in a glimpse of her lingerie as you embrace her. You kiss for a long time, caressing each other, entwined in a hot passion that you wish would never end. Eventually, she pulls away gently and starts to stroke your hair.

"I want you, Cedric," she says fiercely.

"I want you too, Ana."

"I think I love you."

"I think I love you too," you kiss her again, deeply.

"I want you so much, I am aching."

"Me too," you say. Ana smiles.

"Cedric, this is not easy for me, but I need to say something. To let you understand something about me. I am from a different world. I know something about your world from English, from books and movies, you know. My world is different. Do you understand? I am Kurdish woman."

"It's okay, Ana, I understand."

"Please understand, Cedric, I want you, I really... want you. But my world is built on traditions we keep to. This is our way, for the good of our people, our families, and our villages. It is beautiful to us. Important to our identity. How we see ourselves and the way people see us. We can be modern. We love modern things, dancing, clubs—normal things, but we must remember who we are, where we have come from. So, I must wait—you understand—for the man I will marry."

"Ana, I have never met a woman like you."

"What do you mean, Cedric?"

"I mean I want to be with you forever. I will wait forever. I want to marry you, Ana. I have wanted to marry you since the first moment I laid eyes on you. I love you. I am totally, and utterly in love with you."

"You really mean this, Cedric?" she smiles, then laughs. Her eyes widen.

You take her into your arms and kiss her passionately again, and for an eternal moment you dive together into the deepest, star filled abyss.

• • • •

For a while you sleep deeply. You awaken to the patter of footsteps, and the sound of the door closing. Ana is no longer in the bed.

"Ana? Are you there? Ana?"

"Yes, Cedric, I am here." She comes to the bedroom door. She is dressed and holding a paper carry bag.

"I went out for some food. You must be hungry too. No?"

"I am famished."

"Famished?" she laughs.

"Here try this. It is my favorite. We call it Paklawa. It's sweet. Like you." Smiling, you take a bite of the pastry.

"Oh my God, Ana, that is amazing."

"Uh huh. I also bought some other things I think you will like. Come. There is a table out here."

"Sounds wonderful."

She heads back into the other room, and you climb out of bed and get dressed. You have to pinch yourself to make sure that this isn't all some kind of dream.

You really do pinch yourself.

You stand in front of the wall mirror and run your fingers through your hair. You lucky bastard, Cedric. What on earth does she see in me? Whatever it is, you can't screw this up. You meant what you said to her, but you know your future is uncertain right now. God, tomorrow you've got to try to con your way into the Vatican press pack, evade a bunch of unhinged CIA lunatics and sneak onto the pope's plane! It seems impossible. Unthinkable. Ludicrous. You have to win your way through this though, Cedric, no matter what. You can't lose her.

"Are you coming, Cedric?"

"Yes, coming now. Oh Ana, this looks incredible. Wow, it smells amazing. What is all this?" A small banquet for two with flat bread, dips, sweet rice and some fragrant meat and vegetable dishes, have been carefully laid out on the table. Ana lights a candle, walks over to you, and takes you by the hand.

"Let's eat!" she says, her eyes lighting up as she wriggles in her chair. My god, you could just watch her do anything. Forever.

"Ana, about tomorrow—"

"Cedric, let's not worry about tomorrow. We are together now. Tomorrow will be here soon enough, and we will get through it." You detect a sadness in her eyes, despite her brave face.

"There has to be another way, Ana."

"Cedric, I want you to stay, of course I do, but I know that this is not possible. If you stay, there is no chance for us."

"What if we tried to go together. Tonight. Get out of this place, cross the border into Lebanon or Israel."

"Cedric, these borders are heavily secured. We would be shot. I can't leave my people. You must go, Cedric. If we are to be together again, God will find a way for us." Once again, you feel the warm glow inside you, which becomes an aching, tingling, yearning sensation filling your chest and head.

"I can't leave you, Ana."

"You must, Cedric. I will be okay. Don't worry. It will be okay. This is the only way. Please eat. You need your strength. Try it. It is delicious." You take some of the bread and try the dip. It is amazing.

"I wasn't always this way, Cedric. You know... a fighter. I was happy in the village, happy with my friends and my family. When I was little, I wanted to be just like my mother. She is a wonderful woman; she taught me about the old ways and the goodness we have in our hearts. She taught me to dance. To be joyful. I wish you will know her.

"When this war started, I saw real suffering for the first time. I am shocked. You know? I feel something inside me screaming to stop it. I feel injustice. Then I feel the hatred too. The enemy want to wipe us out. They want to live in a world where women have no rights. They want to destroy everything here, to turn the clock back. They are hanging and stoning women to death. Many of my people were forced to leave their villages. They captured and executed them.

"My village was safe from the fighting, but one day they came to ask to us for help, and I know in my heart that I must go. So, I go to the mountains. I learn how to fight, and I learn more about our struggle. I learn about equality between men and women. There is also much, you know, revolutionary talk but I am not feeling strong about this like some people.

"We are many cultures here. Mostly, whenever there has been peace it has been through tolerance for one another. In our history, this is the only way. Religion is beautiful. God is beautiful. But we must tolerate each other's views. I have to defend my people, Cedric. We are always caught in the middle."

"I'm sorry, Ana." You see the despair in her eyes. "No one should have to go through what you have been through. I'm so sorry." She smiles and wipes a tear away with a napkin.

"I got you something Cedric, for your journey." Across the table she passes you a small gift box. It is made of white cardboard decorated with small leaves in gold.

"Ana, you shouldn't have."

"It's just something small. Open it." You open the giftbox and in the dim candlelight you see a small softly glowing crucifix attached to a gold chain. You look up and she is watching for your reaction.

"It's beautiful, Ana. I don't know how to express..."

"God is with you, Cedric. I know this from when I first saw you. You gave me faith again. My heart is full again, like a child. Whatever happens I will always be grateful for this. Because I see in you something true that I never saw in my life before."

"I don't know, Ana, I only know what happened to me. I nearly died on that road, and I think He was there. I'm sure He was. And now it's started something in me. I'm wrestling with all these questions. I can never go back to how I was. I don't know why. Why this has happened to me. I mean, why me? I'm not a good person. I'm selfish, vain, cowardly, I'm afflicted by every deadly sin there is. I'm the opposite of everything I should be."

"Everyone is this way, Cedric. God doesn't come to reward us. He comes to save us."

You look lovingly into her eyes, and she smiles that smile again. You take her hand across the table. She stands and comes to you. She sits on your lap, throws her arms around your neck and you kiss her again.

"Cedric, you must sleep now. We have to say goodbye."

"No, Ana, please stay."

"I can't, Cedric. I want to, but please. I must go."

You look searchingly into her eyes, and you know she is right. You walk her to the door. She turns for one final embrace.

"I will be praying for you, Cedric."

"I will be back for you, Ana."

"Goodbye, Cedric." Slowly she backs out into the corridor and turns to walk away, taking a final glance over her shoulder before disappearing into the night.

Your sleep is fitful. You dream wildly, vividly. The tank again, the maze, Ana. You wake early, as the sun is rising. Her scent lingers on the bedlinen. You lie there in the morning haze longing for her, replaying the night before over and over in your mind, trying to see her—hear her voice. *Will I ever see her again? God the burning passion. Will I ever feel that again?* You take one of the pillows and hold it tight, your eyes closed, inhaling its aroma.

Aching absence. That is all you feel.

You shower, shave, don the disguise, and begin to turn your mind to the day ahead, its menace looming over you like a gigantic black anvil. "We will be guiding you in," he said. *Like I'm some kind of amateur pilot, flying blind.* You wander around the room. Absence. *Ana was right. This is the only way. The only chance for you both. You need to put all your desire for her into this, Cedric. Channel it, turn it into grit. It's the only way forward and the only way back to her.*

I'm going to make this happen.

You gather up your things and shove them all into a small day pack. It's time to get moving. Leaving the room, you glance back one last time at the scene of the greatest night of your life. You close the door and move off down the corridor, taking the elevator down to the lobby. You scan the lounges. There are a few people reading newspapers and having breakfast. You take a seat at one of the small round corner tables. You order coffee and sit there motionless for a while, as though you are on the bank of a rushing river, hunters at your back, no choice but to jump in.

You stand, and without looking around, you head straight for the doors. Out into the morning air, the sounds of the city wash over you. You hail a taxi from the rank.

"Umayyad mosque please."

"Umayyad, yes, sir. Papa, yes?" says the driver with enthusiasm.

"Yes, Papa," you say with a worried look.

The driver is a small local man. The radio is blaring Syrian music featuring high pitched ululations and bagpipes. Usually, you would find this annoying but in your current frame of mind it's somehow energizing, and with your mind desperately clutching at images of Ana, somehow romantic.

You imagine yourself the hero of a spy thriller. Two of the world's great intelligence services in a minor tussle over your safe passage out of the country. You imagine your vehicle being tracked through the streets of Damascus by spy satellites thousands of miles above. Teams of watchers on the ground monitoring your progress through encrypted communications. Would they bother with that, you wonder? Get real, Cedric. This is just a lark for them. A bit of a diversion to test their wiles.

A bit of sport.

The traffic slows and you ask the driver what's going on.

"Checkpoint," he says.

You feel the fear in the pit of your stomach. You're just going to have to push it down, Cedric. You've done this before. You come to a standstill behind a line of civilian vehicles. As you slowly approach the checkpoint the fear rises, and your hands begin to shake. God help me, I don't want to have a panic attack now.

A short middle-aged, moustached, soldier approaches your vehicle and motions to the driver to open his window. The hot desert air evaporates the cool interior immediately. They begin a conversation in Arabic. It seems to go forever. They go silent. The moustache hovers in the window for another moment, and suddenly he waves you through.

"What was that all about?" you ask.

"He want to know where we go. I tell him Papa," he says. "Then he ask me what for. I tell him you here for Papa. Then he ask me why I drive taxi not join the army like him. I tell him I no good for army.

I tell him he has very beautiful moustache. He is very... you know, handsome man. He tell me to move on." He shoots you a mischievous look. "Two more checkpoints. Then you must walk, sir."

The next checkpoint is a non-event, the bored looking soldier barely acknowledging your existence. Nearly there, Cedric.

You approach the final checkpoint feeling reasonably relaxed and confident. A young soldier approaches the vehicle with a steely look on his face.

Your driver winds his window down and immediately erupts into a torrent of condemnation directed at the young officer. Clearly taken aback, the officer hastily looks at your papers, looks around as if to check whether anyone has noticed, and waves you through.

"What did you say?" you ask.

"I say you have important business with Papa and he is holding us up. He ask me for identification and I hit him with many insults, so he is shocked, you know. He is very young, and I put shame on him. I tell him 'What you are doing? This man ambassador. I report on you, you son of a dog. You look like pimp in the road. I am driving here fifty years before you born. God curse on your luck and drop you down from heaven. You stink like old shoe...' This kind of thing," he says with a shrug.

"Very well said," you say with a grin.

"Thank you, sir. Here we stop, you walk two blocks to Mosque." You step out of the car, and he leans out the window.

"Good luck, sir," he calls, swerving the car back onto the road. Why would he wish me luck, you wonder? Hmmm. He's probably one of Schuman's, you think.

There are many people making their way in the direction of the mosque. Families walking together, spilling onto the road beside slow-moving traffic. A party of nuns walk by, singing softly together, all with looks of hope and anticipation on their faces. There is electricity in the air. The shared feeling that one is about to witness something extraordinary. The pope, the Vicar of Christ, is here in the old walled city of Damascus, to meet with Syria's top Muslim cleric. Tens of thousands of Christians and Muslims will be in the crowd for this rare event. All hoping for a glimpse of the two leaders. All praying for peace, unity, and an end to the conflict.

As you advance, the crowds start to thicken. In the distance car horns blare, and the murmur of thousands of people echo through the old narrow streets. The security situation must be a nightmare for Assad, you think, although he seems to have the rebels under control, and fighting is now well away from the city. There could have been no possibility of a visit from the pontiff unless the Syrian government was able to guarantee his security. The security of the pope is one thing, the security of the crowds is another matter. Not something a vain dictator with an image problem would be too concerned about.

As it becomes slower and harder to move forward you start to feel extremely uneasy. You've hit a bottleneck. There's no stopping or going back. The sun begins to beat down and the murmurs of the crowd grow louder.

"Excuse me, how much further is it to the mosque?" you ask a man passing by. The man looks bewildered and clearly does not speak English.

"Papa?" you ask.

"Papa," he says, pointing ahead.

You keep edging forward and after a few minutes the crowd thins out a bit and you start to move freely again as the bottleneck dissipates. You breathe deeply, calming your nerves. Right, you must be getting closer now. God, how am I going to find the bloody press section? It will have to be somewhere near the entrance to the mosque. No doubt the correspondents will have the best view and will be in the best position to record everything the pope says and does. I'll just have to push my way up to the front.

Pausing a moment to survey your surroundings you spot a man dressed in a cream linen suit casually leaning against a wall on the other side of the street. He is holding up a copy of The Daily. Must be one of Schuman's, you think. As you draw closer, he turns, folds the paper, and walks ahead of you, quickly weaving through the crowded streets. You struggle to keep him in your sights but manage to plow on, catching intermittent glimpses of him as you go. After several minutes of dodging and bumping past the slow-moving masses, taking lefts and rights through the labyrinthine laneways, you lose sight of him.

You are on your own again. You look up ahead. No sign of the mosque just yet. Just got to keep going.

These boots are darned uncomfortable. They are chafing your bloody ankles raw. The whole disguise is starting to irritate you. This is madness. What am I supposed to do? Suddenly, your heartbeat quickens. Out of the corner of your eye you see someone who looks very familiar. Wait. Is that Albert? It's got to be him. How is that possible? Could he really be involved in all this? If it's not him, he's the spitting image. Maybe Schuman has found someone that looks like him. That can't be possible. Wait a minute, you're losing him.

"Wait! Albert!" you yell, sensing that your voice is lost in the hubbub.

The tall distant figure lopes through the crowd ahead. Following along, you struggle to make up any ground as you hastily make your way through. You lose sight of him for a while, then suddenly, there he is again, stopped on the next corner. You stop where you are, wondering whether to approach him. Maybe he has a message for me. Or maybe not. Maybe he's just another bystander and you are about to make a complete fool of yourself. Or worse, what if he's not one of Schuman's. What if he's one of Greentree's? He might be looking for me. This puts you in a cold sweat. He does seem to be surveying the crowd. Crap. What do I do?

You decide to proceed with caution, edging slowly closer to the corner while remaining blocked from view by the surging crowd. When you are finally close enough to make out his face, you realize that it is definitely not Albert. Of course, it isn't! What was I thinking!

You try to put on the brakes, but the crowd behind you is jostling you forward. Oh God! They're going to take me right past him!

Suddenly, you feel a heavy bump to the back of your right shoulder that almost knocks you sideways. You look up and see the man in the linen suit again.

"Keep your bloody head down and follow me," he says as he cuts a swathe through the crowd leading diagonally away from the corner.

Reflexively, you pull your cap down over your eyes. Again, he is moving too fast for you to keep up. If he's being observed, he won't want me too close. No wonder he sounded annoyed. You can just make him out in the distance turning another corner up ahead and you hurriedly scrabble your way there.

On the corner is a convenience store. It appears to be closed, and this is confirmed by the small sign hanging from the inside handle. You then notice a poster next to the sign with an image of an Olympic athlete about to throw a javelin. That's odd. Hang on! Bloody hell. You freeze on the spot and your adrenaline starts to pump again.

Go in, Cedric!

You grab the handle, turn, and push the door. It opens and you quickly step inside, closing the door behind you. The quiet contrast of the shop's interior is a relief from the sea of people outside. Okay, Cedric, you need to gather yourself. Surely, Mr. Linen Suit is in here somewhere.

You take a quick look around. It's a perfectly ordinary convenience store. A fridge containing a couple of cold drinks. A few dusty snacks, cereal boxes and essential foodstuffs line the shelves.

The store counter is down the back behind a row of magazines. As you make your way there a tallish, balding Syrian man suddenly appears via some beaded curtains draping a doorway.

"Hello," you say, somewhat taken aback. "Do you speak English?"

"Yes, sir, can I help you?"

"Yes, er, I, I am looking for a friend. He is a foreign gentleman wearing a cream linen suit. I'm a reporter. We are covering the papal visit."

"No, sir. There is no one here. Just me. We have closed early today. Too many people. Everything is gone." Live coverage from the Great Mosque is playing on a small television set that sits on a shelf behind the counter.

"Oh, I see. My mistake, I thought I saw him come in. I should probably go then. I am sorry to have bothered you."

"No bother. No bother. Are you staying in Damascus?"

"Yes. Well, not exactly. Actually, I'm leaving today. I must find my way to the press section. I seem to have lost may way a bit. I saw the sign on the window and just thought that—"

"Well, sir, if you *keep following the signs* to the Great Mosque you will find yourself in the right location," his emphasis provided with a penetrating glare.

"Er, thank you," you reply meekly.

"Sir, perhaps you would like a book for your journey home. To pass the time? We have a selection of English books on the small table over by the magazines."

"That's okay. I really don't have—"

"Some of the finest in world literature, Dostoyevsky, Celine, Twain. Please, sir, allow me to show you." Your book addiction gets the better of you.

Browsing through the titles, you are suddenly struck by an odd one out; *Biggles Cuts It Fine*. You pick it up and before you can open it the man interrupts you.

"Excellent choice, sir. A tale of courage, adventure, and high stakes maneuvers. Perfect reading for a flight back to Europe I am guessing?" Again, the penetrating stare.

"Yes, well. Okay, I'll take it," you offer searchingly.

"Very good, sir. I suggest that you make haste if you do not wish to miss the Holy Father." He graciously escorts you to the door, ushers you out, locks it and is gone.

God, that was weird. Frowning, you quickly flick through the old paperback. Hidden in between the pages is a small bookmark. You take it out and inspect it. A penguin classic promoting *Brideshead Revisited,* one of your favorite books. "Waugh's classic story of Charles Pinder and his infatuation with the Flyte family."

Pinder? That's not right. That should be Ryder. Charles Ryder. You flick through the pages of the book once more to see if you have missed anything. No. Nothing else unusual about the old book or the bookmark. Could be a misprint. Surely not. Charles Pinder. The name means nothing to you. You tuck the book away in your backpack.

Maybe I will read *Biggles* on the plane.

Rejoining the human tsunami, you sense that you are growing ever closer to your destination. Progress is slow now, the crowd inching down the old narrow city street, cloaked by the shade of the old buildings on either side. The noise of the crowd reverberating up and down the ancient pathway, the ebb and flow of the people in the middle, and the pressing of those on the sidewalk to the walls either side, acting like some giant contracting birth canal.

You begin to feel panicked and claustrophobic again as you are swayed this way and that, your movements now well beyond your control. Hopelessly at the mercy of the mingling sea of flesh, you are now actually struggling for breath as people press in on you from all sides. The volume of the crowd noise goes up and up as people start to cry out in fear. Small steps take you this way and that, as you are on the verge of breaking past the upcoming street corners.

Suddenly you feel a mighty surge behind you, propelling you out into the rapidly filling courtyard of the Great Mosque. You are overcome by a sense of relief, awe, and wonder as you are carried forward towards the entrance of this majestic old building, its façade seemingly alive with splendor and personality, gleaming ethereally under a vault of bright blue sky.

Here you are in one of the world's oldest cities, taking in thousands of years of civilization. A place where the Gods of thunder and rain were revered for centuries. A place where early Christians worshipped under Roman emperors and for hundreds of years now, the Muslim faithful have gathered. It takes your breath away.

Thousands of pilgrims stream into the square chanting, singing, cheering and dancing. It is enough to give one hope. Momentarily you are swept up in the joy of the whole spectacle. The anticipation and excitement of the crowd is palpable.

My God, you think. When he arrives, it will be like nothing you have ever experienced.

All sides of the courtyard are lined by security. The Eastern thoroughfare to the Mosque appears clear and heavily guarded. That must be his entry point. You decide to make your way there as best you can.

You begin to work your way through the crowd, inching ever closer to the great archways, domes and minarets soaring above. You have never seen so many Christians and Muslims together in one place, in a spirit of brotherhood. This great peaceful multitude, making no demands of political leaders, no protest, no civil disobedience, no revolution. United by something deep inside them.

You have been in many large crowds before. Music festivals, sporting events, carnivals. But this is different. There is no entertainment factor in two old men in robes greeting one another and exchanging pleasantries inside a holy site where they cannot even be seen. Something mysterious is going on. Everyone knows it, but they cannot explain it. That's why they are here. Just to be. Just to feel. Just to witness holiness. The pinnacle of human experience. Life changing, life affirming, holiness. Like fresh water. It offers renewal.

You've never really understood this. You simply couldn't until now. You look around and it is affirmed in the faces of the many individuals surrounding you. God is a fact of life to them. Like it is to you now. You suddenly feel somewhat inadequate. You're not so special, Cedric, you are just a beginner. An infant. A latecomer to the party. We've lost this in the West. We no longer want to conform ourselves to God. We no longer want to conform ourselves to anything. *Consumption* is the new religion. No wonder it was used to name a disease. It's like trying to fill a bottomless hole. Like feeding an insatiable monster. Never satisfied. Never at peace. Willfully cut off. Proud. Severed. Bereft.

As the courtyard fills, you are virtually conveyed by the hoards behind you to within a short distance from the entrance to the mosque. You will need to move fast to the press section before you are jammed in. You scan your surroundings hoping for another sign from Schuman. Nothing jumps out at you. The man in the linen suit is nowhere to be found. Everyone's in white. It's a bit like playing *Where's Wally*. Bloody impossible to spot anyone in this crowd.

You think of Ana and the wonderful night you spent with her. She was so beautiful. Whatever happens, you are so happy that you found her. Found true love. Your feelings of love for her come welling up inside you again. Standing there, grinning like a fool, you feel so content, so complete, so elated, so filled with joy you want to burst.

God, I feel superhuman right now.

Your moment of rapture is suddenly dampened and replaced by a shot of adrenaline. To your right you notice a familiar face. Where have I seen him before? You rack your brains for a minute. My God, it's that guy from the hospital in Istanbul. It must be him. The one that reminded you of your father when he was young. The one that called you "Tank Man". Bloody hell. It's him. He must have been in on this from the start. He must have a message for me.

You take another sideways glance at him to try and make eye contact. He is not looking your way. He seems intently focused on the entrance to the Great Mosque.

Tentatively, your heart beating faster and your armpits beginning to trickle sweat, you make a move towards him. Just as you make it to within a few feet away, the crowd in the courtyard erupts into an almighty deafening roar like nothing you have ever heard in your entire life. The sound reverberates around you and ripples through the streets for miles, as though the old city itself was crying out for salvation.

Entering the courtyard from the East is a cavalcade of shiny black saloon cars. Two cars from the front, in the back seat of a humble white vehicle that is unmistakably the same make and model as the one you were nearly killed in, sits the figure of the pope.

The outpouring of emotion from the crowd leaves you riveted to the spot. Exhilarated, you watch as the Holy Father exits the vehicle, surrounded by his security detail and high-ranking Vatican officials. He is dressed in his customary white cassock and white ceremonial Mitre. He gently walks up a few steps, turns to face the crowd and raises his right hand to them, index finger crossed over middle finger, in a sign of peace.

The volume of the crowd goes up another level in wild scenes of jubilation as the pope stands there, motionless, acknowledging the crowd with his broad smile, his hands held together in prayer.

Transfixed, and full of adrenaline, you quickly glance to your right again to check whether your man is still there. Yes. There he is. You take a couple of steps towards him.

"Hey! Hey!" you shout, "It's me! Tank Man!" As the man recognizes you, his face turns ashen with horror. He raises his right arm from the invisible depths below. He is holding a handgun. It is now aimed at the pope.

20

C rack! The report of the pistol rings out across the plaza as your shoulder drives into the man's chest, sending the gun flying into the crowd. Crack! You hit the cobblestones hard. Ahhhh! Bloody hell! You are under a stampede of screaming people, being kicked, stomped, and trampled all over. Your hat and wig have come off. You snatch at them, just managing to retrieve the hat before being tumbled along, as though trapped in a giant, inescapable, rugby maul. You instinctively cover-up the way you were taught as a schoolboy, hands clamped over your ears and body in the fetal position. Finally, you find some space and drag yourself to your feet. Battered and bruised you gasp for air as thousands of people, push and scurry in all directions. Many others have been knocked to the ground and are lying around injured. Christ almighty! That madman tried to assassinate the pope!

Still in a state of shock, as though time has stood still, you glance back at the steps of the great mosque. The cavalcade is speeding off. Sirens blaring. In seconds the cars have vanished from the ensuing chaos. You have no idea whether he was hit, or what happened after the gun was fired.

You've got to get out of here, Cedric. They'll all be looking for you now. Even Assad's security services. You decide to drop the hat. If they have any witnesses or CCTV footage your screwed.

You look up. There are cameras in every corner. Heartsick, you crouch down and place your right hand on the ground, hoping that you might become lost in the commotion.

"Cedric, get up... Get up, Cedric. My name is Charles Pinder. I'm here to help," says the man in the linen suit looming above you.

"Pinder?"

"Come with me now, Cedric. We must hurry."

Straining to your feet, you follow him through the crowded square, heading for the nearest alleyway. You limp along after him for at least three blocks amongst the confusion of thousands trying to leave the area. Finally, you stop alongside a bus shelter, and Pinder motions for you to take a seat. Both out of breath, you sit for at least a minute before he asks whether you are okay. You check yourself over and notice a tear in the knee of your trousers.

"I'm fine. Just a few bruises," you reply. "What the hell is going on?"

"I don't know, Cedric, I'm just a watcher."

"They tried to kill him!" you say.

"I don't know if they... I mean I saw, but I don't know what was happening. I was just meant to keep an eye on you and lead you to the press pack if need be. That's my job and that's what I'm here to do. Look, Cedric, the Vatican press will be headed for the airport. We have to get you on their bus."

"Was he hit?"

"I'm not sure. It happened so fast. He lost his hat. Security closed in and the next thing the cavalcade took off. I suspect it was a near miss. You may have saved his life, Cedric."

"But, why? Why was I there? Schuman wanted me there."

"That's above my paygrade, Cedric. Listen, we are going to get you to the Sheraton Hotel. From there you get on the bus with the other reporters. All you need to do is keep quiet and get on that plane. Anyone asks you any questions, use the cover we gave you. Do you understand?"

"Yes. What about the wig and the hat? I lost the glasses too."

"Don't worry about that. Don't worry about your clothes either. Just say you were knocked over in the commotion."

"Look, Pinder, I'm not sure I can do this. You have no idea what I have been through."

"If you want to get out of here alive you will do it."

"What are you saying?"

"Cedric, these people don't ask questions. If they think you are mixed up in something, you disappear."

"Mixed up in what? An assassination attempt on the pope?"

"Look you need to understand their world view. They think world politics, world events, are all guided by the machinations of intelligence agencies. With something like this, anyone out of the ordinary, within proximity is probably a spy. There are no coincidences. You understand?"

"So now I'm a spy?"

"If they catch you, yes. Cedric, I saw what you did. You are brave. You can do this." Suddenly a woman on a motorbike pulls over to the curb.

"Get on, Cedric. Go. I have to get the hell out of here." He stands and walks off.

You look up at the bike. The rider is wearing a black leather jacket, denim jeans and boots. Her large almond eyes observing you through the visor of a black helmet. A mane of wavy auburn hair falls below her shoulders. Her eyes are locked on yours. Business like. She revs the engine. Oh God, here we go.

You climb on the back of the rumbling bike, unsure where to hold on. You feel her hand clasp your left wrist hard and pull it around her waist. You clasp your hands together holding tight as she takes off like a rocket. The roar of the engine echoes through the back streets as she weaves her way across the city. A couple of times she quickly shoots the wrong way down one-way streets to avoid the checkpoints. Holding on for dear life, your cheek pressed to her back, the wind in your hair, you close your eyes and try to stay calm as the bike jerks this way and that, turning accelerating and braking to the extreme. Finally, you feel the bike slow, and you open your watering eyes to the sheltered driveway entrance to the Sheraton Damascus. She pulls up behind a taxi, clasps your wrist again and gently brushes your grip away from her body. You get off the bike, sensing that your legs have turned to jelly. No sooner have your feet hit the pavement, than she is gone in a puff of grey smoke.

Okay, Cedric, steady now. You cannot afford to draw any attention to yourself, which is a little difficult given your rumpled state. You wobble straight through the entrance into the lobby.

Go directly to the bar, you think.

You scan your surroundings. Wall to wall off-white marble with maroon quadrilateral stripes all over the place. Low hanging heavy chandeliers. A line of guests with luggage are hastily checking out at the front desk.

God, I can hardly walk my legs are trembling so much. Got to keep it together, Cedric. Just make it to that barstool you now have in your sights. That's it, just a little further, flaps up, trim a bit, nose down and a Hail Mary, you've landed—right on the cushy red leather seat. For a few seconds you lean both elbows on the bar and hold your head in your hands. A suave barman in a white shirt, dark green waistcoat and bowtie appears in front of you.

"Double shot of Jameson please."

He pours the drink in a flash. You take a big gulp. Hooowee, that burns. You feel every cell in your body jump to attention, as you wait for the calming warm glow to kick in. Christ, what a mess. What an ordeal. I am bloody exhausted, you think. You can't believe you have made it this far, and who knows what peril lies ahead? Maybe you should just throw in your hand and head for the embassy. No, you can't do that. They will definitely have it under surveillance. They'll nab you before you make it to within a mile of the place.

You think back to the look on the man's face, when he saw you in the square, before you tackled him to the ground. A look of shock and disbelief. He lost his breath like he'd seen a ghost. Was this some elaborate set up? Was I meant to find him and neutralize him? How could that be possible? You rack your brains to try to understand how Schuman could have orchestrated it. It doesn't make sense. But if Schuman didn't orchestrate it, who did?

"Whisky Sour please." A deep, male, American voice floats into your head. You look up to see a neatly dressed, middle aged man with longish, greying, brushed back hair and a ruddy complexion.

"Quite a day, huh?" says the man with a shake of the head.

Oh God, I'm not ready for this, you think.

"Er, yes. Quite a day indeed," you bleat. He extends his hand.

"Tom Jarvis. I'm with the Catholic News Service." A shot of fear hits you in the guts.

"A, A, Aaron Rice," you stammer. "Tribune. Just got here in time. I'm covering for Julia Peterson."

"Oh really? I heard she wasn't well. Some of the food here, it's a little exotic. Poor Julia, she's going to be pissed she missed this one." You notice a wry competitiveness to his tone.

"Have you filed yet?" he asks, eyebrows raised.

"What? Oh, no. Not yet. I was... actually, I was caught up at the mosque. You know in the crowd. Took a bit of a tumble. It was a nightmare getting out of there. People fleeing..."

"You were there? What the hell were you doing there?"

"Well, trying to cover the visit. It was just... well mayhem really. Why? Weren't you there?"

"God no, we never go near him."

"What do you mean?"

"Well, it's not worth it. You can never see anything. They always put us down the back somewhere. It's a far better view from the bar," he says pointing to the widescreen TV. Images of the pope's hat being blown off in ultra-slow-motion replay repeatedly, while the scrolling captions provide details.

Attempt on pope's life in Damascus foiled by mystery man. Would be assassin arrested at scene. Pope unhurt, calls for calm, will return to Rome today.

"Of course. Well, I guess my boss wanted me to be in the thick of it," you blurt, cringing in fear at the blurred images of the crowd crudely circled by the news presenter.

"Lucky bastard! Look forward to reading your piece. Listen, we better hurry, I think they want us all on the bus. I'm not sure whether we'll even get on the plane. We'll probably have to schlep it back home. Alitalia or something." He gestures towards the lobby exit. A group of reporters are filing out with their luggage.

The bus, a brand-new luxury coach, is a hive of activity, everyone conversing loudly with the person next to them, or speaking rapid-fire into their phones, hurrying to get seated. All of them intensely dealing with the gravity of the situation.

You take a window seat in the middle of the bus next to Jarvis and try to make yourself inconspicuous. The windows are tinted, so you don't have to worry about being seen from the street.

Bloody hell, Cedric, you made it! You are on the bloody bus! Yes!

You clench your jaw, squeeze your right hand into a fist and smile ever so slightly. You take a deep breath and try to remain composed as you are filled with elation. You hear the loud hiss of the door closing as the bus begins to move off.

You exhale in relief.

Suddenly, the bus driver slams on the brakes, causing everyone to lurch forward. A few laptops and other personal items hit the floor. The doors open again. A tall man in military uniform boards with a couple of others trailing him. He is the spitting image of Assad himself.

There is dead silence.

"Identification papers please," shouts the man sternly. As he approaches, you notice the man's nose is somewhat longer than Assad's. Stop wasting brain power on stupid details, Cedric. You feel yourself sliding in your seat.

The man addresses you bluntly. "Passport." You reach into your dusty backpack and rummage around for it. He eyes you warily. You leave the backpack sitting on your lap covering the hole in your trousers. He checks your details against a list of names. Okay, I'm screwed. He marks the list and looks at you again. You heart beats a million beats per second. Your stomach falls into an abyss of terror.

"Sir, look up please." He holds the passport up as he checks you over.

"Hurry up. We haven't got all bloody day," booms a loud Dutch sounding voice from the back of the bus. "We have a plane to catch, you know." The officer's attention is diverted momentarily to the big man at back of the bus. He looks back at you for a couple of seconds, then hands your passport back. The officer shuffles towards the back and starts a heated conversation with the big Dutchman while the officer's two underlings continue to check passports.

"Classic Vandenberg," whispers Jarvis. "He's the Vatican man responsible for keeping everyone in line. Likes to run a tight ship. Thinks we're all dim wits," he says with a grin, holding up a booklet detailing the Vatican press pack's travel itinerary.

Vandenberg is now red in the face with fury. He is pointing at his schedule and vigorously remonstrating with the tall, skinny officer. After a couple more minutes, the officers get off the bus in a state of high tension, the Assad lookalike hissing some Arabic on the way out and the Dutchman hurling some equally harsh language in his own native tongue. The doors close again, and the bus slowly moves off onto the main street.

Cheers and clapping erupt as Vandenberg settles back into his seat. A look of quiet satisfaction is restored to his large round visage, as the rose remnants of his blushing anger dissipate.

"Good old Vandenberg," says Jarvis. "The guy is hard as a rock. Probably wouldn't bat an eyelid if they ripped his fingernails out," he chortles ruefully. "Nearly caused a diplomatic incident last time we were in these parts. Got into a fist fight with the Imam's security and came back from the mosque with a black eye. The pope, the last one, he didn't mind one bit. He thought it was hilarious. It was a bit different back then. So, what do you usually cover, Rice? How'd you get mixed up in all this?"

"Good question..." you start nervously, "Well, usually I'm on straight news. I'm only here because my boss, well he is a bit sick of the sight of me, you know. I guess it goes both ways."

"Well, I bet he wasn't banking on a story like this when he sent you out here."

"No, I highly doubt it."

"So, what about your piece. Are you going to get something in? Isn't he harassing the crap out of you already?" You imagine Symons giving you the third degree.

"Oh, whatever..." you say coolly. "I'm thinking I'll just write it on the plane. You know a feature article with all the eyewitness stuff. The straight reports are on the wires already. They'll be running with Reuters."

Jarvis nods and smiles. "Well, I hope we have time for a couple more drinks before we get back to Rome sweet home."

"Me too," you say, shifting slightly in your seat. "Me too."

• • • •

As the bus pulls out onto the motorway and begins to pick up speed, you allow your body to relax. Jarvis is now busily responding to messages on his phone. You recline the seat and close your eyes, enjoying the comfort of the brand-new, fully airconditioned coach.

You've always enjoyed bus travel. Sitting high above the traffic, cruising along, you feel safe. Protected. Finally, you are in a familiar environment amongst colleagues. *I like being this Aaron Rice guy. He knows what to do. How to handle himself. You're going to be fine. Just be Aaron.*

Maybe I *will* grow a moustache when this is all over, you think, as you catch a glimpse of your reflection in the window. Although you're not sure whether Ana really liked it. You close your eyes again and try to recall the time you spent with her. It's like trying to remember a dream. No matter how hard you try, you can't recreate it. Her kiss, her body. Her laugh. You can only conjure up an imperfect chimera that just torments you.

A police siren sounds loudly. You open your eyes as strobing blue and red lights flash through the interior of the bus. Oh, God. Here we go again. I knew my luck couldn't last. The bus slows slightly as two police motorcycles pull in front.

"Hey, don't worry, Rice," says Jarvis noticing your trembling hands. "It's just an escort." Suddenly, the bus engine roars as the driver floors it.

"Oh, thank God! I nearly had a heart attack," you laugh. Jarvis starts laughing too and shakes his head as the bus hits warp speed. You settle back into the blissful comfort of your seat.

Finally, you arrive at Damascus International Airport. Here we are, Cedric. This is the endgame. Departing the bus, you are careful to hide yourself amongst the media pack. You follow the herd into the bright lights of the terminal and decide to stick close to Jarvis. He doesn't seem flustered at all and wears a slight look of bemusement.

"Where do we go?" you ask.

"Your guess is as good as mine," he replies. "Usually someone shows up to usher us to the gate. We never know until we get here. They like to keep everything under wraps. We don't get boarding passes or anything if that's what you are wondering."

At that moment a severe looking Syrian woman wearing a crisp white shirt under a grey uniform appears at the head of the pack and begins to escort the group through to a closed off airport security screening station. A couple of security staff move the retractable barrier posts so that a queue can form, and everyone starts to move through.

You shuffle along in a cold sweat, mopping your brow with your shirtsleeve. Like everyone else you pull out the laptop from your bag and place it in a separate tray. You place your bag down next to it and walk through the metal detectors as directed by the surly guards. One of them directs you to await your belongings.

Suddenly the conveyor belt stops and then reverses as your bag goes through the scanner. Oh, no! What is it? Christ, I hope Schuman didn't hide anything in my bag. What if it's that bloody pistol!

"Sir, can you step over here please," says the guard. He takes your bag to a metal table at the end of the conveyor belt. Your stomach drops as the man empties the contents of your backpack onto the table. The man looks at you sharply.

"What is this?" he asks, pointing to the package on the table.

"Oh that? That's just a souvenir I bought." The man starts to unwrap the package.

"It's just an ashtray I sort of liked the look of."

"Why did you buy this?" says the man.

"Well, it's an ornament really—"

"Air Attaché Rick Glaseborn," he says, reading the inscription as he inspects the ashtray from all angles. "Probably an American spy." He shoots you another careful look. Your heart leaps. God he must be able to smell my fear.

"What's this?" he says, holding up the *Biggles* book.

"Oh, just a book for the plane," you say.

"What is it about?"

"Oh, um. It's about a British airman called Bigglesworth, 'Biggles' for short. It's an adventure series. You know, he's a pilot who is asked to do special missions by the secret service. He goes behind the iron curtain, gets into all kinds of scrapes," you say with a nervous laugh. "It's a children's book, really."

"A children's book? Where did you get it?"

"At a convenience store in the old city."

"A convenience store?"

"Yes. They sold some English books."

"Where is this store?"

"It's in the old city. I'm not sure of the address."

"You're not sure?"

"No."

"You don't know where you are?"

"Well, I don't know the street names. No."

"My son is 12. He is learning English. Do you think he would like this *Biggles*?"

"Of course, yes. It would be perfect for him. Hey, why don't you, you know—keep it. I'm sure he would enjoy it very much."

"You think so? You think I should fill his head with this Western propaganda?" He gives you another stern look.

"Well, it's a bit old fashioned. You know, things have changed. The empire it's, well—" The man returns his attention to the ashtray, gives it a shake and replaces it on the table.

"You want to educate me, sir, about the empire? How it has changed? How it has changed hands perhaps?" he snorts, eying you again.

Jesus, Cedric. Just shut up.

"Let me see your passport please." You hand it over and he checks your photo. "Vatican press," he says with disdain, "Too bad they missed him."

Now you are starting to feel some anger boil up. Hold it together, Cedric.

The man holds your gaze again for a couple of seconds and with a sudden wave of the hand he directs you to collect your belongings. You gather them up and shove them back in your bag, hurrying to catch up with Jarvis and the rest of the group. After bounding along a couple of travelators you manage to rejoin them just as they are being directed into what appears to be a private club lounge.

The room is well appointed with tan leather couches, small round side tables and a bar providing snacks and refreshments. The large floor to ceiling windows provide clear views of the aircraft coming and going outside. You sidle over to where Jarvis is sitting and plonk yourself down.

"Ah, Rice. You made it. I saw you got a grilling out there."

"Yeah, he wasn't too friendly," you reply.

"He did seem a little sour faced. How about a drink then?" Jarvis jumps up and heads for the bar. He comes back a minute later with two large gin and tonics. The two of you sit in silence for a while watching the latest news bulletins come in on one of the overhead TV screens.

"You know, I'm not so sure about this guy they picked up," says Jarvis. "I mean he looks like a lunatic. Those crazy eyes and everything, but something seems a bit too... I don't know. Obvious. You know, all tied up with a neat little bow. I mean they say he got two shots off. You could hear them. But they sound different. The second one is louder."

"He only fired one shot," you say.

"What?"

"He only fired one shot. I was there. I saw him with my own eyes. He dropped the weapon after one shot. I heard the other one too. It came from somewhere further away. Maybe a minaret. I mean if you were going to take a potshot from anywhere."

"Jesus. H. Christ. Are you sure?"

"100 percent."

"Okay, Rice, listen. Do not breathe a word of this to anyone. Not until we are out of here. This is dangerous knowledge. Do you understand?" whispers Jarvis.

You take a couple of big gulps of your gin and tonic. That guy was crazy. Literally insane. It probably wouldn't have taken much to persuade him that the pope needed to be killed. A little coercion, validation of the man's paranoid delusions. Clearing things up for him, convincing him the pope is the antichrist. Placing him in the courtyard in broad daylight. A perfect scapegoat. Thousands of witnesses. Including you. The one who was closer than anyone. The one who saw it all unfold. The one who took the guy down. You are surely being hunted. They'll frame me like a picture! What on earth was Schuman up to? He knew I'd spot that guy. I was looking for signs. I wish I had never trusted Schuman! Then again, why would he send me there? An untrained hack reporter being hunted by the CIA? What about Ana? Was she in on this? A honey trap? Maybe it was all too good to be true. You think back to the way she encouraged you to follow Schuman's plan. No. It can't be true. Not Ana. It can't be.

"Ladies and Gentlemen. I have a quick announcement to make," booms the big Dutch priest. "As you are all aware, the Holy Father is fine. He was unhurt, but a bullet passed very close to the top of his head. While somewhat shocked as you would well understand, he has been quick to call for calm and has spoken of the man accused of this gravest act in compassionate terms. Despite the efforts of Vatican security to dissuade him, he has decided that we will all travel home together as we had originally planned." Cheers and clapping break out around the lounge. Vandenberg continues. "We will be boarding the Volo Papale in around ten minutes. Please board in an orderly fashion. I am sure you are all as keen as I am to get out of this wretched backwater."

"Not known for his diplomacy," laughs Jarvis, beaming with delight.

Feeling a little despondent, you reach for your drink. Maybe I'm just being paranoid, you think, staring into space. You don't know what to believe anymore. Maybe you can't hang on to any of it. Not even finding God out there on the road to Damascus. Maybe it *was* just the morphine. Maybe I'm the deluded one.

You close your eyes and try to feel some divine connection again, but you feel nothing. What am I left with? Hope and faith? Again, you feel abandoned. Still, you can't shake this certainty deep inside you, urging you to find your way back. Maybe that's how it's meant to be. Maybe that's what makes life worth living. Maybe that is the mystery that turns life into an adventure, a heroic struggle, that shapes you and prepares you for the end. If true, what could be more beautiful than that?

There must be something behind this material reality. Life is just too bizarre. Human consciousness is just too unique and strange to even begin to explain. All this, all of it is just too impossible to be possible. Again, you try to remember the way you felt out on the roadside as you lay there motionless. Near death you were more alive than at any other time in your life. You felt a certainty that the universe was good. That you were good, and that life was good. Not only was it good, but it was precious beyond belief. Every single life. Yet so many people feel so worthless. Why is that?

That is true poverty, you think. A poverty of spirit that has gripped us and left us starving inside a prison of our own making. And if you say anything about it you will only be persecuted—made out to be some kind of nut. Greentree was right about one thing. Nobody wants to admit they are living in a shared delusion. But it's not even that simple. It's not a competition between world views. Every individual world view is unique. We must accept the world as it is. Maybe that is the only way. With patience, forbearance, tolerance. A messy world made up of messed up individuals. How can we possibly expect a world without turmoil when every individual is on their own journey to enlightenment? Isn't this just all part of the drama, the suffering that leads to wisdom, to eternal truth?

We have to accept this. The stoics were onto something. We just have to keep going and keep trying to do what is right—what we know to be morally right. Maybe that's just wishful thinking.

God, I'm exhausted. I must be losing my mind. You feel like you are on the edge of a nervous break-down. Like the rug of reality as you have always known it has been pulled out from under you. You start to wonder whether Jarvis may have spiked your drink. Everything looks hyperreal.

God, I need to get out of here. I just want to go home.

Doubts gnawing away at your insides like ravenous demons, a wave of nausea starts to hit you. You feel like you are about to vomit.

I have to get to the bathroom.

You make a beeline for the restrooms only to find that they are closed for cleaning. In a feverish flap, you head for the entrance where you came in, only to be stopped by a burly security guard.

"Can I help you, sir?" he says.

"I am looking for a bathroom, I think I am going to be sick." The man looks at your face, quickly leads you out the door, and points to a public lavatory along a stark white corridor.

You stagger along and push through the doorway to the bathroom, breathing heavily. Gasping for air you try valiantly to keep your stomach convulsions at bay. You head straight into a cubicle and standing up straight you try to let the nausea pass. You take in some deep breaths. You run your trembling hands through your hair. Just center yourself, Cedric. You are almost there. Center yourself.

You put the toilet seat down, turn around and sit there for a minute or two with your face in your hands, trying to compose yourself. You have to get back in there, Cedric. You have to get on that plane. It's your only hope.

Finally, you pull yourself to your feet and head back out to the basins. You run the cold water tap and splash water on your face, taking in a few gulps to rinse out your dry mouth. You check your reflection in the mirror.

God, I look terrible. You take some paper towel to mop your face. A toilet stall door opens abruptly behind you and in the mirror, you recognize with horror, a familiar figure.

"Hello, Cedric," says Greentree with that familiar smirk of his, communicating far more than a greeting. Lost for words, you just stare back at his image in the mirror.

"Feeling a little sick, are we? Like poor Julia Peterson? I have to hand it to young Schuman. This is quite a plan he cooked up on the run. Shame to see his gifts go to waste."

"How did you—"

"We've hacked all the cameras. Biometric surveillance, Cedric. Heard of it? Impervious to fake moustaches. We use it to find bad guys in a crowd. Facial recognition, gait recognition. Welcome to the wonderful world of AI," says Greentree leaning casually against the bathroom wall.

"Okay, let's get this over with, Greentree. You've really had your fun with me now," you reply wearily.

"Well now. You are a most wanted man here, Cedric. You should be pleased to see me. I am the lesser of two evils, so to speak. Much lesser. One phone call to Syrian Security Services and I can wash my hands of you."

"Look, I'll do whatever you say, Greentree. Just promise me you will leave Ana alone."

"Ana? Oh yeah, that girlfriend of yours. The one that kicks like a mule."

"If you hurt her, I'll—"

"You'll what?" laughs Greentree. "You think she really gives a damn about you, Cedric?"

You grasp at the cross hanging around your neck. Yes, you think. You know she does.

Suddenly the bathroom door flies open and smashes into the wall with an almighty crash.

"Put your bloody hands in the air," says a man in a long Arabic dress shirt, pointing what looks to be a long walking stick at Greentree's face.

"Schuman," says Greentree, raising his hands. A dark figure in full burqua enters the room behind him. "And let me guess, Ana Karenina. How did you two get in here?"

"A limp helps to beat the cameras," says Schuman sharply.

"What's this? Something out of your Cold War closet?" says Greentree gesturing towards the cane.

"Well, as a matter of fact we do keep it in a closet, with our poison umbrellas. You never know what the weather may bring," replies Schuman.

Still frozen to the spot, you look up at Schuman.

"Schuman, this is crazy. What happened today? Why did you send me there? To the Mosque. I could have been killed," you utter.

"Cedric, I had no idea this was coming. No idea. You have to believe me; I had nothing to do with it. This guy, I am not so sure about, though," says Schuman waving the stick at Greentree.

"You really think we would be involved in something like this, Schuman? A hit on the pope? Come on. Really?" says Greentree raising his eyebrows.

"I don't know who to believe anymore," you say.

"That makes two of us," says Schuman. He turns his attention to Greentree. "Okay, Greentree, where do you want it?"

"Ouch! You f..." Whomp. Greentree hits the floor like a sack of cement. A dart protruding from his right leg.

"You'd better get moving, Cedric, I'm not sure whether horse tranquilliser has a use-by date."

Ana removes her veil. "Cedric, come quickly with me now," she says, her voice ringing through you. She grabs you by the hand and you scurry down the hallway in a state of confusion to the door leading into the lounge. You stop there and she takes you by both hands.

"When I saw what happened, I knew I had to be here for you," Ana whispers gently. "What you did was incredible. You are a hero, Cedric. My crazy hero. Go now, Cedric. I will wait. I love you no matter what." She throws her arms around you and kisses you passionately.

"I'm coming back, Ana. I promise."

"I know, Cedric. Go!" she exclaims, her beautiful eyes flickering. She quickly shoves you through the door and runs. Stumbling into the lounge, you look up to see that the last passenger is boarding.

"Rice! Where did you go? Hurry up and get on!" calls Jarvis. A shot of adrenaline and endorphins pump through your system.

She loves me. She really does love me! Run, Cedric. Run onto that plane now!

21

As soon as you step into the cabin the flight crew close the door behind you. The plane immediately begins to taxi out onto the tarmac, as you and Jarvis hurriedly make your way to your seats.

You stow your bag and sit down in a window seat with an excellent view of the left wing. Jarvis plonks down next to you and buckles his seatbelt. As the plane readies for take-off, you press your head against the plexiglass window, hoping to catch a glimpse of Ana or Schuman. There is no sign of either of them. You hope to God they have managed to escape.

Suddenly you notice a couple of vehicles heading out towards the plane. They look like military jeeps.

"That was a close one, Rice. We nearly left you behind," shouts Jarvis as the aircraft's jets begin to roar.

Hurtling down the runway now, the Volo Papale leaves the two jeeps trailing a mile back and lifts off into the clear blue sky.

Gasps of relief are audible and the passengers adjacent to you, a young Latino woman and a middle-aged African man, are smiling with happiness. The old city below slowly disappears, and within minutes the Mediterranean Sea comes into view. Cloud banks engulf the aircraft as it steadily climbs ever higher into the heavens.

"Hey, Jarvis. Did you pack a parachute? I think I see a Russian MIG tailing us," bellows the African man in a warm South African accent.

"Just another escort," laughs Jarvis. The young woman starts to giggle, and the African man laughs a hearty laugh. You and Jarvis start to laugh too.

Oh my God. I made it, you think. I bloody well made it.

"Uh oh, look out," says Jarvis. "Vandenberg has busted out the Krug." Trays of champagne flutes are passed around the cabin and everyone is partaking in the celebration. You can hardly hold your glass; your hand is shaking so much.

"Hey, Jarvis. Get this," says a man holding up a copy of the International New York Times. "Donald Trump says that if he wins the White House, the first thing he's going to do is meet with Kim Jong Un. He called the guy a genius. How do you like that?" shouts the man across the aisle.

"Are you sure that's not a copy of Pravda?" says Jarvis. "Holy Mother of God, what next?"

Leaning back in your seat. You let that news sink in. This could be good for you, Cedric. Maybe Greentree and his cronies will let things slide. They'd be crazy to start something up with Russia and North Korea that might explode in their faces. Maybe this whole thing will blow over. Maybe they've already moved on. Schuman had the upper hand back there at the airport. Still, the safest bet will be to look out for Schuman's exfiltration man in Rome. The CIA will either be waiting for you, or they won't be.

Jarvis has borrowed the newspaper and is quietly skimming his way through it. The drinks start to take effect, and you finally have a chance to process all you have been through.

What an adventure. The adventure of a lifetime. Never in your wildest dreams did you think that anything like this would ever have happened to you. A bloody coup, a terrorist attack, a crazy CIA plot, an attempted assassination of the pope. And in the middle of it all, love. Real love. Love for a beautiful, brave, amazing woman. And love for life itself. A reverence that will abide in you forever. A transfiguration. A renewal of the mind. A change in consciousness that has opened your eyes to a new reality. You have suffered. But now you can see that suffering for love is happiness. Genuine happiness.

Knowing that you are loved and valued deeply and personally, no matter what. That is genuine happiness. Really there is nothing else you need. You don't need to do anything. You don't need to say anything. You don't need to make anything happen. You don't even need to know anything. Just look up in wonder. Like a child. It's all perfect. It's all true. It's all beautiful. It's all good. It's all divine. We need to hang onto that, you think. If only people could see that.

It's the materialistic mindset that results in war, destruction, and complete disregard for the sanctity of human life. This is the ultimate tragedy. A mindset where we are nothing more than organisms, here for a short and brutal moment. This makes life a living hell. An empty reality fueled by human arrogance. A world where divine love itself is ignored, shut out, and totally forgotten.

How are you going to keep living in a world like this? How are you going to survive the sheer folly of human existence without going insane? All you can really know is that you will spend the rest of your days yearning for the peace you found on that roadside. A peace that really is beyond all understanding and impossible to hold onto in this crazy world. But you will never forget it. It will always be there, deep within your soul. Always.

At that moment, the curtains to the front cabin, the pope's cabin, are drawn back. In full regalia, the Holy Father takes a few careful steps along the aisle and comes into full view. He exudes peace. He smiles. The cabin erupts into warm applause.

"Thank you," he says nodding gently.

"Holy Father, how do you feel after what happened today and what will this mean for the peace process?" shouts a young man now standing in the opposite aisle.

"As you would understand I am very saddened by today's events. Very saddened. I am sure you all have many questions—questions that I will answer in good time."

"But Holy Father—" the young man continues.

"I will release a statement from the Vatican when we have arrived back safely," says the pope, holding his hand up. "By the grace of God, I am intact. In body, mind, and spirit, I remain intact. The church remains intact. My hat and my cassock require some repairs. But that's okay," he says with a laugh.

"I will say one thing. We must not let go of hope. When we look at the world around us, we are holding a mirror up to ourselves. We must, every single one of us, find our way back to God. We have a long way to go. It seems we stray further every day. We must help one another to heal. We must keep striving for peace. We must love one another. Even our enemies. This can only come from within. Do not expect governments or charities or even churches to make this happen. You must make it happen. You, in your heart, must want it to happen. Pray, grow in God's love, join with others and your fruits will be bountiful. It is you who will lift us out of the darkness and into the light. Even if it is only for a fleeting moment, somewhere, somehow... May God bless you all."

The Holy Father makes the sign of the cross and whispers a brief benediction. His smile is radiant. He turns and shuffles back behind the curtain.

My God, you wonder. *Was I sent to Damascus to rescue the pope, or was the pope sent to Damascus to rescue me?*

You feel a tingle make its way from the back of your neck up to the crown of your head, spreading a wonderful sensation throughout your entire body. There is only one word to describe it.

Joy.